# Don Pendleton's Mack
# Bolan®
## Cold War Reprise

A GOLD EAGLE BOOK FROM
# WORLDWIDE®

TORONTO • NEW YORK • LONDON
AMSTERDAM • PARIS • SYDNEY • HAMBURG
STOCKHOLM • ATHENS • TOKYO • MILAN
MADRID • WARSAW • BUDAPEST • AUCKLAND

Recycling programs
for this product may
not exist in your area.

First edition July 2009

ISBN-13: 978-0-373-61530-8

Special thanks and acknowledgment to
Douglas P. Wojtowicz for his contribution to this work.

COLD WAR REPRISE

# Kurtzman looked concerned

"Hal won't be particularly pleased with you hitting up old contacts."

Brognola was the least of his worries, Bolan mused. With a death squad on the loose in the streets of London, the Executioner knew that it was time to load up for bear.

In this particular case, the ursine was a breed the Executioner had hunted before, a ghost species he'd hoped had disappeared with the fall of the Berlin Wall.

Unfortunately, the Soviet Bear was still a living, vital threat, and its predatory hunger had claimed the lives of two of Bolan's old allies.

Hunting season was on again.

SERIES

Oh for a lodge in some vast wilderness,
Some boundless contiguity of shade,
Where rumour of oppression and deceit,
Of unsuccessful or successful war,
Might never reach me more.

> —William Cowper
> (1731–1800)

It would be nice to shut out the evils of the world,
but my conscience demands that I search for the truth
of every rumor of oppression and deceit, and try to
head off all wars to make them unsuccessful.

> —Mack Bolan

## CHAPTER ONE

Mack Bolan was no stranger to the London night, having come to the grand old city early in his war against organized crime and returning for multiple engagements since. Yet the Executioner was not on a hunt this night, nor was he being pursued.

Bolan had the collar of his black wool long coat turned up against the cold, his arctic-blue eyes scanning the dock for trouble. He was walking with a light load, relatively speaking, carrying only a Beretta Px4 Storm in his shoulder holster, with a compact version of the same model tucked into his waistband at the small of his back for backup. The two sidearms accepted 17-round standard or 20-round extended magazines, equaling the firepower of his usual standard, the Beretta 93R machine pistol, while fitting into a smaller profile.

With his instincts at full alertness, Bolan spotted ordinary potential threats—drunken soccer hooligans, knife-armed thugs on the prowl for mugging victims and smugglers awaiting their contacts. The London dockyards were a wilderness, but as long as the Executioner was there to keep an appointment, he had to maintain a low profile.

Bolan sidestepped a pair of drunken sailors who staggered out through the door of a musky-smelling dive. Sweat, alcohol, cigarettes and even a few whiffs of marijuana thrown in for good measure assaulted Bolan's nostrils as he went into the dockyard bar. The crowd turned its attention to the newcomer, who was over six feet tall, powerfully built, clad in black with chilling blue eyes that cut like lasers through the gloom of the tavern. A jukebox and a television set struggled against the undercurrent of slurred and hushed conversations, failing to do more than contribute to the wall of white noise. That was the point, though. No one sound carried farther than a tabletop, allowing plotters to plot and cheaters to cheat without being overheard by interested parties.

A stocky Slavic man gestured from his corner booth. Two shot glasses bracketed a bottle of clear liquor in front of him, and to one side, an ashtray was overflowing with crushed-out butts. Bolan knifed through the bar as the Slav poured the booze into his shot glasses, pushing one of the little servings of the clear stuff to what was to be Bolan's seat. Bleary, smoke-stung eyes looked up at the Executioner.

"Mikhail Belasko," Vitaly Alexandronin greeted, lighting another cigarette as Bolan slid into the booth.

"The name's Cooper, now," Bolan corrected, taking a sip. It was a bitter, foul version of vodka that tasted as if it had been filtered through sweat-crusted socks. "Couldn't find anything better?"

"Tastes just like the crap I distilled in Afghanistan," Alexandronin replied. "Except British feet stink a bit more."

Bolan chuckled. Alexandronin offered him an unfiltered cigarette and Bolan accepted it. The Russian's lighter fired it up, and Bolan took a single puff before resting the cigarette between the knuckles of his left hand. He didn't want to offend Alexandronin's hospitality, and Bolan had the discipline to avoid slipping back into a nicotine habit. "Bad booze and worse cigarettes? This is war mode for you, Vitaly."

"Why else would I invite you by for a drink?" Alexandronin asked. "It's not for my health."

Bolan frowned, but he wouldn't interrupt the Russian, breaking the rule of polite conversation by going for hard data right off the bat. He could see that Alexandronin was ragged, his jowls hanging loosely as if he hadn't eaten for a month. The Russian's fingertips were completely bronzed by nicotine stains, but the last time Bolan had interacted with the defected former KGB agent, his skin had been a healthier shade due to quitting smoking. Lack of sleep darkened Alexandronin's eyes into an impenetrable shadow. "Is it about Catherine?"

Alexandronin took a long pull off of his cigarette, blowing the smoke through his wide, blunt nostrils. His brow crinkled and Bolan knew he'd touched a raw nerve. "The pitiful excuse for lawmen in this damned city claim that she was jumped by soccer hooligans. The thugs broke Catherine to pieces, and she lingered in a hospital for the last of her days."

Catherine Alexandronin was not a name on the

Stony Man watch-list database, but Bolan cursed himself for not keeping an eye out for her. He had last known her as Catherine Rozuika, a TASS journalist who had helped Bolan and Alexandronin derail an effort to turn back the democratic processes of the early Commonwealth of independent states. The hard-liners were not willing to give way to the end of the old Soviet Republic and freely and blatantly killed anyone in their path. The Executioner had stopped the plot and through his Stony Man contacts, had arranged for a new life for the pair in London.

Catherine had been a beautiful woman. Back then, Bolan had enjoyed a few moments of tenderness with the lady reporter. The news of her death by a brutal beating was like a knife in the soldier's heart. Something, though, had sparked Alexandronin's paranoia. "You said the police 'claimed.' You don't buy that story."

Alexandronin knocked back his glass of vodka. "The law looks at the ambush of an investigative reporter as just another case of drunk sports fans. But this was not the work of alcohol-besotted misanthropes."

A stack of photos plopped in front of Bolan and he leafed through them, studying the photographic records taken at the emergency room and during her autopsy. Bolan's sharp mind already spotted inconsistencies between the police reports and reality.

"Pay attention to the broken right arm," Alexandronin said.

"The end result of a standard Spetsnaz cross-forearm disarmament snap," Bolan replied. "Using one limb as a fulcrum, the gun hand is deflected, the force shattering the ulnar bones. Catherine was armed, and she pulled her weapon to defend herself."

"We have enemies," Alexandronin replied. "Mere hooligans would have just picked up the gun and shot her with it."

"They were sending a message," Bolan suggested. "Stop snooping. Question is, what was she snooping into?"

"The newspaper she worked for 'misplaced' her most recent notes," Alexandronin added. "None of her coworkers will even stay in the same room as I am in."

Alexandronin opened his shirt. A bloody bandage was on his upper chest. "I'm still snooping and I nearly caught all six inches of the blade that did this."

"You find out anything about what she was looking into?" Bolan asked as the man buttoned his shirt.

"It was initially a fluff piece, allegedly, talking to Chechen refugees who had emigrated here to England. They're trying to escape the troubles back home," Alexandronin answered. "But she confided in me that the refugees were scared."

"Of the Russian government or their own people?" Bolan asked. "Chechen rebels are hardly saints, even if the world is admitting that Moscow is longing for the good old days of the cold war."

"Russia has changed some, but not enough," Alexandronin said. He poured himself a fresh shot of vodka, then hammered it down in one gulp. "There is a group in Moscow, a highly trained antiterrorism special branch."

"They call themselves the Curved Knife," Bolan mused. He flicked a tower of ashes off his untouched cigarette. "Doesn't take too much imagination to see that the Curved Knife is an allusion to the old Sickle that crossed the Hammer as the symbol of the Communist party."

"The Sickle symbolism is not lost on anyone who's aware of them," Alexandronin said. "They are no more than the midnight knockers from the old days of the KGB. They are the same type of bastards who picked up those considered unfaithful to the Party and helped them to disappear."

"Usually with a bullet in the head, and a trip to the bottom of a bulldozed pit," Bolan added. He took a token puff on the cigarette, washing the foul taste away with the bitter liquor. He looked down at the glass, then held it out for Alexandronin to refill.

"The stuff grows on you," the Russian noted with a chuckle, pouring another round.

"Helps to keep the bad taste of this news out of my mouth," Bolan answered. "Catherine lived a few days after the beating?"

Alexandronin nodded. "She never recovered consciousness. Internal hemorrhaging finally took its toll. I told the doctors to pull the plug. Russians live, or Russians die. The limbo of being trapped in a coma is neither, and it traps the soul in a broken sack of flesh."

Bolan nodded. "She never said anything about what happened to her in that case."

Alexandronin sighed. "She didn't even say goodbye. Not out loud."

He pushed an envelope toward Bolan. The name "Mike" was scrawled on the front, a reference to his old identity of Mike Belasko, long since discarded. In the dive, its scene of strawberries was an island of freshness. "She wrote one for me, as well, my friend. I didn't look at yours."

Bolan glanced down at the slender envelope, then sliced it open with his pocketknife. Catherine's strawberry-scented perfume filled his nostrils, bringing him back to their time together, entwined in each other's limbs. There was a small, folded slip of paper within.

"'My soldier, I could never replace your lost rose. May you someday find peace, and never forget the night we shared. Cat.'"

Bolan folded the slip and put it back in its envelope. He fought off the heartache those simple words left in their wake. He met Alexandronin's gaze.

"It was never a secret that you two had been lovers," the Russian told him. "That didn't mean she was less of a devoted wife to me."

"I feel your pain, Vitaly," Bolan told him. "And I'll help find her murderers."

"No, comrade. I will help you," Alexandronin replied. "My race is nearly run, and I miss Catherine far too much to want to live in a world without her."

"That's the melancholy talking, Vitaly," Bolan said, but not too forcefully. "Keep her memory alive."

Alexandronin's attention was seized by movement at the door. His hand slid off the table, resting on his belly, just above his belt line. Bolan looked at the reflection of the two men in the surface of the vodka bottle. They both had Slavic features and were dressed in black. Their hawk-sharp eyes scanned the bar patrons, seeking out their designated prey.

"I assume you are armed, Mikhail," Alexandronin said.

Bolan nodded. "The two at the front are just the flush team. If we cut through the back, we'll run straight into the trap team."

"Sharp as always, my friend," Alexandronin mused. "So we go through those two?"

"Provided they don't have someone hanging back behind them. They could be supported by another trap team or even snipers," Bolan said. "That's how I'd do it if I were setting this trap."

"So what is our plan?" Alexandronin asked.

"Let me talk to those two," Bolan told him. "Maybe I can head off any violence. This place isn't choir practice, but I'd hate for bystanders to get hurt."

"As is your way, comrade. Precision and concern for those around you," Alexandronin stated. He patted the old Heckler & Koch P7 stuffed into his belt. "Respect for accuracy is another thing we have shared, my friend."

"Can the past tense, Vitaly. The Russian government has an agency off the leash, so I'm going to need your help," Bolan admonished. "You get killed, who do I tap for intel?"

"Remember Kaya?" Alexandronin asked. "She's still with the government. Russian Intelligence."

Bolan winced. "Do you really want to risk her life?"

"She risks it keeping in covert contact with me, Mikhail," Alexandronin explained.

"Three heads are better than two. Stick with me."

Alexandronin's eyes narrowed, his lips turning up into a smile. "You have done more with much less, Mikhail."

"Focus," Bolan warned.

Alexandronin nodded. "I am."

Bolan stubbed out his cigarette, burying it with the other stubby butts in the pile flowing over the top of the ashtray. The soldier palmed his shot glass and got out of the booth. The two black-clad Slavs eyed Bolan suspiciously, confirming to the Executioner that the men were professionals. They focused on him like anti-radiation missiles launched at a radar installation. The pair wore their jackets loosely in contrast to Bolan's snugly fitted wool long coat. The custom-tailoring of Bolan's coat hid his two Berettas completely, but the lumpy loose jackets worn by the two Russians indicated that the pair were armed with more than flat, sleek auto pistols. Their eyes locked on the glass in Bolan's hand.

Bolan passed between the pair, shoving them rudely aside. His elbow connected with something big and heavy hidden under the lapels of one jacket. Bolan cursed the pair in Russian. "Move aside, you sons of whores. I need more vodka!"

"Fucking bastard," one of the professionals snarled, returning his response in Georgian-accented Russian. "Who do you think you are?"

Bolan met his gaze. "A thirsty man in front of two jackbooted thugs. Two pathetic leftovers of a dead regime if my eyes serve me right!"

"You don't look Russian," the other hardman said in English. His accent was flawless, further proof that these men weren't just pulled off the street. "What relation are you to Alexandronin?"

"Brothers in blood," Bolan returned. "What is your interest?"

"That man is a traitor," the Georgian gritted in Russian. "And if you consider him your brother—"

"Shut your mouth!" the English speaker said to his companion. He glared at Bolan. "Walk away from this if you value your life, 'brother.'"

Bolan smirked. "I was just about to suggest the same thing to you."

Behind him, Bolan could tell that Alexandronin was moving because the Georgian's interest was suddenly locked on to the booth.

"Trying to distract us?" the Georgian asked.

Bolan snapped his arm straight, the palmed shot glass shattering against the Georgian's cheekbone. Broken glass slashed ragged wounds through his eyeball and cheek. The other hardman stepped back, driving his hand into his jacket for the heavy chatterbox concealed beneath. Bolan kicked out, catching the English speaker in the side of his knee, folding the man's leg with the crack and pop of dislocating cartilage and unsprung tendons.

The background drone of the bar suddenly went silent as the millisecond of explosive action brought a spray of blood and the ugly crunch of a shattered knee joint to the patrons' awareness. The Georgian screamed, half blind from the broken splinters sticking out of his punctured eyeball. Alexandronin slipped up behind him, grabbed a handful of collar and twisted. The tightened neck of his shirt smothered the Georgian hit man's agony as fabric garroted across his windpipe.

The blunt, short barrel of Alexandronin's P7 jammed into the Georgian's kidney. "You reach for the weapon under your coat, and your kidney will end up decorating the floor."

Bolan helped his broken-kneed opponent to both feet, reaching under the man's jacket to use the grip of the harnessed machine pistol he wore as a handle to maneuver him. From feel, Bolan recognized it as an Uzi of some form. A good tug let his captive know that Bolan had command of the situation.

The bartender looked under the counter at some form of fight-pacifying weaponry, but the sheer speed and violence of action dissuaded him reaching for it. Whoever the barkeep thought Bolan was, he had the reflexes to counteract anything that he kept under the bar. "Please, guv'nuh, take it outside."

"That was my plan," Bolan told him.

Alexandronin tossed some folded pound notes in front of the bartender. "Another bottle of potato juice for the road."

The Georgian gurgled as the bartender put a bottle on the counter. Alexandronin leaned in toward his captive, smiling. "Grab my vodka for me, friend."

The Georgian picked up the bottle and the four people left the confines of the bar. Both Bolan and Alexandronin held their prisoners directly in front of them as human shields. By the time they were outside, Bolan had his man's Uzi well in hand and down by his thigh, safety selector clicked to full automatic.

"Let your rifleman know that he'd better hold his fire," Bolan warned as they stood under the bar's overhang. "Unless you wouldn't mind having a new orifice torn in you."

The limping, agonized Slav spoke into a collar microphone, speaking quickly. The hardman was straightforward, as Bolan had proven his fluency in Russian, making it clear that any deception would be futile. Bolan couldn't hear the other end of the conversation because his prisoner wore an earphone, but the hostage explained that he had been compromised.

"Where's your shooter?" Bolan asked.

"There are two of them," the hobbled prisoner replied.

"The bar's quiet again," Alexandronin noted. He pocketed the bottle of vodka, no longer needing a chokehold on his prisoner as the man was busy holding the tattered remnants of his glass-shredded face together. "The backdoor team is likely moving up."

"Point the way," Bolan ordered. "Vitaly, stay sharp."

*"Da,"* Alexandronin said.

A distant rifle cracked instantly, and the black-clad human shield jerked violently against Bolan. The prisoner's blood gushed out of a hole torn into his breastbone, arterial spray spurting through the centralized chest wound like a fountain. Now a deadweight in Bolan's arms, the corpse still provided some use as a protective barrier, and the Executioner pushed out into the street. Alexandronin forced his prisoner ahead of him, as well, but the riflemen focused on Bolan, their bullets crashing into the unfeeling form of the dead man.

Bolan spotted a muzzle flash, lined up his Uzi and fired the submachine gun. The chatterbox had a range of 200 yards in trained hands, and no living man was more familiar with the stubby Israeli machine pistol than the Executioner. The distant gunmen stopped shooting, but Bolan didn't feel as if he had scored a hit. Suppressive fire, however, still was worth the spent ammunition, and Bolan looked for the second rifleman. Alexandronin stumbled, the Georgian bending backward as the Russian's P7 discharged. Alexandronin's claim of spraying the hit man's kidney across the bar floor didn't quite come true as the 9 mm round missed the organ completely. The deadly slug, however, still tore through Alexandronin's opponent, slashing a stretch of aorta apart.

"Vitaly!" Bolan called.

"Their round went through my thigh," Alexandronin said, limping to cover.

Bolan began snatching items from the dead man's pockets, spare magazines and a radio specifically. He let the body tumble lifelessly to the ground as he rushed to scoop up his ally. Together they ducked between a couple of buildings. The leg injury was a shallow furrow along the outside of Alexandronin's thigh. The bullet had struck far from the femur or the femoral artery, meaning that the man could still walk, though his leg was drenched. Bolan recognized the smell of the rotten vodka they had been drinking. A bone injury would have been crippling, but had the blood vessel been nicked, Alexandronin's life would be measured in seconds. Bolan looked his friend in the eye. "Bad news. You lost the vodka."

Alexandronin grinned. "A tragedy, Mikhail. I can still walk."

Bolan dumped the spent magazine from his Uzi, feeding it a full one he'd plucked from its former owner. The savvy warrior also took a moment to secure the earpiece and the body of his hostage's radio to his harness. Being able to listen in on the conversation of his enemies would be a force multiplier.

The bar front opened and Bolan caught a glimpse of four men bursting through the doors, scrambling to cover. Bolan fired off a short burst that sent the dark-clad assassins deeper behind their cover.

"Get to a safer position," Bolan ordered Alexandronin. "I'll cover you."

The Russian shook his head. "This is my fight, too, Mikhail."

"You're hurt and slowed down," Bolan argued.

"I can turret," Alexandronin replied. "You can still move quickly. Together we can surround them."

Bolan didn't have time to argue about tactics, especially since Alexandronin was right. He handed his friend the Uzi and the remaining spare magazine. "Don't die."

The Russian smiled. "I have men to kill before I rest, Mikhail."

"Remember that," the soldier said, drawing his Beretta.

The Executioner raced across the street, covered by a spray of rapid shots from Alexandronin.

Once more, London was a host to Bolan's cleansing flame.

## CHAPTER TWO

Alexandronin's first burst of Uzi fire kept the assassins' heads down as the Executioner charged around their flank, Beretta Storm leading the way. Bolan held his fire, his Russian ally leaning on the trigger to keep the enemy focused away from him.

"Which of those two idiots lost control of his Uzi?" one killer snarled in Russian.

"Probably both," another answered his comrade. "They were both human shields, remember?"

"Longbow to Tomahawk, be alert! One operator moved around to your side of the street," another, presumably a sniper, informed the hit crew. Bolan was glad that he'd taken the time to relieve his former prisoner of his comm link. Aware that the enemy was on to him, Bolan sidestepped into the open and fired four quick shots at the squad in front of the bar. Two of his shots struck one gunman center mass, but the impacts had no affect on the would-be murderer.

Bolan snaked back behind cover as the Russians' Uzis crackled, ripping the air he'd stood in moments before. The assassins were wearing body armor, good stuff, too, as Bolan had Dutch-loaded his Beretta with high-velocity hollowpoints and full-power NATO ball ammunition. The high-pressure ball rounds were effective against a good deal of ballistic vests, meaning that the killers had expected heavy opposition. The corner that Bolan had ducked behind was chewed up as a trio of submachine guns tracked to keep the big American pinned.

Bolan ran a mental countdown to the moment when a "Flying Squad"—Scotland Yard's version of SWAT— showed up to the scene of a raging gun battle on the bank of the Thames. The Executioner knew that he had minutes, but with the skill and professionalism of the assassination cadre, he'd need every second of that Doomsday countdown to put the killers away. Now, Bolan not only had Alexandronin's life to worry about, but also the British policemen who would be caught in the cross fire.

Three weapons in the front meant that the rest of the team was swinging around the back to strike at the Executioner from behind. Bolan charged to the back alley, Beretta leading the way. His suspicions were confirmed when he heard the whispered announcement of "in position" from a new speaker on the communications hookup.

Bolan whipped around the corner, his Beretta's muzzle jammed into an assassin's face, breaking his nose. The soldier's off hand slapped the gunner's Uzi against the wall and though the hitter triggered his subgun, the rounds spit through empty air. Bolan triggered his Storm, the solitary 9 mm round blowing off the back of the killer's skull, disgorging a cone of spongy brain matter and blood into the face of the second man with them. The remains of the dead man's skull contents turned the assassin's shooting glasses into a blood-sprayed mess he couldn't see through.

The Executioner tossed the corpse of the point man aside and pivoted the gun in his hand to strike the surviving killer in the head. The Slavic gunman stepped back, tearing his glasses off, the motion helping him to avoid the weight of the handgun as Bolan's swing jammed it up against the wall. Now able to see, the Russian killer lunged forward, forearm trapping Bolan's gun hand against the wall.

The close-quarters gunfight suddenly turned into a brawl as the assassin chopped at Bolan's neck, but the soldier deflected most of the lethal precision with his shoulder. The neck-breaking blow degraded to a clumsy slap that cuffed Bolan's head above his ear. The gunman tried to bring his Uzi to bear, but the Executioner had trapped the subgun between his hip and the wall. The frustrated hitter tried to nail his opponent between the eyes with a backhand stroke, but Bolan took the blow on the crown of his head. The curved surface of his skull denied the murderer a solid hit, sparing Bolan anything worse than scalp abrasions.

The soldier snaked his foot behind his enemy's ankle and with a surge of strength, barreled the gunman backward and off balance. The assassin stumbled onto his buttocks, the Uzi wrenched out of his grasp. No longer restrained, Bolan had both arms free to tackle the killer prisoner. He dropped on the gunman, knees slamming into the hardman's shoulders with jarring force, pinning the man to the ground under his 200-plus-pound frame. Bolan fired off a hard punch to the prone assassin's jaw, a knockout blow that jammed the mandible into a heavy juncture of nerves at the side of his neck. The Slav wasn't rendered unconscious, but neural overload left his eyes glazed over, staring glassily into the murky, starless night sky.

"Kroz! Report!" a voice over Bolan's radio demanded. The stunned Russian groaned incoherently as if to answer the broadcast order. Bolan took a moment to pull his Combat PDA, activating its 8 megapixel digital camera to record the gunman's face, just in case this particular prisoner had as short a shelf life as his last one. Bolan punched the assassin once more, and the stunned, glassy eyes closed with unconsciousness.

Bolan brought the microphone to his lips. "Kroz can't come to the phone right now. However if you leave a message at the beep…"

"Shit! Shit!" the Russian on the other end swore. "Switch frequencies! Channel B!"

The alternate frequency plan might have worked, had not Bolan captured not one but two different radios. Bolan checked Kroz's unit for indications of the secondary communications frequency and found that Kroz had scratched his dial to mark the next channel. The soldier plugged his earphone into Kroz's unit and clicked over to the frequency.

"…fucking guy?" one of the conversants complained in Russian.

"Maintain radio discipline," the leader of the death squad ordered.

Sowing panic among his enemies was a good weapon for evening the odds against superior numbers and firepower. As it was, the assassination team was down four shooters in the space of a few minutes. With two sharpshooters and three gunmen on hand, that was nearly half of the Russian force.

"Central says to abort!" another voice cut in. "The mission has been compromised."

So, the assassins have a coordination and operations center, Bolan thought. If they're going to cut and run, there's a chance that they could give me a better look at who ran this op.

Bolan scurried back to the front of the bar, listening to the Russians as he did so.

"Principal target still breathing. Cannot disengage anyhow," the hit team's commander returned.

"Scorch the earth," the coordinator snapped. "Principal is no longer an issue. Avoiding his partner is!"

"Confirm command scorch," the leader said.

"Burn it all down!" the commander bellowed.

Bolan snapped open the stock of his Uzi. He wasn't certain of the extent of the firepower the death force had on hand, but the people in the dive were at risk. He used the Uzi's butt to punch out a window into the bar.

Inside, patrons huddled close to the floor, terrified of the rattle of full-auto weaponry ripping and roaring outside. Though there was a likelihood of the presence of murderers and other scum being among this crowd, Bolan had little proof of their collective guilt, let alone knowledge of actions warranting death by high explosives. He fired a burst into the ceiling and the crowd rose as one, a human tide breaking for the back door, shoving out into the alley. No one wanted to go out the front, which would take them right into the middle of the current firefight. It was better than giving away that Bolan was listening in on the Russians' party line by shouting a warning to the bar bums.

The first thunderbolt impact blew the doors off the dive, tearing them off of their hinges. Splinters and shrapnel forced the Executioner to duck out the window to avoid being sliced by the rocketing wave of debris. He popped back up and saw that the panicked patrons had managed to evacuate long before the interior of the bar was turned into a blast crater. The force of the explosion informed Bolan that the enemy had resorted to RPGs, rocket-propelled grenades that could be reloaded quickly and were devastating to a range of 300 yards.

Bolan snaked through the broken window with whiplash speed, dropping to the shattered floor as the next 77 mm warhead impacted at the corner he had been hiding behind earlier. The concussive fury of the thermobaric warhead was so violent, Bolan could feel it through the brick wall. Had he delayed in leaving the causeway beside the bar, he would have been pulverized by the fuel-air explosive's radius of ignited atmosphere. As it was, Bolan had to shake the cobwebs from his head.

He hoped that Alexandronin had retreated to more solid cover when the death squad broke out their heavy weapons. Bolan rushed across the explosion-ravaged bar and vaulted over the counter. He look around swiftly to see what kind of crowd-calming firepower the bartender had. Crouching behind the bar, he was at eye level with the shelves beneath the counter and saw a bolt-action Enfield sitting on a shelf. A box of .303 stripper clips sat next to it. It was an unusual combination for bar-room defense, but the SMLE had been sawn down to a fourteen-inch barrel for faster handling in the bartender's area. The sawed-off Smelly was a better option than a cut-down shotgun, and even at fourteen inches, the .303 rounds would cut through body armor and put a man down like a sledgehammer. It would also be more than sufficient to counter the enhanced reach of the Russians' snipers.

Bolan stuffed the stripper clips into his pocket, then chambered the first round on the rifle. He couldn't expect razor-fine precision with an untested set of iron sights, and an unregulated load of ammunition, but the soldier's years of marksmanship gave him enough experience to be able to hit a man-size target at three hundred yards with bone-smashing authority.

The Enfield's stock took out a window behind the bar, and Bolan slithered out into the next causeway. The handy little bolt action was short enough for the soldier to maneuver through the narrow passage and he poked around the corner. He was barely visible at the range the enemy rocketeers were firing from. The smoky trails of the RPG-7 shells cut across the dock front, pinpointing the enemy's position about two hundred yards downrange.

Bolan could see Alexandronin's former hiding spot had been hit by a rocket grenade, but there was no sign of his Russian ally. The soldier hoped that his friend's leg injury hadn't slowed him so much that he hadn't reached safety before the 77 mm warhead impacted.

Suddenly an Uzi crackled close to the Russians' position. Bolan saw the stocky outline of Alexandronin leap back behind cover. While Bolan had engaged the other team of gunmen, Alexandronin had to have scrambled to flank the death squad.

Bolan shouldered his Enfield and fired, his first .303 shot missing the head of an Uzi-wielding gunman by inches. However, the powerful rifle round tore into the upper chest of a Russian holding one of the rocket launchers. The sharp-nosed slug excavated a gory tunnel through muscle, organs and bone, dropping the rocketeer in a messy pile of dead, twisted limbs.

That caught the attention of the death squad survivors. The shooters turned their Uzis and remaining sniper rifle toward him and fired where Bolan's last muzzle flash had flared. A hail of bullets tore into his old position, but the Executioner had gone back into the bar via the broken window and crouched in the smoky wreckage of the building's rocket-shattered doors. Focusing on the distant muzzle flashes and adjusting his hold for his last known miss, Bolan fired, working the bolt with lightning quickness. The Enfield had more than enough power to kill a man at two hundred yards, and over the radio set, he heard two agonized grunts, one of which dissolved into a death rattle.

Bolan stuffed the stripper clip into the top of the Enfield and shoved its ten trapped rounds into the deep reservoirs of the rifle's magazine.

"Get that RPG on the bar again!" the field leader growled.

"Arkady's dead! The fucker killed Arkady!" another hitter snapped.

"Shut up and stay focused!" the commander ordered, frustration in his voice.

Alexandronin's Uzi snarled again in the distance, and Bolan's ally had to have hit the man who'd picked up the RPG. The 77 mm shell speared up into the night sky on top of a column of rocket exhaust. It peaked at three hundred meters before gravity overpowered the exhausted, sputtering rocket engine. The grenade spiraled as it descended, smoke spilling out of its tail and etching the warhead's course back to ground level. The heavy explosive load detonated on impact with a bright flash. The fireball's brilliance flashed into a smoky cloud that obscured Bolan's view of the enemy kill force. Since visibility was a two-way street, the Executioner charged toward the opposition's last known position, trading his Enfield back to the fully charged Uzi.

"Report! Report!" the field commander bellowed.

"I've got movement on the walkway!" one Russian answered. "Gregori's down!"

"Stop the gunman!" the commander urged. "Fire!"

There was a grunt over the radio, the sound of a fist striking flesh. Somewhere in the foggy haze, Alexandronin had hurled himself into hand-to-hand combat with the last of the enemy assassin's hit men.

THE RPG BLAST LANDED so close to Vitaly Alexandronin that it shocked the Russian expatriate to the core. Shrapnel had opened several lacerations on his head, arm and torso. Pain burned through his stocky body, but it was only a background ache, adrenaline numbing him to his body's protestations. His fist throbbed from where he had punched the reporting gunman in the ear, carpal bones cracking against hard skull. It was a clumsy attack, but the hard-liner thug had been knocked off his feet. Blood poured from the hit man's ear where the ruptured eardrum drained out.

The man's head hadn't flexed like a jaw would have, and the result was broken knuckles and fractured hand bones. Alexandronin dismissed the self-diagnosis. Catherine, the love of his life, had been shattered far worse by scum such as the one he had struck.

Alexandronin speared his fist under the sternum of his stunned opponent, driving the breath out of the assassin's lungs. As the gunman folded up in pain, he dropped his Uzi. Alexandronin chopped down hard on his downed foe's throat. The killer's trachea collapsed, accompanied by the sickening crunch of his larynx. Blood poured over the dead man's lips, his eyes bulged out by the force of the blow.

"Two bastards I give in your memory, my love," Alexandronin rasped. As he spoke, he tasted blood in his mouth. A cough pushed up a mouthful of sticky crimson. He was so high on adrenaline, he had ignored the pain of a piece of shrapnel that had cut between his ribs and penetrated deep into one lung.

It was bad, he knew, if he could fill his mouth with blood on one weak cough. But Alexandronin was not dead yet. The man he knew as Belasko would need a prisoner or two to continue closing down the foul conspiracy that had taken Catherine away from him.

The team commander's attention had been drawn by Bolan, the two men maneuvering around each other, Uzis snarling and cracking in a leaden debate of point and counterpoint. It was a ballet of bullets and dodges between the two men.

Alexandronin scooped up the partially spent Uzi of the man whose throat he had crushed and reversed it into a club. The assassination team's field commander didn't notice his primary target's sudden charge until the eight-pound mass of the submachine gun hammered between his shoulder blades with stunning force.

The commander folded to the ground, insensate as Bolan held his fire.

"You're hit," Bolan noted, ignoring the unconscious prisoner that Alexandronin had just taken.

The Russian smiled, putting his best face on the lie. "It is far from my heart, Mikhail."

The buckle of the expatriate's knees betrayed the truth, however. Bolan reached out and caught his ally before he collapsed to the ground. The soldier lowered Alexandronin to a reclining position. He looked for the injury that had caused him so much weakness. Bolan ripped open his friend's shirt and saw the ugly, puckered gash over Alexandronin's ribs.

"Lung hit," Alexandronin explained. "Not near heart…probably pleural artery… Can't control that kind of bleeding in the field…"

"Quiet. Save your breath," Bolan ordered.

"Adrenaline…pumped oxygen through blood…" Alexandronin continued. "No breath left to save. I'll be gone in…minutes. You have…last gift."

"Vitaly, damn it!"

Alexandronin cupped Bolan's cheek, smiling at the big American. "Don't mourn for me, Mikhail. My comrade, my brother, I had already died the day Catherine did."

Bolan pressed a button on his PDA. "I've already transmitted a call for an ambulance. Hang on and the paramedics can stabilize you."

"It would just be surviving, my friend," Alexandronin told him. "Not living."

He coughed, blood foaming on his lips. Bolan stroked the dying man's forehead, frowning. "Give Catherine my love when you see her again, Vitaly."

Alexandronin smiled weakly. "The dead all know the love meant for them unspoken in the hearts of the living. We do not need revenge to prove that fealty."

"What plot these men are protecting, it needs to be stopped," Bolan said. "I'll end it."

Alexandronin clapped Bolan on the shoulder. "It is your way. It's why I called you. You will protect others from suffering as I did when Catherine was taken away from me."

Sirens sounded in the distance. "Take your prisoner, Mikhail. Those are police, not paramedics."

Alexandronin closed his eyes, his last breath a deep sigh.

"Sleep well, my friend," Bolan whispered, lowering Alexandronin's head gently to the ground.

The Executioner hauled the unconscious assassin over his shoulder and darted down a causeway to reach his rental car. He left behind the ghosts of the friendly dead to their much delayed reunion.

The warrior intended a different gathering for the damned souls he was about to pass judgment on.

## CHAPTER THREE

Opening up the interface to the Russian Intelligence Agency's GUI system, Kaya Laserka noted that she had twenty-four new e-mail messages. The field agent, assigned to the Moscow Organized Crime Interagency task force, clicked on the tool bar, taking her to her electronic Inbox. Most of the mail was one form of memo or another, mostly tedious reminders and uninspiring trinkets like tenure awards or daily positive reinforcement sayings.

The header of one e-mail, however, brought a chill to Laserka's spine.

"Catherine was murdered," it read in bold, blocky font.

Laserka waited what seemed an eternity as her slow T1 connection, burdened by the equivalent of Third World technical issues, struggled to load the message. There was a link to a London newspaper Web site that carried the report of a brutal, coma-inducing beating of Catherine Rozuika Alexandronin. There was also an appended note that she had been taken off her life support when her husband, Vitaly, was informed that she had been rendered brain dead. The return e-mail was to a free online service, one she didn't recognize. However, the title Outcast1995, contained the year her mentor and training officer, Vitaly Alexandronin, left Russian Intelligence amid a government scandal. Laserka had no doubt who the sender was.

Almost a decade and a half before, Laserka had been a fresh young rookie to Russian Intelligence, and Alexandronin had given her a wealth of lessons and experience that carried her across the intervening years. Laserka fired off a response e-mail, but the server spit back a "message not deliverable" response.

The mail had been sent four days earlier, Laserka noted. She had been stuck on an investigation and away from her work terminal. She'd only just returned to Moscow the previous night after a week in the field, running a surveillance operation. She'd had no urge to go to the office. She had been tired, sweaty and hungry, and only wanted to scrub her auburn hair clean of the stink of perspiration, stale coffee and an ever-hanging cloud of cigarette smoke trapped in her locks. Laserka was as fit and trim as when she was just a raw recruit, but closing in on the latter half of her thirties meant that she didn't have the same reserves of energy to make a quick trip down to the office after the end of a stakeout detail.

Running her knuckle across her full, wide lips, Laserka tried to interpret the disappearance of Alexandronin's e-mail account. It was probably a security ploy on her old mentor's part, using a one-time temporary address, then closing it down. Alexandronin was still a reviled name in the halls of the RIA because of his interference with an effort to put things back to what many KGB veterans felt was a finer time and way of doing business. Laserka had escaped the prejudice of the old hard-liners by being young, pretty and a hard worker. A short hospital stay during the time Alexandronin was offending the old guard also conveyed a cloak of anonymity to the lady agent.

Whenever Alexandronin wanted to get in touch with his former student and partner, he would create a temporary, easily disposable and recognizable e-mail address that would last only long enough for a brief, anonymous exchange. This kept Laserka from getting into trouble with her superiors, but kept the friendship the pair shared alive and vital. Sometimes, the two gave each other news of prevailing politics that would affect her career or his exile, as far as they could determine.

The death of Catherine did not appear to be a random act of violence. That Catherine and Vitaly both were targets of bitter old enemies was not news to Laserka. Husband and wife both kept themselves armed, contrary to Great Britain's inane and ineffectual firearms laws. Laserka had noted several instances of violence over the years that the English nanny legislation had failed to prevent.

On a whim, Laserka performed a quick search, entering the keywords "Russian, violence and London" into the news database. Almost instantly, several article links popped up on the screen, detailing a violent battle that had left eight dead in the London docks, only a few hours before. The only person with identification was a Russian national. The name was not a surprise to Laserka, though reading "Vitaly Alexandronin" plunged a dagger of sadness between her ribs. She tried to blink away the beginnings of tears, swallowing hard to remove the knot of a forming sob from her throat.

Laserka closed the search engine and hurried to the washroom after shutting down her computer.

Though they had been separated for almost fifteen years, the man had been like a surrogate father to her. She barricaded herself into the toilet stall and took a seat, allowing the tears inspired by the death of a dear friend and his wife to flow. Being in the minefield of RIA office politics had given her the ability to smother her sobs to inaudible squeaks and deep breaths, but her eyes cast forth a torrent of weeping. Laserka was glad that department regulations frowned upon the wearing of mascara at the office. At least now she didn't have to mop streaks of black left in the wake of her tears.

She could imagine Alexandronin chiding her for being so lazy and mannish about her appearance, happily giving in to regulations rather than spend a few moments beautifying herself in the morning. A chuckle broke through where sobs had been held silent and at bay. Her mentor had always been one to find the positive in life. It was a trait that the cold war veteran had developed to keep himself sane through years of Soviet oppression. The gentle memory of friendly admonishment felt like a message from the ghost of her mentor, reaching between the worlds of the living and the dead to give her a bit of comfort.

It took a few minutes for the tears to pass, toilet tissue sopping the wetness from her cheeks. Finally, Laserka took a deep breath, checked her reflection in the mirror and returned to her desk. No one paid attention to her; a pair of reading glasses swiftly perched on her nose hid her eyes somewhat. They wouldn't have a good chance to see the redness in them. She fired up her computer again, keeping herself buried out of sight inside her drab, gray cubicle.

Laserka had paperwork on the surveillance operation to complete, and the sooner it was done, the sooner she could go back home to her Spartan apartment and mourn for her friend and mentor, preferably with a bottle of vodka. The quiet goodbye ceremony would be a proper send-off for Alexandronin and his beloved wife.

Laserka opened her notebook to enter her data into the GUI when she noticed a small warning flag on her screen. She clicked on it and opened up a new window.

"Unauthorized Web search activity, Laserka, K., scanning articles pertaining to Vitaly Alexandronin," the pop-up declared. Laserka bit her lower lip in concern, cursing her curiosity and decrying the snoopiness of the RIA information technology team.

"Report to Supervisor Batroykin for debriefing," a new pop-up informed her.

Batroykin was a bastard and a half, stuffed into a half-bastard-sized container, she thought. The old-school KGB veteran was five feet tall and nearly five feet in circumference, a bald little blob of rice pudding packed into a polyester tent of a cheap suit. For the illustration of the pathetic old guard who clung to the ideals that Alexandronin betrayed, Laserka didn't have to go much farther than the bloated, multiple-chinned official.

Laserka took a damp kerchief and pressed it to her eyes to lessen the bloodshot qualities of her whites. The cool water from her glass helped to ease the burning irritation behind her lids, but not the irritant that now started to fester under her skin, the irritation of Batroykin. She frowned, looking at her eyes in the small mirror she kept in a drawer. They still looked reddened, but there was no sign that she had been crying. It was more as if she had just suffered a small allergy attack. Many of the things in her office, from the hand-sanitizing gel to shavings from her pencil sharpener could have given her eyes her current amount of discoloration.

She gathered her nerves, then walked into Batroykin's office. The bald, pasty gnome glanced up at her, his beady eyes looking at how her skirt hugged her athletic but still curvaceous hips, eyes lingering down to her feet clad in short-heeled pumps.

Laserka cleared her throat. "You called me, sir?"

"Have a seat, Kaya," Batroykin offered, waving his hand to a chair in front of his desk. He made no bones about the leer he directed at her toned, muscular calves.

Laserka took the offered seat, in no mood to raise a fuss over his obvious sexual harassment. In fact, she was hoping to capitalize on it to keep her out of trouble. For the man-blob's sake, she even crossed her legs to give him a good show. It was callous to appeal to Batroykin's lechery to lessen any harsh punishment she may have incurred by snooping online for news about Vitaly Alexandronin and his wife, but surviving in a Russian bureaucracy was a deadly chess game. "You sent a warning to me about a news article I looked up? The murder of Vitaly Alexandronin?"

"Actually, it was the article about the brutal attack on a defected reporter in London," Batroykin said. "A hyperlink in an e-mail you opened today."

"Oh, because I had done a little digging. Alexandronin was found dead earlier this morning," Laserka replied.

Batroykin showed interest in the form of a worm-like white eyebrow arching on his puttylike brow. "So you weren't contacted by the traitor? He didn't try to ask for your help in determining the assassination of his wife? After all, you had been his partner for the first year of your career."

"My training officer, not my partner, sir," she lied. "How would you like being condescended to every day for eight hours?"

"How am I sure you're not talking down to me right now?" Batroykin asked.

Laserka sighed, letting her so-called superior get a look at the low neckline of her blouse, purposefully unbuttoned to reveal her freckled cleavage. She caught a glint of delight in the old gnome's eye, his pink, slug-like tongue glistening as he licked his lips. She spoke again, drawing his attention back to her face. "Because, sir, we have always had a good relationship. Or your approval of my performance has lead me to believe."

She threw in her best seductive smile, then gave her lower lip a light bite.

Batroykin watched her with rapt appreciation, then

cleared his throat. "So, do you know who had sent you the article about Catherine Rozuika?"

"I had asked when he first started these updates, but he evaded the question," Laserka continued to lie. Having had over a decade and a half to develop a good cover story for the mystery e-mails, should they have been discovered, gave her more than sufficient practice to let the misinformation roll off her tongue. She hated to be duplicitous about her connection to Alexandronin and his wife, but the truth might cost her more than a paycheck.

She could always get another job, but she only had one brain for an irate hard-liner to put a bullet into.

"Any suspicions?" Laserka asked.

"Many loyal agents were purged from Russian Intelligence in the wake of Alexandronin's exile," Laserka said. "I have a list of four possible former operatives who would rightfully bear a grudge against him. It's on my computer."

"You mean this list, Kaya?" Batroykin asked, handing her a slip of paper. He had likely hoped to surprise her into revealing any inconsistencies in her story, but Laserka had purposefully constructed the list and her notes to maintain her secrecy with Alexandronin. "It is a very thorough research on your part."

"I wanted to be able to present the bona fides of these e-mails if they resulted in something important," Laserka explained. "I know how you prefer to have solid intelligence from reliable sources. Your thoroughness is legendary, sir."

Batroykin showed a flash of ego gratification at her statement. "You are an excellent agent, my dear. I'm certain that I can make your inappropriate Internet usage into some vital information that I required. After all, what is your job?"

"Intelligence agent, sir," Laserka answered, putting a small tinge of bubbliness into her voice.

Batroykin nodded, the magnanimous king of this particular cubicle farm, passing his approval down to a loyal serf. "Precisely, my dear."

He got up, waddling around the desk to rest his plump hands on her shoulders. Laserka tried not to laugh at the similarity of this situation to western "sexual harassment training" videos. He gave her shoulders a squeeze that was likely meant to be sooth-ing and seductive, but it was more like a mentally challenged farm boy trying to cuddle a kitten and crushing it inadvertently to death. She winced and re-strained the urge to rake his face with her fingernails. For all his apparent softness, the squat gnome of a man had a grip like a vise.

"Why don't you take the rest of the day off, Kaya?" he suggested softly. "Perhaps go shopping for some-thing nice to wear this weekend."

"Why? What's happening then?" Laserka asked, genuinely curious.

"I have to attend a formal gala for a ranking party member," Batroykin replied. "It's mostly an official in-vitation. I'd prefer to have a winsome, but skilled op-erative with me than my wife. In case the Chechens decide to cause unnecessary drama at the event."

Laserka resisted the urge to roll her eyes. She and other female agents had been on these "escort mis-sions" before, and they always ended up with skimpy dresses and unwanted gropes under their skirts. "I'm honored, sir. But my paycheck has already been spent."

Batroykin returned to his seat behind the desk, pulling out a small plastic card. "Since this is an official sortie, you can use an agency purchase card."

Laserka raised an eyebrow, taking the plastic.

"Dismissed, Kaya," Batroykin said. "Oh, and my preference is for red, backless dresses. And make it a good one. These are important people, and they'll know cheap off-the-rack crap at first blush."

"Thank you, sir," Laserka replied, wondering how she could get out of attending the function.

TRYING TO FIND A TRENDY and affordable backless dress in Moscow was hardly something that Kaya Laserka was familiar with. She would have had better luck locating a five kilogram package of Afghan Black Tar heroin or a cache of smuggled Heckler & Koch submachine guns. She sent out a few calls to friends on her cell phone, but the circles she ran in on the few brief moments she spent off the job were equally clueless about where to find something scarlet, slinky and fashionable. Finally, her friend Bertie gave her a suggestion that bordered on life saving.

"Why not give one of your informants a call? They should know where to find at least knockoffs of big-name dresses," Bertie said. "Your boss wants skin and curves, not a label. He wouldn't know Dior if the designer himself bit him and sang a chorus of 'I'm a fancy dress I am!'"

"My hero," Laserka said.

So here Laserka was, standing outside a warehouse

that was a covert marketplace for smuggled goods from outside of Russia. Though capitalism and western retail had invaded Moscow with a vengeance, despite the political backslide of the current administration, the black market was still prosperous, usually having better prices than the state- and foreign-owned department stores, as well as a better selection. Laserka had changed out of her office wear, which would have labeled her as a government official of some sort. Instead, she wore a black turtleneck, a hooded sweatshirt with an unauthorized rhinoceros logo on one lapel, and a pair of knockoff jeans that hugged her long, athletic legs. She kept her pistol on hand, in a small black leather purse just large enough to hold the compact weapon and two spare magazines.

There were a couple of burly men at the side door to the warehouse, their build and alertness pegging them as former Russian army, probably hired as much for their size as for their military training to serve this particular clandestine market. Laserka walked up to the pair as they glowered at her. "Is the store open?"

One man's eyes narrowed as if rusted gears struggled to motivate in his primitive skull. "Are you police?"

It was a standard challenge. If a buyer entered, denying his or her law-enforcement status, any evidence gathered on such an excursion was considered inadmissible to the well-bribed Russian judiciary. If Laserka did admit she was a cop, any purchase she made would be used against her by proprietors if she had to testify against them.

Since Laserka's department dealt mainly with narcotics and military-grade weaponry, not jeans or watches, she grinned. "Off duty. I need a dress."

The two hulking goons looked at each other, then chuckled. "Come on in, Off-duty."

"Make sure you give us a good look when you try your dress on," the other said with a leer.

Laserka winked and squeezed past the two hired muscle and entered the warehouse.

Inside, all she found were empty tables. Confusion seized Laserka for a moment. Certainly the proprietors toured a series of abandoned buildings to keep ahead of the Moscow police, but her informant, Vladimir, had said that the bazaar would be at this location today. It took only a few heartbeats to scan the empty warehouse for signs of life, and she whirled toward the doorway she'd just entered. She saw one of the six foot ex-Army hulks blocking the doorway, a wicked spring-blade knife locked in his hand.

Laserka leaped over an empty table, knowing she couldn't get to her concealed Makarov in time. The sound of the knife spring echoed in the old warehouse as a four inch spear-point blade rocketed out of the handle. The razor-sharp tip plucked at the hood of her sweatshirt as she dropped out of sight.

"You and that spring knife!" the other thug snarled, shoving his way into the warehouse. He held a suppressed pistol.

"Mine makes less noise," Spring-blade said, but he traded his empty handle for a more standard blade, a wickedly curved jambiya Arab-style knife.

The gunman grunted and triggered his handgun, bullets chasing after Laserka as she kept low, scrambling along the aisle of abandoned tables. "Stand still, Off-duty! It won't hurt so much!"

The off-duty RIA agent flipped a table on its side as a barricade against the pistol-toting killer. Robbed of power by the suppressor they passed through, the slowed bullets plunked limply against the aluminum tabletop. The shield gave her the time to pull her Makarov from her purse. With a flick of her thumb, the pistol was live and ready to fire. She rolled out into the open and sighted on the gun-toting assassin. The gunman hadn't expected Laserka to take the low road, firing from prone. He had been waiting for her to pop over the top of her barricade.

The Makarov barked twice, bullets punching into the would-be murderer's center of mass. The hot little 9 mm rounds cracked the big man's sternum, but their impact only seemed to stagger him. Laserka swung her aim up to the middle of the stunned thug's face and cranked off two more shots that obliterated the goon's face.

The table barricade rattled loudly as it was slapped aside by the burly knife man.

"You're supposed to die, bitch!" the thug roared, lunging at her.

Laserka rolled, firing one shot at the blade-wielding killer as her Makarov passed across him. She was rewarded by a cry of pain from the raging slasher. The big killer landed on the concrete floor, the jambiya jarred from his fingers as he landed. Laserka was struggling to her feet when a massive paw wrapped around her gun hand.

Training took over and Laserka let herself be pulled

in closer to her large opponent. With his strength adding to her momentum, she powered an elbow into the hollow of the burly assassin's throat. The jolt was enough to shock him into releasing her arm. Laserka stumbled back, raising the Makarov again.

The pistol barked three times, recoil trying to wrest her off target, but Laserka held on tightly, punching the last of her magazine through her opponent's face.

Panting, Laserka denied a wave of relief that wanted to pass through her. She reloaded her gun quickly.

Batroykin and Vladimir had set her up to be murdered.

## CHAPTER FOUR

Bolan slapped the cheek of his prisoner, trying to get him to wake up. It was a relatively gentle action, but the assassination team leader bit down hard. The head killer had only started to blink with returning consciousness when something crunched in his back teeth. The sound of the breaking capsule, combined with a sudden fit of convulsions had Bolan rushing to pry the man's mouth open. It was too late, almond-smelling foam bubbling out of the dead man's mouth.

The corpse's eyes rolled up in his head, and Bolan cursed that he didn't have time to retrieve the other unconscious death squad member that he had left behind the bar. Taking a paper towel, Bolan cleaned up the dead man's mouth, wiping bubbling drool from his lips. Pulling out his PDA, Bolan clicked a picture of the lifeless face. As an afterthought, he took the dead fingers and dipped them into ink from a broken pen and used a sheet of complimentary stationery to record the corpse's fingerprints.

Bolan looked over the Uzi and the magazines he'd

confiscated in the assassination attempt. He took some clear adhesive tape and laid it along the bodies of the magazines, then laid out the strips on more plain white paper. Close examination of the tape picked up three or four good, readable fingerprints. The warrior took a moment to compare the results with the prints taken off the corpse sitting limply in the chair. To his sharp eyes, they appeared different enough to be worth copying and transmitting back to Stony Man Farm. Thanks to the science of forensics, Bolan was able to disprove the adage, "dead men tell no tales."

Bolan linked up with Aaron Kurtzman at Stony Man Farm in the electronic ether utilizing his wireless secured broadband connection from his laptop.

"I thought you told Hal that you were going on vacation," Kurtzman said without preamble.

"It turned into a busman's holiday," Bolan confessed. "A friend of mine ended up on the receiving end of a Russian-speaking murder team."

"Russian speaking? That will narrow down the database to compare these faces to," Kurtzman replied. "Oh, you've got fingerprints, too?"

"Grabbed some enemy weapons. The prints came along with the spare ammunition," Bolan explained. "Scotland Yard have anything yet on the bodies I left at the docks?"

"The dead are at the morgue at the East Metropolitan Police crime laboratory," Kurtzman said. "Eight, including your friend. You said you left another behind? There aren't any reports of suspects in custody."

"Run the latent prints first, then," Bolan requested. "The magazine came from his harness. It might help me track him down."

"Running them through both IAFIS and its Interpol counterpart," Kurtzman replied, referring to the Integrated Automated Fingerprint Identification System maintained by the Federal Bureau of Investigation. "Think of any other databases to check them against?"

"These people were well-trained, so try to hack into the Russian Defense Department," Bolan suggested. "All records, even the closed files."

"That would take a lot more time," Kurtzman said. "We're not dealing with a state-of-the-art U.S. agency's computer system."

"I figured as much," Bolan answered. "I'm going to check with a few friends I have here in the Metropolitan Police. Maybe they have some suggestions for London's Russian immigrant crime problem."

"Hal won't be particularly pleased with you hitting up old contacts. You're not supposed to exist, Striker," Kurtzman warned.

"Then don't tell Hal. I've been around the globe hundreds of times. The folks I've met are the same people who make me seem almost omniscient," Bolan said. "Computer hacking and satellite photography aren't the only ways for someone to gather information."

"What about your prisoner?" Kurtzman asked. "Is he doing any talking?"

"Only if Hell has its own version of Saint Peter as a receptionist," Bolan replied. "He bit down on a cyanide capsule."

"That's old-school," Kurtzman commented. "Haven't seen a Russian bite down on one of those in ages."

"He woke up as my prisoner, wrists tied. Plus, we were in a dark garage," Bolan pointed out. "He probably thought I was going to hook his nipples or testicles up to a live battery."

"Water boarding is the new vogue," Kurtzman said. "Less painful and less chance of death."

"Neither way is my style," Bolan countered. "But how was he to know that?"

"Truth told," Kurtzman said. "The Russian defense records are a garbled mess. I doubt the programmers have even heard of indexing software. That even presumes all of those fingerprints are stored electronically and not in metal filing cabinets."

"What about IAFIS and Interpol?" Bolan asked.

"Scan's still running," Kurtzman replied. "This is real life. These checks don't happen as quickly as a commercial break, Striker."

"Give me a call on my PDA, then. I've got people to run down," Bolan said.

"Keep your powder dry, Striker," Kurtzman said, logging off.

Bolan went to the car and took out his standard concealed carry harness, replacing the Storm with his familiar Beretta 93R machine pistol and the rifle-accurate and powerful .44 Magnum Desert Eagle. With a death squad on the loose in the streets of London, informed of his interference, the Executioner knew that it was time to load up for bear.

In this particular case, the ursine was a breed Bolan had hunted before, a ghost species he'd hoped had disappeared with the fall of the Berlin Wall.

Unfortunately, the Soviet Bear was still a living, vital threat, and its predatory hunger had claimed the lives of two of Bolan's old allies.

Hunting season was on again.

THE LADY DETECTIVE was still pretty, Bolan reflected as he folded his tall frame into the passenger seat of the compact car she'd driven to the rendezvous.

"Gunfight at night, then you ring me up. There's got to be a better way to arrange a date with me," she said.

Bolan smiled. "I missed you, too, detective. How's your partner?"

"Back at the station. Care to mention anything about the bodies you piled up?" the detective inquired.

"Russian speakers. Well-armed and coordinated," Bolan said. "They were skilled, too."

The detective shrugged, brushing back her golden hair. "Not skilled enough. You're alive."

"They hit their intended target," Bolan confessed. "Vitaly Alexandronin."

"Familiar name. I didn't catch that particular case, but his wife was a reporter who ended up beaten into a coma," the lady cop replied. "Case ended up with dead ends, but it stunk like a pile of rotted fish."

"Vitaly told me he felt she was assassinated because she was snooping into Chechen refugees, picking up stories about the government's crackdown on the rebels," Bolan told her. "I didn't leave too much behind, but you examine those guys. There might be links between them and Catherine."

"They took out the wife in a beating, but brought machine guns and rockets for the husband?" the detective asked. Her lips pursed in disbelief.

"Vitaly was KGB and Russian Intelligence. He spent time doing all manner of dangerous things for his country before he offended the old guard," Bolan explained.

"That begins to make sense," the cop said. She sighed. "I remember when I got involved in one of your operations. My sister ended up dead and we had to drop my partner off at an emergency room. I still feel the ache in my ribs when it gets rainy and cold."

"Rainy and cold in London? Ever think of moving to Jamaica?" Bolan asked.

"Sure, and then you show up down there hunting heroin smugglers, and zombie lords pop out of the woodwork," the detective mused out loud. "Running afoul of Bloody Jack was enough horror movie for one lifetime, thank you."

Bolan shrugged. "Is the coroner still our old friend from that case?"

"No, he retired," the lady cop confessed. "It'd be a new guy who might actually be fooled by your identification."

"Is he skilled, though? I'd hate to run a wild-goose chase because I couldn't get the right info from forensics," Bolan replied.

"Metro Homicide's medical examiners aren't complete primates in comparison to your flashy American crime solvers," the woman quipped. She took a deep breath, looking out the windshield at the alley they were parked in. "I'm sorry I exploded all over you that night, Cooper."

Bolan rested a comforting hand on her shoulder. "I know exactly how you felt. Remember, I had my sister murdered, as well."

"Do you need any hands-on help with this?" she asked.

Bolan shook his head. "I don't have any support on this one. It's a personal mission."

"So then you do need an extra gun hand," she offered.

"I appreciate it, but I've seen enough friends die in the past few hours. The next time I blow through London, I promise if it's a quiet trip…"

"We'll have tea together?" the detective asked. She drew Bolan in for a tight hug. She felt the bulk of Bolan's gun under his jacket. "Your life never works out that way, Cooper. Even if you do make it back here, you won't have quiet time to spare."

Bolan nodded. "True. Just take care of yourself, Mel."

"I'd say the same for you, but…" She handed a small notebook to the warrior. "This is everything our Russian mob expert had on the local families. Might want to check out the Borscht Bolt. It's a restaurant-turned-club for the Slavic set."

Bolan smiled. "This won't get back to your superiors?"

"After our last dance through this town, I'm bulletproof." She started the car as Bolan climbed out.

She sighed. "Don't make too much of a mess for me, Cooper."

Bolan waved to the woman as she drove off. She was one hell of a good cop. He wished her safe travels until they met again.

THE EXECUTIONER PULLED UP to the London Metropolitan Police Crime Laboratory and Forensic Science center. He secured his car and slipped his identification from his war bag. The badge identified him as Special Agent Matt Cooper of the FBI. Brognola would be put out to know that Kurtzman and Stony Man coordinator Barbara Price had set him up as being an interested party in the deaths of suspected Russian organized crime figures in London. His cover was that he was part of an Interopol task force tracking *mafiya* activity across Europe and the British Isles.

There was indeed such a task force. Price meticulously kept abreast of major organized investigations around the globe, thanks to her liaisons with the international intelligence community. Fostering an encyclopedic knowledge of national and international events allowed her to slip Bolan, Able Team and Phoenix Force into operational positions with a minimum of intrusive appearance. Stony Man Farm was able to place its operations teams quietly and efficiently with the establishment of such a road map.

Bolan doffed the Beretta 93R machine pistol and its shoulder holster. While it was hard to imagine a federal agency approving a mammoth handgun like the Desert Eagle, it was still not outside of the ordinary. Contrarily, an extended-magazine, suppressed machine pistol was over the top for even the most paranoid of gunslingers. Bolan solved the dilemma of a backup pistol with the Compact Px4, supplemented by three spare 20-round magazines.

Ready for action, Bolan entered the crime laboratory. The Metro cops waved him through after a thorough examination of his credentials and a frisk that revealed Bolan's personal arsenal. Given that he was an American FBI agent, and their familiarity with the Bureau's mandate of two service pistols at all times, the London cops cleared him through the medical examination wing.

"Just let us know if you need a rocket launcher down there," the bobby at the desk told him.

Bolan laughed. "That's why I pack this bazooka." He patted the Desert Eagle.

That elicited a grin from the traditionally unarmed British peace officer. "Oh, good. Usually you Yanks don't pack your senses of irony for a trip over here."

"I found room in my carry-on bag," Bolan returned with a smile. The light banter helped Bolan fit in despite the firepower he was packing. A little humor was one of the Executioner's favorite tools for forging a quick friendship. The shared joke now could mean a vital trust gained later on.

Bolan slowed down as he saw a trio of men wearing coveralls and carrying toolboxes cross an intersection ahead of him. While it wasn't uncommon to see maintenance men walking through the halls of any building, there was something in the brief glimpse Bolan had caught that set his neck hairs to stand. Though not a student of metaphysics and the scientific explanations for sixth senses and danger precognition, the soldier was aware that the subconscious mind had a vastly more powerful means of analyzing potential threats. He was aware simply because he had experienced it on countless occasions, to the point that he trusted his hunches as much as the latest satellite or radio intelligence.

Doing a quick review of his memory of the three men, he envisioned them in his mind's eye. His subconscious mind opened up and that was when Bolan pegged the trio as Slavic men with traditional *mafiya* tattoos visible on their necks. The precise formation that they walked in pegged them as military men and their coveralls were loose, yet lumpy enough to be concealing more than just cell phones and pocket-knives.

Bolan picked up his pace, rounding the corner in time to see the three men halted at a checkpoint just outside of the morgue. The policeman at the entrance was asking for their identification. Bolan's combat computer kicked into overdrive as one of the "workmen" knifed a rigid hand into the peace officer's throat. He charged down the hall as the British cop seized up. Bolan recognized the blade hand technique as being a Spetsnaz unarmed attack meant to collapse a person's windpipe.

The cop had only a minute left in his life as he would choke to death. The trio of assassins pushed past him into the morgue. Bolan plucked his pocket-knife out of its sheath and skidded to the police officer's side. "I need a straw or a pen!"

The order was brusque and direct, and while the sudden bark was stunning and confusing, one of the nurses caught on to him, spotting the bruise rapidly forming on the policeman's throat and the knife in Bolan's hand. "A tracheotomy!"

She plucked a pen from her pocket, biting one end, then the other off. Bolan held the policeman still, kneeling on the man's forearm to keep him from blocking the incision. To punch a knife point through the tough, fibrous material of the trachea was difficult, but could be done quickly. Bolan speared the blade in vertically, along the grain of the windpipe, rather than go crosswise. Air suddenly hissed out through the blood-burbling wound, and the nurse pushed the hollow body of the pen tube into the cut.

"I'm going after the men who did this," Bolan told her. "Keep him stable!"

Before she could even sputter "be careful" the warrior pulled his Desert Eagle and charged after the covert kill squad. Bolan couldn't spare any more time than was necessary to rescue a fellow warrior from choking to death on a collapsed airway. The cleanup crew was on a kill mission to eliminate the evidence of their conspiracy.

More people would end up dead if the Executioner didn't act quickly.

LUKYAN BELKIN, THE LEADER of the cleanup crew, rubbed his sore fingertips after spearing them into the throat of the nosy, interfering bobby in the role of "rental cop" outside the morgue. He noticed a blur of movement from down the hall, but not seeing a gun in the running man's hand, he pushed into the crime laboratory's medical-examination ward. "Lock the door behind us."

One of his companions leaned into the heavy steel door and threw the bolt. The squad member jammed a desk against the door to further hamper pursuit through the doorway. Once it was secured, Belkin reached into his toolbox, casting aside the drawer of utensils. Screwdrivers and hammers clattered onto the floor, revealing an area denial mine inside the case. The bomb was basically a canister of flammable fuel that could be dispersed by a nonincendiary charge. Once the fuel spread into a room-filling cloud, a spark would ignite the airborne droplets. The resultant fireball would incinerate everything in the morgue.

Obviously, Belkin didn't intend to stay in the area when the blast occurred. His other companion cuffed a white-coated woman in the head with the butt of his machine pistol. The woman collapsed to the floor, staggered by the force of the blow. Belkin set about placing the trio of thermobaric charges at various points in the morgue to insure maximum devastation. The ally who had barred the doors threw open cabinets in the wall where the corpses were laying in cold storage. Their orders were to eliminate any evidence of the dead assassins found at the docks.

The fuel-air explosives would render everything in the morgue a useless, pulped and scorched mass. No chances were being taken in this regard.

A .44 Magnum round smashed through the lock that had just been secured. The metal door shuddered, and Belkin froze in surprise. He hadn't seen any gunmen in the hall, and few London cops had handguns. Fewer still carried hand cannons with the power to penetrate a fireproof door. A powerful shoulder forced the door open, hurling aside the desk that was supposed to have barred it shut. Whoever was interfering with the cleanup crew had to have had prodigious strength. Belkin unslung his MAC-10 machine pistol from its coverall concealed holster, then fired the weapon at the door.

A spray of 9 mm rounds splashed off of the steel panel of the bashed-open door. A huge muzzle flash filled the air where the door had opened, and Belkin grimaced as he took a thunderbolt to his chest armor.

The other two Russian hitters whipped their MAC-10s up in response to the Desert Eagle's roar, but the Executioner had already slithered through the narrowly opened doorway, dropping prone to the floor. He was behind the cover of a countertop and cabinets where coroners would store their surgical supplies and wash up in the sink. The heavy countertop and the strong wood needed to support it gave the interloper considerable protection from the lightweight machine pistols that the team had brought with them.

"Get the woman!" Belkin shouted. "We need a hostage!"

The Russian operative winced as he crawled behind an overturned autopsy table. Being struck in the chest with a .44 Magnum slug, even while wearing body armor, was not one of the things that Belkin had ever wanted to experience. He was fairly certain that the bullet had broken a rib or two. He looked to see where his compatriots were and what they were doing. The unconscious morgue attendant laying on the floor stirred, but the two cleaners were cut off from her as the man behind the counter pinned them down with blazing fire from his entrenched position.

"I have a clean shot at the woman!" Belkin announced loudly. "Desist and pull back, or I'll kill her!"

A smoking hole punched in the steel of the autopsy table, the bullet having penetrated mere inches from Belkin's head.

"You try making that shot, your body won't have to be taken very far," Bolan returned. "Your choice!"

Belkin snarled. It was a standoff, and the timers on his bombs were counting down.

Only two minutes remained before the morgue would disintegrate in a fireball.

## CHAPTER FIVE

Mack Bolan reloaded his Desert Eagle, fitting a carefully calibrated stack of antiarmor loads. His initial shot against the leader of the cleanup squad had been with his conventional 240-grain hollowpoint rounds. They had been enough to tear through the fire door or the relatively slender metal of the autopsy table, but against Kevlar and trauma plates, the Executioner needed something with a lot more punch. This magazine was filled with 350-grain, tungsten-cored .429-inch slugs that Bolan kept on hand for when he had to take on criminals in an armored personnel carrier or corrupt thugs hiding behind the protection of million-dollar, tank-skinned limousines. The copper skin wrapped around the hardened cores would protect the gun from the steel-mauling tungsten centers, and the powder charge was balanced to cycle the action of the big Israeli autoloader. Once he caught a glimpse of one of the coverall-clad foes, they would be dead, no matter what they wore.

During the reload, Bolan spotted a munition placed

on the floor off to the side of the autopsy room. He recognized it as a fuel-air mine, designed for destroying
enemy forces or stockpiles of ammunition and arms
inside cave complexes. The FAE mines would also
work with deadly efficiency to turn every ounce of or-
ganic material inside the morgue into charred ash.
From the look of the one he saw, it was on a countdown
timer, hence Belkin's urgency to get a hostage. Bolan
didn't know how much time he had left, but considering the speed and precision of the Russian crew, it
couldn't be much longer than a minute.

The enemy gunmen were reloading their machine
pistols, contemplating their options as the doomsday
numbers ticked down. One of the shooters swung into
view, his MAC-10 blazing. Another raced into the
open, rushing toward the stunned woman they had
pegged as their hostage.

Bolan dived out onto the tile floor, 9 mm rounds
plucking at his sleeve and pant leg as the enemy gunner sprayed to keep him contained. Sheer quickness
had taken him outside the shooter's line of fire, and he
hit the ground in a slide. The second gunman was in
full charge toward the fallen morgue attendant, not no-
ticing the Executioner until a .44 Magnum armor-
piercing slug smashed through his vest, coring deep
into his heart as if he were clad only in tissue, not
trauma plate.

"Son of a bitch!" Belkin snapped, watching the spray
of arterial blood gush out from both sides of his dying
comrade's perforated torso. The man's forward momentum gave him two remaining steps on his final run before he crashed face-first to the floor in a boneless heap.

"Bastard!" the other Russian gunman shouted, swinging out into the open to get a better angle on Bolan.

The Executioner's next shot tore through the vengeful Russian's shoulder, blasting the muscle, bone and cartilage of the joint in an explosive detonation. Blood sprayed from the horrendous injury, and the limb sagged on the few remaining ligaments of sinew that hadn't been destroyed by the Desert Eagle's rocketing talon of copper and tungsten. The shooter folded in pain, his gun hand pinning the dangling arm in place. Bolan ended his suffering with a third shot that caught the Russian at the bridge of his nose. It was as if someone had taken a hatchet to a melon, the top of the man's skull flying backward in a spraying volcano of brains and gore.

Two down, one to go, but there was also the threat of the thermal charges. Bolan charged toward the overturned autopsy table that the team leader had taken cover behind. On the run, he spotted a second of the mines in the far corner of the morgue floor. Given their size and the number of toolboxes that had been brought in by the "maintenance men," he estimated that there was a third atmosphere-destroying bomb that had been brought in by the cleanup crew. As one part of the brilliant combat computer that was the Executioner's brain contemplated minimizing the damage, the rest of his consciousness was focused on bringing down the last of the lethal conspirators. With a vault, Bolan leaped over the upturned table. He spotted his opponent in midair and, using the edge of the table as a fulcrum, he steered himself feet-first down into the cleaner's gut.

The air exploded from the Russian's lungs and his head slammed back against the steel tabletop.

Bolan kicked the machine pistol out of the stunned man's hand, skittering the weapon wildly across the tile floor. Belkin reached up and grabbed Bolan's belt. The soldier responded with the heavy trapezoidal wedge of the Desert Eagle's muzzle, lashing it across the man's jaw. Having incapacitated the last of the conspiratorial gunmen, Bolan holstered the Desert Eagle and rushed to the closest mine.

The Executioner had hoped for a control lever that would allow him to disarm the explosive, but the enemy had sabotaged the mines' control panels. The disengage mechanism had been destroyed.

Plan two, Bolan thought. The destructive power of the mines wasn't a factor of the amount of explosives in them, but a mechanism of the fact that their concentrated fuel was dispersed through the atmosphere in an aerosol suspension that made the oxygen in the air into additional reactant for the secondary spark. By denying a large area of combustible air to the devices, they could be significantly defanged. It would require an airtight, heavy steel container to minimize the blasts.

Luckily, the refrigerated, hermetically sealed body-storage drawers in the morgue were exactly what Bolan needed. He shoved the mine into one shelf and swung the heavy steel door shut, snapping down the locking bolt. There was a brief sigh from the metal panel as the cabinet sealed itself, the airtight closure sucking into place.

"What…what's hap…" the woman said, finally able to speak and move after her ordeal. Bolan scooped up a second mine from the tile floor.

"You need to get out of here," Bolan ordered. "These are bombs."

The morgue worker's eyes widened. "Those drawers are under negative air pressure."

Bolan paused for a half step. "Can you kill the ventilation?"

He continued his quick rush to stow the bombs away, parking the second mine into another empty storage drawer. Again, the door slammed shut, the locking bolt snapping into place just before the hiss of the air seal slurped the door tightly closed.

The woman limped toward a wall panel. She was bleeding from the forehead where the skin had been split, and it was likely that she had suffered head trauma when the Russian had struck her. "Ventilation shut-off…"

Bolan hauled the last thermic mine into his grasp and saw that there were no more empty shelves. He rushed to one of the sliding drawers where a dead Russian lay, his body riddled with bullet holes. Bolan grabbed the corpse under the arm and dragged him off the metal sliding slab. A spill on the floor would likely contaminate whatever evidence was on the body. If the mine detonated, it would kill dozens of people in the halls outside of the morgue.

The corpse flopped on the tile and Bolan shoved the mine in place. Slam! Latch! Hiss! Sealed.

Bolan spun away from the wall and dived toward the emergency ventilation cutoff. He punched the button hard enough to open a laceration on his palm, and the whole morgue seemed to gasp as if it were a living creature. Bolan scooped the woman into his arms and tucked her tightly into the corner, using his broad back to shield her. He'd equalized the pressure in his ears before firing the first shot from his bellowing Desert Eagle, so any explosion wouldn't rupture his eardrums. He hoped that his body was enough to shield the morgue attendant, his hands cupped over her ears to protect them.

Belkin moved groggily, reaching for the handgun tucked under his coveralls. "Fucking...interloper..."

Those were the conspirator's final words. If he had a thought behind them, it was cut off. The whole wall of the morgue devoted to body storage shook as if a train had crashed into the building. The hatches that contained the bombs were torn off of their hinges. One of them pulverized Belkin as it rocketed off, powered by the force of the explosive mine. The concussion wave bleeding off the wall hurled bodies to the floor, both the living and the dead. Bolan and his charge had been lifted off their feet by the heaving wall, but the soldier twisted so that the morgue attendant was cushioned by his body.

The storage drawers had done their job perfectly. Despite the wreckage wrought by their blasted hatches and a few fluttering pieces of burning paperwork that had been stored too close to the wall, the murderous power of the bombs had been smothered.

Bolan helped the woman to her feet, one hand under the back of her head to keep her stable. "Are you all right?"

"I'm Annette Brideshead," she answered, large brown eyes blurry and unfocused. "I'm the medical examiner in charge of this shift."

Bolan supported her, sliding his arm under her shoulder to keep her upright. Obviously she was mentally disconnected, not answering the question offered. "Can you walk?"

Brideshead's unfocused eyes danced across Bolan's face. He knew that her head would be wobbly atop her neck if he hadn't been holding her. "I'm forty-five years old. I've been walking most of… Oh, dear."

Bolan turned and saw that the leader of the cleanup crew was sandwiched between a storage hatch and the twisted wreckage of an autopsy table. At least Bolan assumed it was the leader. The ragged, bloody stump of a neck was all that remained above the shoulders. "Sorry for the mess, Annette."

"The doors… You said those were bombs. Poison gas doesn't act like that when it's released, does it?" Brideshead inquired.

"Not gas, not like you thought. But it was good that you shut down the negative air pressure in the drawers," Bolan replied. He didn't want to think of the destruction that would have occurred if the aerosolized fuel had spread to the ventilation system, sucked up by the intake valves.

A policeman, the one Bolan had joked with only moments before, entered. He had a Glock 17 in hand and was ready for action. The bobby relaxed upon seeing Bolan ministering to Brideshead. "I thought you were only kidding about rocket launchers."

Bolan looked around the corpse-strewed, blast-shaken morgue. He sat Brideshead down and folded his jacket to cushion her head. "Someone didn't want me looking at the bodies stored here."

"Haven't these chaps heard of court orders?" the bobby asked as he holstered his pistol.

"That's not the way these people operate," Bolan replied. "Are there paramedics on the way?"

"Yes. Was that you that gave me mate a straw in the neck?" the officer asked.

"Headless over there crushed his trachea. He all right?" Bolan asked.

"Well, he was already laying down when the building bounced. He's mighty thankful to you, Agent Cooper," the cop said. Looking around at the mess, he sighed. "And for saving the rest of us from a right nasty bump, I'm adding my thanks, too."

Bolan nodded in appreciation. "The sad thing is, I'm not done here."

The British cop chuckled. "If it's all the same, I won't go running to any Russian restaurants for a while, Mr. *Mafiya* task force member."

Bolan managed a weak smile for the officer. He patted the notebook in his pocket, unable to keep such a promise.

IT HAD TAKEN HOURS for Bolan to be cleared after the battle of the morgue. It took that long for the London Metropolitan police to be convinced of the order of events, especially the slicing open of the windpipe of a fellow officer, even with a crushed trachea. It also took that much time for the lawmen to return Bolan's Desert Eagle, not that the Executioner hadn't had spares stored back at his safehouse.

At least Bolan got a couple of mugs of coffee out of the interview process, which he followed up with an order of fish and chips to fill his empty stomach. Bolan tossed a French fry out the car window and picked up his PDA, dialing the Farm.

"Talked your way out of another mess, Striker?" Hal Brognola's voice came over the line. Brognola was the director of the Sensitive Operations Group, based at Stony Man Farm, Virginia.

"Can't go running to Daddy every time I stub my toe. I handled it," Bolan replied. "I suppose Aaron let you in on my progress so far."

"Two gun battles in less than twenty-four hours. He couldn't keep me out of the loop after that. I'm sorry, Striker, but as much as you want to keep this away from government interference, this has become an issue of national security," the big Fed told him.

"What have you picked up on this thing?" Bolan inquired.

"The two faces you sent Aaron belong to Spetsnaz troopers reported killed in action by the Russian Department of Defense," Brognola stated. "Officially, you didn't kill anyone."

"So I'm fighting the Special Forces of the living dead?" Bolan asked. He couldn't keep the sarcasm out of his voice. "I knew the trend in horror movies was for smarter and faster walking dead, but they're as much corpses as I am, Hal."

"Now they really are dead." Brognola sighed. "Of course, you remember your friends in Russian Intelligence."

"Friends for real, Hal?" Bolan asked. "I'm a little too tired for wordplay."

"No. Real friends," Brognola emphasized. "A Russian Intel operative named Kaya Laserka just avoided being killed by a couple of thugs."

"Laserka? She was Alexandronin's trainee and partner. Did she get an e-mail from Vitaly?"

"Apparently so. She reported the incident and a friendly operator to Stony Man gave the report to us," Brognola said. "She couldn't get directly involved, and I don't want to compromise her identity."

"A friendly Russian agent?" Bolan asked. That lifted his mood some. "And a woman, so that really doesn't narrow things down. Where is she?"

"Well, she's holed up in her apartment for now. She was given a quick 'how-to' on going to ground. Barb gave her the lesson."

"Barb" was Barbara Price, mission controller at Stony Man.

"And my description, so she doesn't put a bullet in my head?" Bolan asked.

"Yes. I've got a flight for you leaving in two hours," Brognola said.

"Get me one around midnight, Hal," Bolan requested. "I've got one or two more stops to make here in London."

"Damn it, Striker. What now?" Brognola complained.

"One of the men who was sent to kill Vitaly got away last night," Bolan said. "He's the only living witness that I have to what's going on. I need some answers."

"And you can't let a guilty party stroll away from a murder attempt on a friend," Brognola added.

"If I can't protect the people who I care about, I can

at least make certain that those who meant them harm get the punishment they deserve," Bolan said.

"Does it quiet the ghosts?" Brognola asked.

"It placates my guilt," Bolan answered. "Some."

"All right. The plane will wait as long as it takes for you to show up, Striker. It's a private charter, so he can delay for you," Brognola told him. "Good hunting."

"Thanks, Hal," Bolan said. He closed the PDA, fired up the engine and drove toward the next battle in his War Everlasting.

KAYA LASERKA PUT the phone down after the call from the woman named Barbara. She had arranged for a hotel room, quietly, and informed Laserka to expect to meet with a man who went by the identity of FBI Agent Matt Cooper. The Russian woman didn't like that idea. "There was one man, several years ago. His name was Belasko."

"You'll find that Cooper is everything you're expecting from Belasko," Price told her.

"Everything?" Laserka inquired. "I doubt that anyone could match the man I knew. All right, what does Cooper look like?"

"Six three, black hair, powerful build," Price rattled off.

"And cold blue eyes?" Laserka asked.

"Exactly."

Laserka smiled, recognizing the general appearance of the man she had known as Belasko. "He'll do fine, then."

"I'm glad we understand each other," Price replied. "Don't worry. Help is on the way."

Laserka packed a bag, slipping her Makarov back onto her belt's inside-the-waistband holster. She draped her sweater over the handgun's butt to conceal it, then she tucked another weapon, a tiny Glock 26, into her purse. She added two spare 15-shot magazines originally designed for the slightly larger Glock 19. Technically, the tiny Austrian pistol was considered a better design than her trusted old Makarov, smaller in length and height, chambered for a more powerful cartridge, and holding eleven shots. Still, the Russian Mak was flat, and its butt had room for all of her fingers on its comfortable grip. It just felt nicer than the teeny Glock. The 9 mm Mak had never let her down. Laserka knew sentimentality toward a tool meant to keep her alive was considered foolish, but she had an attachment that translated into comfort and superior skill.

Barbara had the right idea. Sticking around her apartment would only make her a sitting duck. If the men sent to kill her could find her while she was hunting for a dress on the black market, then they could easily be able to make a move on her in her own home. She tucked her purse tight under her arm and was ready to leave through the front door of her apartment. She heard the floorboards creak on the other side.

Since she wasn't expecting visitors, she pivoted, scooped up her overnight bag and rushed for her window. A shadow fell across the fire escape and she put on the brakes, reaching for her Makarov. She looked toward the kitchen and saw that the light through the window in that room remained unbroken. Of course there wasn't a fire escape at that point on the ledge, but Laserka hustled into the kitchen, drawing the sliding door shut behind her.

As it closed, she heard the front door rattle violently under a ferocious kick. She moved to the kitchen window. The front door shook again. When she heard the window just off of the fire escape rise, she opened the kitchen window at the same time. From the front, she heard the apartment door crack on the third kick. She saw the back of a man pulling through the fire-escape window as she slid out onto the ledge.

Laserka's overnight bag was small and light, thankfully. If she'd been burdened with heavier luggage, balancing on the slender lip of cinder block would have been impossible. She let it hang on its shoulder strap, freeing her hands to grab the railing on the fire escape. She swung her legs down to the next landing, lowering herself to stand on the rail. Popping in front of the window that the second intruder had just gone through would have just been asking for a fight. She braced on the wall, then stepped onto the landing with a minimum of rattling metal.

"Where the hell is she?" she heard one man grunt.

She paused. "Oleg, is there anyone on the street?"

"The kitchen!" another voice swore. Whoever these men were, they had coordination, but no inkling of operational communications security. Laserka padded down the fire-escape steps, putting layers of grating between herself and her apartment. Laserka's legs ached from the tension between speed and stealth on the metal steps. Still, she reached the bottom, apparently without being noticed. She clambered down the ladder, then cut away from the street, aware that Oleg and his friends might be watching her from above.

She walked four blocks before she walked down

into the subway. By the time her hunters finished clearing her apartment and surmised that she was in the wind, she was stepping onto a train car, heading for the hotel to await "Special Agent Matt Cooper."

Then, she'd start her own hunt, turning the tables on her tormentors.

## CHAPTER SIX

Mack Bolan was dressed to impress underneath his trench coat and wide-brimmed hat. Underneath the loose overcoat, he was snug in his skintight blacksuit and battle harness. The high-tech polymers of the uniform conformed to Bolan's musculature, a blend of fibers that provided the Executioner protection from burns in the middle of fires and offered a modicum of defense against small arms. Its composition also enabled it to protect him from the elements, insulating him from all but the most chilling cold and blazing heat. Aside from accentuating his phenomenal physique, the snugness of the uniform prevented him from snagging on anything in battle. His holsters for the Beretta 93R and the Desert Eagle hung on his battle harness openly, allowing him swift access to both handguns, while slit pockets and belt pouches bulged with compact munitions, impact weapons and other tools of his warrior trade. He'd blackened his face with greasepaint, affecting a terrifying war mask that was shaded by the wide brim of his hat. A war bag concealing a pair of Uzi submachine guns dangled from his gloved hand.

The Russian club was a compact urban fortress with small windows and heavy doors. Guards stood on duty at the front, and they were alert for potential threats. The *organasatya* gangsters were on edge now that the man known to some as "the American" was stalking them in London. Bolan had given them a bloody nose in this city on an earlier visit, so he was not an unknown quantity. He was as fresh in the memory of the few survivors of that encounter as a tidal wave or monsoon.

Bolan was here to tie up a loose end, and the remaining assassins were his last link to the old confederation that was willing to commit murders in two world capitals and attack the London Metropolitan police headquarters with blatant terror. Though he had transformed himself into a dark specter of vengeance, his plan was to cow their resistance through intimidation. Too many leads up the ladder had been lost over the past day due to unrestrained violence. Fear was going to be his primary weapon now.

Half a minute's work with a lock-pick gun gained him entry through a side door.

Bolan passed the maître d's podium and walked into the restaurant proper. Dozens of sets of eyes turned to look at him, frozen in the shock of his presence.

Nobody seemed quite certain what to make of the Executioner, although they all kept their hands well away from their weapons. Hopefully, Bolan would be able to keep his Scotland Yard ally from cleaning up another huge mess. That all depended on how hard

Bolan could ride the wave of intimidation he'd been surfing for the past few minutes.

Bolan reached into the gym bag, pulling out the empty Uzis by their barrels. "Yanos Shinkov. Would you explain where these weapons came from?"

The dozens of faces turned, almost in unison, toward a man sitting in a booth, stirring tea in a glass mug with a silver spoon. Shinkov tapped his spoon on the glass, knocking moisture from it, then he set the utensil down. He was a blunt-faced man with a mane of black hair that flared up from a widow's peak like a fountain of dark silk that stopped below his collar. The Russian mobster sighed, then held out his hand. "Take a seat, American. We can discuss this with civilized tongues."

Bolan strode through the restaurant, then dumped the Uzis in the middle of Shinkov's table. He took a seat across from the mobster. "Civilization is not something I trust in, Shinkov."

"Please, calm yourself. We are still hurting from the last time you visited vengeance upon us."

Bolan looked around. "Over twenty gunmen shows you have some fight left in you. And the Uzis I took from your men—"

"No," Shinkov replied, cutting him off quickly. "Those were not my men. Those who would work for us have no love for any person claiming authority back in Moscow."

Bolan frowned, keeping his glare cold. Shinkov was sweating and he took a quick sip of tea, as if to wash a lump stuck in his throat. "Are you not the leader of London's *organasatya?*"

"That I am, but the *mafiya* is not a tool of the Kremlin," Shinkov explained.

Bolan looked around the room. "Then why do half the faces I see in here belong to veterans of KGB operations in Great Britain?"

Shinkov cleared his throat. "These were men who had nothing after glasnost, the great peace accords between enemies separated by the iron curtain. They had no home to return to, so they needed someone to give their lives order and structure."

Bolan nodded. "And you needed more bullies to terrify the immigrants."

Shinkov winced at the accusation. "When Rastolev came here, he threatened us. He promised that he would drop the sky on us."

"What did Rastolev want from you to have peace?"

"Guns. You are right, those are my weapons," Shinkov said, sounding genuinely ashamed. "He also wanted protection and a safehouse."

"For fifteen men," Bolan said.

Shinkov's eyes widened at the estimation of Rastolev's forces. "Yes."

"So there are four left," Bolan said.

"Including Rastolev," Shinkov replied.

Bolan ran through his mental roster of cold-war era enemy operatives. Rastolev was the code name for a young, up-and-coming hard case who had allegedly been killed in action during the final, painful days of the Soviet occupation of Afghanistan. There had been rumors of his presence in various operations in the Commonwealth of Independent States, but unlike the Executioner, the rumors of Rastolev's existence were relegated to the same veracity as sightings of dinosaurs in the Congo. "Rastolev's supposed to be dead."

"The same could be said of you, American," Shinkov replied. "It's just that we are so familiar with your footprints, especially since they are still fresh on our necks."

"I would be flattered, but I didn't come here to have my ego massaged," Bolan growled.

"You came for answers," Shinkov said. "You want to know where Rastolev is, and who he could be working for."

"I already know about the Curved Knife and their operations in Chechnya," Bolan cut him off.

Shinkov swallowed hard again. "We do not say their name lightly."

"Of course not," Bolan replied. "They are a return to the bad old days of the KGB. They are the monsters who knock in the night and who make families disappear into meat grinders. They are the ones who taught the Middle East how to truly use terror as a weapon because they held all of the Soviet Union in check with a steady whip hand. They are the ones who gave a bottom-feeding minority the ability to order a billion believers into silence with their violence of action."

Shinkov sighed. "We are not saints, but we love our country. The Curved Knife is a return to the days of Hammer and Sickle. Once they get the Russia they want, things will be difficult for all on both sides of the law."

Shinkov slid a sheet of paper to the Executioner. He smiled. "The enemy of my enemy can be my friend."

Bolan looked at the address, memorizing it. "The London *organasatya* isn't my friend, Shinkov. But for now, we are sharing an enemy."

Bolan touched the address slip to a candle, then set the burning paper on his plate, watching the golden flower consume it, leaving behind only ashes. "Remember, you live because you're the lesser of two evils. You are the devil I know. Try not to become more familiar to me."

With that, the Executioner left the club, disappearing like a vengeful shadow into the cold, dark night.

THE NIGHT BEFORE, the hostel had been bustling as the Curved Knife operators were packed two to a single room, ready to go at the drop of a hat. Now the building was quiet, only three other tenants sharing the structure with Rastolev. He sighed, lighting another cigarette. He couldn't believe that the precision strike on the morgue to eliminate the captured bodies of their fallen comrades had been so completely derailed. Belkin was too skilled an agent to have been foiled by an unarmed London policeman whose only combat experience was a drunken skirmish after a soccer game. Whoever had interfered with that mission had to have been more than just some simple civil servant. That's why, as Rastolev smoked, he kept an Uzi submachine gun in his lap, fully loaded with the safety off.

Koriev entered after a polite knock. "Sir, the others have arrived with our reinforcements."

Rastolev smiled, stubbing out his cigarette. "Good. If our visitor arrives on schedule, he'll be expecting only a handful of men."

"Sir, these are not Spetsnaz assault troopers," Koriev countered. "They're just French Muslims. These are men who the French government forced to flee."

"Not the French," Rastolev answered his subordinate. "One Frenchman who thinks he's a lone action hero. They will go back to their cowardly ways once the Knife caresses that fool's throat."

Koriev shifted one foot to another. "Benik is handing out Glocks to the French. I wish they had more brains so that we could give them something that was actually effective…"

"They are here to add bodies to our numbers. Their extra presence will obfuscate the true odds and allow us to maneuver around the American," Rastolev explained. "While he is busy dealing with the Muslim hooligans, we will outflank him and catch him by surprise."

"More guns didn't mean a thing against *him* down in Mexico a few months back," Koriev said.

Rastolev rolled his eyes. "The American may have the *mafiya* pissing in its pants, frightened of its own shadow, but he is still just a human being. He may be skilled, but so are we. We are the cream of the crop, the force so special that we do what cannot be done by lesser men. We are the Curved Knife. We are the sickle that reaps the enemies of the proper leaders of our nation, and clears the chaff from the field. He won't be able to anticipate us."

Rastolev looked at his laptop. Thanks to a wireless network of security cameras, he could see all around the hostel with a single glance. The busload of young hooligans was spreading out to the positions pointed out by Benik. Rastolev didn't expect the undisciplined Muslim gang members to stay at their posts once the American started his attack, but the dispersal of their numbers would allow a steady stream of pressure against the interloping American long enough to buy Rastolev's surviving team time to surround, pin down and eliminate him.

If Rastolev could take out that kind of a threat, his position in the reorganized Russian government would be elevated to near godhood.

He took a sip of tea, trying to calm himself.

The American is not dead, Rastolev thought. Not yet.

THE EXECUTIONER WATCHED as the reinforcements slid into place around the battered, rundown apartment flats. There were two dozen young Arab and black men brought in, and the soldier recognized their type as one of the Russians handed out Glock handguns to each of them. They were refugee Muslims who had scurried away from France's initial crackdown on the riots inspired by their disenfranchised brethren around Paris. The French president had driven them into hiding. One of their bolt-holes was London, but other major European cities had communities that accepted their ostracized criminal brethren. While a vast majority of the disenfranchised youth were only manipulated to violence by silver-tongued demagogues, these young hooligans were part of a hard-core minority, people perfectly willing to kill, rape, burn and pillage with the flimsiest of justification.

These particular young men had cold, soulless eyes and scars on their faces and hands, the souvenirs of their lives of brutality. The healed cuts and abrasions on their hands were leftovers from inflicting harm, split knuckles from punching victims in the head, and crisscrossed palms and fingers showing healed lacerations left over from their grasps dislodging on knife handles as they stabbed those they considered prey.

The injuries on their faces came from their victims, scratch marks wrought in cheeks and foreheads where the battered and the murdered clawed out, using their fingernails as weapons. Bolan could tell from a glance that the men admiring their new combat pistols were as far from innocent angels as Bolan himself was from an ordinary soldier. Unlike the questionable patrons of the bar the night before, the warrior had proof of their activities scrawled in scar tissue on their skins and gleeful reaction to new weapons. A new means of killing had been handed to them along with the promise of murder before the rising of the sun. Their blood thirst would be sated this night, at least that is what the Russians had promised.

Bolan hated to dump another mass murder into Scotland Yard's lap, but twenty-four gunmen with an itch for homicide required a form of scratching that only the Executioner could provide. Bolan left his machine pistol, a Fabrique Nationale P-90 with a barrel-mounted suppressor, hidden under his duster. He pulled his double-bladed fighting knife, knowing that if he cut loose on full-auto and inspired a cross fire, the apartments around the hostel would catch bullets through their windows. The P-90 might have had a nominal "silencer," but it would still make noise and ruin the element of surprise he'd have over the Russian assassins.

Like it or not, the young bloods on hand were meant

to be cannon fodder and noisemakers, to buy the professionals time to outmaneuver Bolan. Taking out the would-be murderers with only a fighting knife would be next to impossible, but the Executioner had to even the odds with a minimum of fuss, as well as contain and eliminate the violent hooligans who would cause mayhem to spill over into the lives of innocent Londonites.

If Rastolev was setting up a trap specific to the Executioner, the Russian couldn't have constructed it better. The Executioner's fighting prowess was not to be matched, but his concern for innocent bystanders was paramount. In the midst of a residential neighborhood, Bolan's options were limited, hampered by his basic concerns for noncombatants.

Hand-to-hand combat would limit stray shots and noise, and even in the event of a firearm discharge, Bolan would be in their midst, so their bullets would be aimed inward, not out through windows. That would mean that the warrior would be in the heart of Rastolev's trap, surrounded by thugs and trained, motivated commandos, all the while pinned down and unable to use full-auto and grenades to even the odds. He'd have the focus of a swarm of bloodthirsty maniacs if he played the odds correctly.

To do that, though, Bolan had to make a near suicidal run. He rested his binoculars on the passenger seat of his car, turned off the interior dome light and exited his vehicle under the cover of darkness. With the Applegate knife tucked against his forearm, he headed for a causeway two doors down from Rastolev's headquarters. The black phosphate finish on the blade kept the fighting knife from being noticeable against his limb, just in case there were thugs on hand to patrol the whole block. In the gap between apartment buildings, Bolan sheathed the knife and peeled out of his duster. His blacksuit, snug against his chest and powerful limbs, was snag-free to allow him swift and unhindered movement. Bolan hopped up, bracing his hands and boots against the brick walls on either side of the causeway. The narrow passage gave him enough room to climb up between the two structures. It was a physically demanding crawl up four flights, but the Executioner's magnificent physical conditioning was up to the task. His arms and legs burned from the exertion, and he paused at the roof, not wanting to cause too much of a disturbance by flopping over the top of the building.

The brief respite helped to relax his muscles. Bolan kicked off one wall, dragging himself to the roof and slithering down like a snake in an effort to minimize his profile. If Rastolev had posted someone atop the hostel, they had to have had an excellent hiding spot. Bolan checked the rooftops carefully, letting his eyes, ears and instincts stretch out for indications of an enemy sniper hidden amid the chimneys and low walls around the roofs. The chimneys would have granted a good amount of cover and concealment, but the length of a marksman's rifle would still poke out, noticeable in the rooftop shadows. That was one thing in the Executioner's favor, but given compact weapons like the Uzi or Bolan's personal P-90 PDW, there could still be lethal firepower up here, fifty feet above the London streets.

Bolan got up, racing across the roof in a swift run. His dark silhouette was far from invisible, so he hoped that his sudden dash would attract the attention of any hidden enemies. At this height, a stray bullet would sail over innocents in their homes. It was a calculated risk, but no enemy rounds sought him out. With a leap, he crossed between buildings easily, landing in a momentum-bleeding somersault that brought him safely to a halt. Gathering himself, Bolan looked around for signs that his presence had been observed. So far, he was still unnoticed, but that could change at any moment.

A second leap brought him closer to his ultimate goal. He scanned for any changes in the roof line. No differences showed, but Bolan wasn't going to take a single thing for granted. He stayed low, scanning and seeking out opposition. The next leap would bring him down on top of Rastolev's headquarters, but each previous hop had raised a ruckus on the prior rooftops. A quieter landing would be required, or else the Russians and their called-in reinforcements would rush up to the fourth floor and start shooting.

Bolan paused at that realization, mentally going over the angles. At this level, an all-out gunfight, going straight up and down, would keep stray bullets from going toward neighboring buildings. He would have the battle focused on him and not on the other flats. It would entail extra risk on Bolan's part, but he would have the protection of ceiling and roofing materials that would slow down enemy bullets.

Bolan launched himself, his two hundred-plus-pound weight thumping on Rastolev's roof. Shouts arose from below. Almost immediately, an enemy handgun cracked, tar paper jerking as bullets sliced up through it.

"He's here! The American is here!" came an angry cry in Russian just before an AKM assault rifle opened up. Heavy steel-cored rifle bullets shattered through wood and plaster as if it were papier-mâché, the line of incessant, full-auto fire chewing closer and closer to Bolan as he struggled to his feet.

## CHAPTER SEVEN

Rastolev and Kroz heard the sudden crackle of weaponry two rooms over. Kroz, his face covered in bruises from the knockout blows he received the night before, lunged and scooped up an AKM folding-stock rifle.

"He's here," Rastolev growled, catching a second AKM tossed toward him by Kroz. "And the bastard has set the fight so that he can control it."

"The man is a sorcerer," Kroz replied. He unfolded the stock and lead the charge toward where the Muslim teens had opened fire through the ceiling. In counterpoint to the rapid cracks of the young men's pistols, Kroz could hear the footfalls of a large man on the roof. He swung the rifle up and sprayed the ceiling. There was a loud thud as the American leaped for cover.

Kroz milked the trigger, sweeping the ceiling with heavy, powerful rounds that went through treated wood, tar paper and plaster as if it were tissue paper. Full-auto and deep penetration gave him the ability to cut through the intervening material with a hope of catching the interloper with a lucky bullet or two. So far, he could still hear the enemy running on the roof. Rastolev came in and directed two of the young hoodlums to the window.

"Get to the roof!" Rastolev ordered in French. The Russian triggered his own AKM, then waved to Kroz. "Go with them."

Kroz dumped his partially empty magazine and replenished its ammunition reservoir with a fresh 30-round banana magazine. "Keep us covered."

Rastolev opened fire again, a short burst that cut into the ceiling above. "Go! Kill that bastard!"

Kroz slid out through the window, seeing his two young allies clambering up to the roof with monkeylike agility. Kroz reached up, hooked the top of the window frame and hauled himself up, using his feet on the sides of the window to brace himself to climb farther. In a single kick, he launched himself over the edge of the roof just in time to see one of the radical young Muslims tumble back into the gap between the two buildings. A quick glance back showed that the bloodyshirted corpse bounced from wall to wall before crunching in a grisly mess at the bottom of the causeway.

Kroz threw himself behind a chimney as the American's machine pistol wheezed out suppressed auto fire. Bricks chipped off the chimney and Kroz thrust his AKM over the top of the rectangular column. He triggered a burst of 7.62 mm ComBloc rounds toward his enemy without exposing himself to incoming fire. The other Muslim sent up to support Kroz fired around an air-conditioning unit, trying to catch the Executioner in a cross fire. The young man jerked violently as a burst of 5.7 mm rounds tore messily through his gun arms and shoulder. Muscles torn and bones shattered by high-velocity slugs, the radical dropped his Glock. Kroz ignored the wails of agony of his ally and scurried closer to the American's position. The Curved Knife operative was shielded behind a skylight, sliding flat just as the big man triggered his silenced P-90 toward him. The AKM was thrust upward again, and he milked another burst at his enemy's position. The "Hail Mary" shooting didn't have a chance of hitting a skilled, agile opponent, but as suppressive fire, it was able to keep Bolan off balance.

"Round two, American!" Kroz bellowed. "This time will end differently!"

No answer. Somewhere out in the darkness, he heard the plastic on plastic clatter of the P-90 being reloaded. Kroz took a moment to feed his hungry and depleted AKM with another 30-round stick. Running out of ammunition in the middle of a firefight would end his bid for personal vengeance against his enemy far too soon.

Glass shattered and Kroz popped up to see Bolan drop into the skylight he was hiding behind. Kroz triggered his AKM, trying to catch the warrior, swinging down to the roof below in an effort to take his target on the way down. Instead of the scream of an American, he heard only curses in Russian.

"Kroz! You idiot! We're still down here!"

This man truly was a sorcerer, Kroz thought. But his magic will have to run out sooner or later.

THE EXECUTIONER TUMBLED backward the instant he landed from his drop through the skylight. The acrobatic maneuver hadn't occurred a moment too soon as 7.62 mm steel-cored slugs tore through the ceiling and punched into the floor he'd occupied a moment before. The other Russian and his radical backup erupted in curses of complaint and panic in a medley of languages. Kroz's attempt to nail Bolan had come just a little too close to their heads for comfort. Coming up in a crouch, Bolan focused on a section of wall, drew his Desert Eagle and hammered four thunderous shots that tore through the plaster and drywall as if they were no stronger than gossamer.

One of the Muslims screamed, coughing blood as he staggered into the open, lung and throat torn by 240-grain hammer blows. The young man crumpled to the floor and Rastolev cut loose with his AKM through the intervening barrier, hoping to catch Bolan. Powdered plaster clouded the air as Bolan put his Desert Eagle away and reached for a stun grenade on his harness. He pulled the pin and lobbed the thunder bolt through the doorway. The Executioner needed prisoners, Russians in particular, so using the deadly guns was out of the question. The flash-bang went off, producing a senses-shattering sheet of light and sound that knocked the men in the next room into stunned states.

Bolan charged through the doorway as Kroz opened fire, raining steel-cored bullets through the ceiling in a desperate attempt to catch him again. With a diving roll, Bolan kept ahead of the stream of full-auto death. He swung up his P-90 up and raked the ceiling, the hard-punching 5.7 mm rounds cutting through to the night sky, losing a lot of their energy, but still maintaining enough force to elicit a cry of pain from Kroz. The man growled in agony, but the AKM continued to roar. Bullets chopped through the ceiling and shredded a stunned and blinded Muslim gunman only a few feet away from the Executioner.

Bolan lunged and seized Rastolev in a headlock. With the insensate Russian team leader under control, Bolan hauled him into the hallway instants ahead of a scythe of AKM rifle rounds pouring down in a brutal rain of death. The assassination mastermind struggled to get away from Bolan, but a hard fist under the sternum took the fight out of him. Bolan shoved the man to the floor and brought his machine pistol up again as he heard someone drop through the broken skylight to join him on this floor.

"Come on, scary man! Quit running and fight!" Kroz challenged.

The FN P-90 chattered to life, sweeping the section of wall where he'd heard his Russian adversary. The slender 5.7 mm bullets cut through wood and drywall, chewing a line through the material. Bolan grabbed a fistful of Rastolev's collar as a handle to drag the Russian down the hall while the SMG in his other hand laid down a blistering salvo of suppressive fire. The hardline assassin's rifle went silent as Kroz tried to dodge. Having put the Russian on the defensive, Bolan tossed the unconscious Rastolev into a hall closet. Feet pounded up the stairs at the end of the corridor, so he drew a pair of stun grenades, hurling them after popping their pins with his thumbs.

The downstairs backup and Kroz all caught faces full of shock wave that stopped them cold. This gave the warrior a moment to check Rastolev's mouth for a cyanide pill that might have been hidden in a hollow tooth. Bolan found it and yanked off the false cap. The pill tumbled out of Rastolev's mouth and into the warrior's palm; he threw it away. The Russian began to stir, recovering his consciousness, but the Executioner anchored him in place with a tap of the P-90's steel-reinforced stock against his temple. AKM fire chattered through the wall, signifying that the Russians had recovered from the effects of the stun grenade. Bolan shut Rastolev in the closet, even as rifle bullets ripped the air over his head.

Bolan didn't want to lose another prisoner, so he scrambled toward the steps, drawing attention away from the closet. He rushed to the top of the stairs just as the hired guns showed signs of recovery from the stun grenade. The warrior triggered his P-90 machine pistol on the run, cutting into the lead young tough at the top of the staircase. The riddled gunman toppled back into his two allies, their handguns thrown off target. A volley of 9 mm rounds zipped wildly past Bolan's legs with inches to spare.

Russian curses erupted from the stairwell below the snarl of bodies suddenly entangled at the top of the steps. Bolan leaped and brought both feet down on the chest of the man he'd just shot. With the addition of his hurtling weight, an avalanche of human bodies slammed down into the Russian conspirator who was trying to get to the Executioner. The landslide of living and dead men threw the assassin back down the steps, flattening him against the landing between floors.

One of the hired gang members reached up, clasping the strap that held Bolan's hip holster tight against his thigh. It was a wild, one in a million grab, and with a hard yank, Bolan was wrenched bodily into the railing and flipped over to the third-floor landing. It took all of the Executioner's physical conditioning and remarkable agility to avoid breaking his neck, but he landed hard enough to jar the submachine gun from his grasp.

Bolan struggled to his feet, looking up at the landing to see his three prior opponents attempting to unsnarl themselves from their lifeless comrade. The warrior whipped out his Desert Eagle and fired a .44 Magnum round through the features of one hired gun who had gotten hold of the Russian's AKM. The young radical's skull exploded as the Magnum hollowpoint round tunneled through bone and brains at 1400 feet per second. The cup-nosed heavy slug exited through the shattered dome of the corpse's head and tore through his partner's thigh, rending a cruel furrow through muscle.

The injury inspired the hired gun to drop his Glock, both hands flying to his torn leg. The Russian assassin wrenched the nearly headless corpse in front of him, blocking Bolan's next devastating Magnum shot when Kroz's AK roared from above. The 7.62 mm rounds snarled through the ceiling above Bolan's head, forcing the warrior into retreat. Aside from a spray of splinters and a covering of plaster dust, the Executioner had avoided the effects of Kroz's latest murder attempt.

"Kroz! You crazy bastard! Check your fire!" the Russian behind the headless human shield bellowed, even as Bolan fired through the ceiling with his Desert Eagle. The big Israeli hand cannon locked empty and Bolan stuffed the weapon into its holster, transitioning to his Beretta. He couldn't punch through the ceiling with the 9 mm hollowpoint bullets, but the ball rounds loaded between the combat ammo could reach Kroz on alternate shots, if necessary.

Bolan dumped the Dutch-loaded magazine and replaced it with one filled with twenty NATO pressure full-metal-jacket rounds to give him a better chance of cutting into Kroz through the intervening ceiling. Flicking the selector lever to burst mode, he ripped off a trio of rounds into the air before the sound of footfalls behind him set off his instincts.

A swung box cutter hissed through the air, barely missing the back of the Executioner's head so closely that wisps of hair hung in the air in the wake of the slash. Bolan whirled under the blade-wielding thug's back swing and rose, putting all the power of his legs and back behind the rising fist that he plunged under the attacker's jaw in a bone-shattering uppercut. As the stunned blade man staggered backward, Bolan dug his heel deep into the youth's exposed sternum. Ribs splintered under the force of the savage kick, jagged shards of bone slicing through lung tissue as if it were melting butter. Bolan put a single Beretta round through his dying opponent's forehead to prevent any unnecessary agony that the gasping youth would have suffered. As the crack of the mercy shot faded, movement in his peripheral vision warned him of the two Russian death dealers in the stairwell, on their feet and armed.

The Executioner spun, his Beretta burping tribursts

through its attached suppressor. Kroz dived out of the way, but his comrade jerked violently, bullets chopping his heart and lungs to pieces. The Russian collapsed, vomiting blood as his AKM triggered, due to a death seizure. Even as he moved sideways, Kroz cut loose with his rifle. Bolan was moving, too, just stepping out of the way of the stream of wall-tearing slugs that rose a chorus of death screams that would have been his if not for a sudden stride out of the way. Kroz was helping to even the odds against the hired guns with his scything sweeps of full automatic fire, but Bolan triggered the Beretta at him again. He tracked the tear of AK bullets through the wall in an attempt to catch the one that escaped the night before.

Kroz's AKM ran dry from the sound of it. The floor suddenly erupted in the room that the Executioner was in, an assault rifle and a set of handguns spitting bullets up through the carpet as the men on the second floor strove to kill him. Bolan leaped onto a bed, the frame and box springs shielding him from the handgun rounds. The rifle, on the other hand, chewed the floor he'd been standing on moments before, reducing much of it to splinters. The warrior filled his Desert Eagle with a fresh magazine now that he was behind cover, and he closed the open slide on a .44 Magnum shell in the breech. He poked the hand cannon over the floor and fired four rapid-fire rounds into the room beneath him. A scream of agony split the air, rewarding Bolan for his efforts.

The AKM below snarled again, and Bolan rolled back between the bed and the wall. Rifle slugs punched up through the mattress, snagging the pouches on the back of the Executioner's belt as they penetrated the floor and bed. The warrior relaxed as the chatter of the enemy rifle ended. Bolan pushed off the wall and dropped to the floor. With a hard kick, he dived out of the room and into the hall.

Only the Glocks of the hired gunners followed the Executioner through the floor; the fourth of the surviving assassination squad members obviously reloaded his rifle. Bolan spotted Kroz with more hired thugs at his side. The two professional soldiers opened fire on each other. As they raced for cover, neither had a good shot at their opponent, but Bolan noted that Kroz wasn't using his AKM, and the Beretta and Desert Eagle elicited grunts of dying agony from the imported French outcasts. That was a good thing for the Executioner because even though Kroz's Glock had a high-capacity magazine, it lacked full-auto fire and saved Bolan from a room-sweeping swathe of rifle rounds. Unfortunately, even the 3-round bursts of his own Beretta were far too precise and short to chase down the enemy Russian, leaving the belligerent assassin alive and kicking to continue this battle.

The gunners who were backing up Kroz were not so mobile and aware of incoming fire, and thus suffered the brunt of .44 Magnum and 9 mm rounds that tore through their chests and took them out of play. Bolan cursed as the hallway floor erupted beneath him. The other Russian and his young-blood backup hosed the ceiling with their weapons, a round slashing up through his calf. Fortunately his boot sole deflected the hit and turned it into a mere flesh wound, not a crippling leg-breaker or muscle-slicing injury. The Executioner returned to the bedroom he'd evacuated and pulled a stun grenade off of his harness. He dropped it where the floor had been weakened by the scores of AK and Glock rounds, then lunged back into the hall as the streams of fire followed the sound of his feet into the bedroom. The concussion blast shook the building, and Bolan returned to the bedroom. A chunk of floor, damaged by the high-powered rifle's wood-splintering onslaught, had been torn free by the shock wave of the grenade. Bolan leaped into the hole and dropped to the ground with the agility of a hunting cat. The thud of his arrival caught the attention of half a dozen men who had been expecting the gunfight to spill down the stairs, not drop through the ceiling.

Bolan fired two bursts from his Beretta, tearing the face of the Russian leader and coring the chest of a radical street punk to his left. The 93R locked empty now, but the rest of the hired malcontents scurried for cover, giving the warrior time to reload. He stuffed another 20-round magazine into the empty machine pistol. The floor creaked above Bolan, and the warrior scrambled away from the shadow of the hole. In the same moment, Kroz's pistol flashed through the gap. The Executioner fired his 93R into the ceiling, forcing Kroz's retreat. Unfortunately, the Executioner's evasive maneuvers had brought him closer to his other enemies.

One of the young thugs lashed out, wrapping muscled arms around Bolan's head and neck. The man's weight pulled Bolan off balance, but the warrior used the shift in his momentum to his advantage. The big American's body sandwiched the grappler against the wall. Putting his whole body's weight behind his shoulder, Bolan felt his opponent's rib crack from the impact. The tough's arms flopped from around Bolan as agony sliced through his chest. The Executioner seized the stunned grappler and swung his body around in time to shield himself from the spray of two Glocks. Bolan hurled the bullet-riddled corpse toward the two shooters, flattening one of the youths under the lifeless weight. The other had managed to sidestep the flying body, but ended up with a face full of Beretta bullets.

A fourth gunman whipped around a doorway, Glock tracking. The Executioner grabbed his wrist and yanked the hired muscle into a pistoning knee. Breath exploded from the youth's lungs as Bolan's kick stabbed deep into his abdomen. He finished him off with a brain-scrambling elbow to the ear, dropping his limp form to the floor in a crumpled heap.

The last of the hired gunmen on this floor were still standing. The third, pinned by the corpse of his ally, looked out with them as they gawked at the Executioner in disbelief.

"Run away," Bolan said in the smattering of French that he knew.

The three conscious survivors scrambled down the stairs in a frightened panic, one tripping and bouncing off the landing, but scurrying down the rest of the stairs in a wild crawl.

That left Kroz still in action, plus whatever gunmen were still intent on earning their pay but stationed on the first floor. There were a couple of wounded and incapacitated foes still alive on the higher floors, as well.

Glass crashed in the room that Kroz had last occupied. Bolan whirled and rushed to the sill.

The Russian had escaped down the causeway, the warrior catching one last glance of the man's heels as he dashed around the corner.

Bolan knew this wouldn't be the last of Kroz, and the warrior could only hope that he could get another shot at him further on in this mission. He walked back up to the fourth floor and went to the closet where he'd deposited Rastolev. Lifeless eyes stared from the darkened closet, a deep furrow carved through his forehead with an AKM round.

Bolan let out another sigh. Kroz could have simply gotten lucky, or he'd fired his rifle on the closet door deliberately to shut down a potential source of intel on the conspiracy that Alexandronin and his wife had been murdered for. The pink froth of churned brain tissue bubbled and trickled down Rastolev's forehead. Scorched earth, with three of the four escapees was all that had been accomplished this night. Police sirens howled, cutting through the night, meaning that he wouldn't have time to toss the building for computers or files.

On a hunch, Bolan frisked Rastolev's corpse and found a small Web-capable smartphone in one of the dead man's pockets. The wireless hand-held device would be able to provide morsels of data if he could hook it up to Stony Man Farm's cyberstaff via uplink. Finally, Bolan hadn't come up empty in this chess game of fight and feint with the conspiracy. He might even catch a clue about the next stage of this mission.

Bolan left the building and was down the block before the first squad cars showed up. He'd even retrieved a battered old raincoat in olive drab from the front hallway to conceal his blacksuit and arsenal of weaponry and spare ammunition. Instead of a grim warrior, he was just another stroller on the streets of London. He entered his rental car and watched the building and its neighbors.

Citizens came out onto the street, frightened and disturbed by the gunfight, but no one came out begging for an ambulance or mourning a dead flatmate.

Satisfied with the battle being contained only to Rastolev's men and hired thugs, Bolan pulled out.

He had a fast plane to Moscow to catch.

## CHAPTER EIGHT

In the back of the chartered Gulfstream jet, Mack Bolan awoke from a two hour catnap. The brief respite helped the warrior replenish his mental batteries.

Bolan retrieved Rastolev's smartphone from his pocket and located a USB port on the side. The compact keyboard-bearing device was half the size of the Combat PDA that Hermann Schwarz had designed for Stony Man's action teams. The phone had a built-in flash memory drive that could hold two gigs of data, and was able to connect wirelessly to the Internet. Using a USB cord from his laptop, Bolan plugged the smartphone into his Combat PDA. The bulkier device had a more powerful processor, a better digital camera, secure and more powerful wireless connections and a massive flash memory core that was packed with utility software designed by the cybernetic wizards of Stony Man Farm for hacking almost any operating system on the planet. Bolan pulled up the Vulcan Probe, named by Schwarz for a popular science-fiction character's telepathic interrogation technique. The utility went to work, digging into the smartphone's electronic mind, smashing through encryption security that would have kept the device locked up and useless to an unauthorized user such as Bolan. The Vulcan Probe was a power tool without peer, having the irresistible force of a freight train but the finesse of a master pool player.

Rastolev's smartphone held dozens of stored photographs and a hundred "secure" e-mails. Bolan examined the photos, which were grainy, thanks to their 2.1 megapixel resolution, but the subjects of the photographs were unmistakable. They were of various people in London backgrounds, including Vitaly Alexandronin and Catherine Rozuika. The pictures had been sent from other phones equipped with cameras as they were in an automatically generated folder labeled "received images." The photos initially were observations of the pair's daily activities, and people Rozuika had spoken to. There was a folder that was labeled "Captured Images" and there were four pictures in there. There were only four, and they depicted Catherine, her face a bloody smear, laying in a pool of blood after her cruel beating.

These photos had to have been taken by Rastolev himself. They had been stored as proof positive that he had completely destroyed an unarmed woman, dooming her to an existence as a human vegetable for the few remaining days of her life. The sight of the Russian reporter, horrifically smashed by trained martial artists, was a cold slug of ice spearing into Bolan's heart of hearts. The cruelty of the attack had been carefully measured to provide a deadly warning to anyone trying to follow in Rozuika's footsteps.

Bolan felt a salving calm come over him, his anger and pain at her treatment mollified by the memory of Rastolev sitting in the closet, his skull shorn open. It was only a small measure of satisfaction, but the death of the Russian team leader helped sooth raw nerves as the memory crept through Bolan's mind. The knowledge turned bitter when he realized that the men who had sent Rastolev were still alive. Though they had not personally touched Catherine, they had taken satisfaction in seeing her mangled body laying on a London sidewalk.

Bolan had work to do to find these cruel conspirators. He scrolled through the e-mails on the flash memory, reading the Cyrillic script as best he could and looking for clues as to the identity and location of the masterminds of the hideous attack. But his knowledge of the script was too limited. He'd leave the e-mails to Kurtzman and the Stony Man team, who would break down the e-mails, their path through the Internet, and base Internet service providers to track down the men who had been willing to murder to further their political ideals. He tapped his stylus on the screen of the Combat PDA and forwarded the contents of Rastolev's smartphone to the Farm in a high-speed dump.

The PDA warbled. Kurtzman was on the other end.

"We just received your electronic care package, Striker," Kurtzman said.

"Good. See if you can break down any patterns of communication," Bolan requested. "This seemed like more of a last-minute kind of operation on their part."

"How could you tell?" Kurtzman asked.

"There were only a few days of observation and

communication before the first attack," Bolan surmised. "Generally, Russian kill teams like to take at least a week to make certain they can pull off the kill with deniability and a minimum of risk."

"Sounds like a reasonable assumption," Kurtzman said. "We've got information on that runaway from the docks."

"Give it to me," Bolan told him.

"The man's name is Viktor Krochina," Kurtzman explained. "He was part of a Russian embassy in France. He'd been pulled over for a traffic violation, but since he was a guard assigned to the embassy, he got off on diplomatic immunity. Interpol kept his fingerprints on record."

"But someone tried to erase them," Bolan said.

"How'd you know?" Kurtzman asked.

"Simply because you have that little smug lilt in your voice that you always get when someone doesn't clean up their hacking well enough," Bolan explained.

Kurtzman laughed. "Apparently the hackers that are in the employ of this conspiracy are very skilled and quite thorough. It was only through digging down into the deepest backups of the Interpol computer that we were able to find the records."

"Any word on his current affiliation?" Bolan asked.

"The choir invisible," Kurtzman answered. "Allegedly he was assassinated by a Chechen terror cell that he was trying to bring down."

"Chechnya?" Bolan pressed.

"Nope. This was around Moscow," Kurtzman explained. "He was given a funeral, closed casket because the car bomb didn't leave much of a face behind for loved ones to look at."

"It sounds like a fabrication," Bolan noted.

"Yeah, Krochina seems to have been sanitized. Stripped of an identity and background, he's a good, deniable blunt instrument to send overseas, or be used in the Kremlin's backyard."

"Still the Kremlin?" Bolan asked.

"The new Kremlin, at least according to the rumors that are passing through the Chechen refugees," Kurtzman clarified. "There's an organization that has been called the Curved Knife."

"Yeah. Discussed it with Alexandronin," Bolan answered.

"Well, get this. There's a faction of the Chechen rebels who call themselves Iron Hammer," Kurtzman replied.

"Hammer and sickle," Bolan mused. "Surely they wouldn't be that obvious."

"Iron Hammer is a known quantity. Curved Knife is just a rumor that's being fiercely denied by the administration in Moscow," Kurtzman explained.

Bolan squeezed his brow. "Makes sense. Has Iron Hammer been a particularly effective branch of the Chechen rebellion?"

"They've claimed responsibility for twenty car bombings in the past two years, and have been instrumental in the assassinations of over a dozen public officials," Kurtzman confirmed. "They operate in Moscow and in Grozny."

"So there's a chance I might run into them when I go to pick up Laserka," Bolan noted.

"We weren't exactly quiet about arranging the charter flight for you, Striker," Kurtzman admitted.

"That's perfectly all right," Bolan replied. "I wanted it that way. It gets bothersome actually running after the bad guys. Setting myself up as bait…"

"They drop into your lap, giving you a lead on the next rung of the ladder," Kurtzman concluded. "If you want, I'll have Laserka meet you at the airport."

"No. I'll go to pick her up," Bolan said. "Trouble might try to follow me. I'll take my time and scope them out. I don't want to bring any drama to Laserka's doorstep."

"Sounds like a plan," Kurtzman replied.

"I'm going to catch a little more sleep before we land," Bolan said. "I have a feeling that there's going to be more than enough excitement in the coming day."

"Have a good nap, big guy," Kurtzman said, then signed off.

Bolan turned off his Combat PDA and slipped it back into his pocket. He closed his eyes and drifted off into a sleep that he hoped would be dreamless.

KAYA LASERKA HEARD her cell phone blurt, awakening her from a fitful sleep. She snatched up her pistol and scanned the hotel room. Her heart thumped as she made the connection between her sudden awakening and the electronic chirping of her phone. She flicked the Makarov's safety back on and leaned to pluck the portable phone off her bed table. It was the American woman who had introduced herself as Barbara.

"Cooper will be landing in a couple of hours," she

told Laserka. The Russian Fed looked out the window. The sun had risen, but only barely.

"Will he come here, or should I see him at the airport?" Laserka asked.

"Cooper said to maintain a low profile. Order some room service and pay-per-view on the TV," Price suggested. "Unless you've already caught a case of cabin fever…"

Laserka debated answering sarcastically, but sighed. "I'll get some breakfast. What the hell, it's not my dime."

"That's the spirit," Price told her. "Cooper's bringing some equipment and some data for you. He also has a smartphone that we're cracking the hard drive on. I'd want to run a few names past you, but Cooper wants to be in the room with you and ask the questions himself."

"If he's anything like Mike Belasko," Laserka said, pausing to let her irony sink in, "he's a hands-on sort of man. I thought he was coming by sooner."

"He had an errand to run," Price explained. "Unsurprisingly, that's where he netted a Russian's smartphone."

"And he thinks I'd be familiar with who the conspiracy might be?" Laserka asked.

"Not personally, but agencies have rumor mills," Price told her. "You'd be surprised."

Laserka took a calming breath. "Not anymore. Not since the two attempts on my life."

"Yeah, sorry about that, Kaya," Price said. "One thing Cooper wanted me to ask you was if anything had come to your attention in regard to Chechnya before the whole mess with Vitaly."

"Well, the department had me do some surveillance of weapons buys," Laserka replied. "Guns and ammo meant to go to Chechen insurgents, straight from old military stockpiles."

"Anything unusual in that?" Price asked. "Were you working with Curved Knife?"

Laserka felt like she'd been punched in the stomach. "I better call for some breakfast."

"We're monitoring the cell signal for other listeners, Kaya," Price reassured her. "You're alone with me on this line."

"Yeah? Well, forgive my skepticism, okay?" Laserka asked. "Those bastards tracked me down through a trusted informant and got him to send me into an ambush. Then two more big goons came to my apartment to finish the job. Have you ever been driven out of your own home? Or been paranoid about your own coworkers?"

"No to the second question," Price confided.

"Sorry, Barbara. First, one of my friends dies, and now I'm on the run and my only hope is…you know who," Laserka said. "A man I wasn't even sure was on my side when we met a decade and a half ago."

"He was on your side," Price said firmly. "And he still is."

"I know." Laserka sighed. "Anything else?"

"Not unless you want to talk about Curved Knife," Price suggested.

Laserka looked around the hotel room. "Perhaps someplace less public. When Cooper arrives."

"Understood," Price said. "Be careful."

Laserka smiled weakly. "It's far too late for that."

KROZ FIT HIS NEW NAME and lack of identity as if it were a second skin. His original name, Krochina, had been erased from most of the Russian government's records, and it would require a very skilled and determined investigator to learn anything about him, thanks to Curved Knife's hackers. Rastolev and the others had been buried, their birth names having been scourged from minds, though the mastermind of their field operations had become famous in intelligence circles. As a hollow name, Rastolev's notoriety hadn't been a handicap, and in fact had become an asset when dealing with the easily cowed *mafiya* expatriates around Europe and the Middle East. Kroz stuffed his empty Glock into a garbage bin, and pulled out his cell phone for one last communication. He pressed the speed dial.

"This better be good," came the voice on the other end.

"I'm the only one left," Kroz said.

"Any other prisoners taken?"

"No one from our close family. Maybe a few of the French hirelings, but they're clueless. The American tried to take Rastolev, but I emptied my magazine into the closet where he'd been stuffed," Kroz explained.

"Who knew about the rental apartments?" his commander asked brusquely.

"Our lost cub, but if the American had gotten that out of him, then we'd have been visited sooner, rather than our maid service encountering him back at the morgue," Kroz explained. "I know for certain that the bastard hadn't followed me."

"Yes. I heard about the incident at the forensic sciences lab," came the reply.

Kroz held his tongue, not wanting to say Bennorin's name over the phone. The Russian commander was another "dead man" in the same vein as Belkin and Rastolev, but he was a whole level higher on the food chain than them. Bennorin was nearly as much a legend in Moscow as the hunter Kroz had just escape from. Very few men had been there for the American's rampage against the old guard of the KGB and fewer still had been able to pull off an operation under his nose. Bennorin had not only succeeded in his goals, but had escaped. Granted, he had the shadow of a more blatant plot to draw the American's attention. That kind of luck and skill made Bennorin an honored figure in the cover community. "Have you gotten all the news of his visit to our house?"

"Ever since last night, we've had resources monitoring the London law," Bennorin explained. "You are correct. Rastolev was quieted by one of your bullets, unless the American executed him with an AK."

"He didn't," Kroz answered. "But you already knew about that."

"Of course. We also heard that a private charter flight took off four hours ago, headed for Moscow," Bennorin said. "I've already arranged for your next ticket."

"Back home to Moscow?" Kroz asked.

"You don't have a home," Bennorin corrected. "I'm sending you on ahead to Grozny."

"With *him* on the way to Moscow?" Kroz asked.

"He'll be on his way to Chechnya in no time," Bennorin said. "And you are long overdue for your duties in Grozny anyway."

"You'll let the American go unhindered?" Kroz pressed.

"What do you think?" Bennorin countered. "I'll throw what resources I have in Moscow at him. But I have no doubt that he'll survive to be an interference in Chechnya. The American is not stopped easily."

"Already fatalistic about failure?" Kroz replied. "That doesn't sound like you—"

Bennorin cut Kroz off. "Try not to remind me that you are the sole survivor of a *failed* operation that has compromised my security and the secrecy of our plans, exposing us to discovery by one of the greatest threats that the Russian people have ever faced. Because, right now, no one would cry for you if I personally scooped your brains out through your left eye socket with a rusty spoon."

"Understood," Kroz said. "My apologies, sir."

"Prepare for interference on the Chechnya end of things and attempt to contain the damage when he appears," Bennorin ordered.

"I'll do what I can," Kroz replied.

"Time to let the Chechens get involved in covering our asses. Let them know that the American will interfere with their fight for freedom," Bennorin said. "We put him between two forces, he will be kept off balance. The conflagration sparked when our people and the Chechens go after him, as well as the conflict here in Moscow will create a sufficient amount of strife to advance my plans."

Kroz cleared his throat. "So he'll be even better than a bomb going off in Moscow."

"I've been in the path of this storm before," Bennorin replied. "Survival and thriving is possible, but you have to know how to handle him. Going directly toward him is not a successful strategy. He's a force of nature, and all that can be done is to let him do his thing to his satisfaction."

"And he will exacerbate the situation, like Hurricane Katrina did. The storm that stripped the city of New Orleans of its civilization, turning it into a war zone," Kroz said. "Grozny will be torn asunder when we unleash the Iron Hammer on him. Even if he destroys them completely…"

"Martial law will still be declared. That is why I have local Iron Hammers going after him here in Moscow," Bennorin said. "When life sends you a lemon, squeeze it over your fish and keep eating."

Bennorin hung up.

Kroz threw the phone to the ground, then smashed it to splinters under his heel.

He waved down a taxi. Bennorin told him that he had a plane to catch. Kroz didn't feel like frustrating the Russian spymaster anymore….

KAYA LASERKA HAD FINISHED her breakfast when her phone rang. She looked at it for a moment, wondering who else would be calling her. The hotel room had been equipped with a disposable cell phone that had been her secure umbilical to Stony Man Farm, but this was her usual cell. She picked it up, then saw who was calling.

Batroykin. Her throat tightened, and she pocketed the phone. She didn't want to get into too much trouble, but she knew that taking the call in the room could possibly give away her position. Laserka left the hotel, walking six blocks before she turned on her cell again, and dialed Batroykin back.

"Kaya? God, woman, I was worried about you!" Batroykin said over the phone. He sounded genuinely concerned, but Laserka had experienced enough over the past couple of days to be warranted in her paranoia.

"Sorry, sir," Laserka apologized. "I went to ground."

"Because of the attack?" Batroykin asked. "I've got members of the department working with the Moscow police trying to figure out who was after you. We've got forensics going over their bodies. Do you feel like you need protection?"

Again, Batroykin's earnest worry translated over the cell phone. Laserka began to feel some guilt, though her cautious side wondered if that was Batroykin's goal. "I'm sorry, comrade. There was another incident."

"Yes. Your apartment was turned upside down. When you didn't show up this morning, I sent some officers over," Batroykin said. "There wasn't any blood, but you had me worried."

"No, I'm in good health," Laserka answered. "I just found someplace to lay my head that no one else in the world would ever know about."

"Smart girl," Batroykin said. "Listen, if you want, meet me at the café, in person. This way we can talk without compromising your position."

"Compromising my position?" Laserka asked.

"Just hang up and turn off your phone," Batroykin ordered. "You never know who might be trying to track you down via the GPS signal in your unit."

The line went dead, and Laserka looked at the cell phone for a long moment.

She turned it off, then took out the battery, sliding it into a separate pocket from the phone. She fished in her pocket, got some change out and hunted down a pay phone.

"Hello?" Batroykin answered.

"Won't talk long," Laserka said. "You're worried that people are trying to track me down?"

Batroykin took a deep, nervous breath on the other end. "It's no coincidence that someone wanted you dead after looking in on Alexandronin's death. They tried twice so far. I want to talk, in person, and make certain that you and I are on the same page."

"But, sir..." Laserka began.

"Listen. I know that you think all I want from my pretty young agents is a little handful of ass, and yes, that is true," Batroykin said. "But damn it, you are one of my people. And you do good work for me. I want you to be safe, and no one is going to fuck with my department if I have any say in this."

Laserka swallowed. It would be so easy to dismiss this as an appeal to her doubts and confusion. Being pulled to the coffeehouse where the agents usually went to get a stiff drink after work would bring her in the line of sight of a lot of people. But Laserka was all alone, despite the assurances from across the Atlantic that "Matt Cooper" would be riding to her rescue.

"Besides, if I let you get killed, that'd be one less beauty I could leer at," Batroykin added. "It's a lose-lose situation for me if I let you get hurt."

"Fine, I'll come to the coffeehouse..."

. "The café," Batroykin corrected. "You're too well known at the house."

Laserka had to think, then remembered what Batroykin was talking about. He was talking about a buffet-style restaurant that was usually packed during a lunchtime rush. It was an out-of-the-way place that had enough bodies in it to make routine surveillance all but impossible. Even a wire hidden under clothing would pick up only noise and static. "Oh, there?"

"The crush of bodies will be good insulation," Batroykin said. "We have arrangements to make, Kaya. I still need you for tomorrow night."

"You want me at a party when I'm being hunted?" Laserka inquired.

"I've got word that something serious is about to go down," Batroykin said. "I'll bring something for you to the café. Be careful, Kaya. I'll see you at twelve-thirty."

Batroykin hung up. Laserka looked at her watch. She had five hours before her meeting with her supervisor. Maybe that would be time enough to meet with Cooper. She wouldn't mind having some backup with her if this were indeed a trap.

## CHAPTER NINE

Bolan, fully rested after his second catnap on the plane, arrived in the lobby of the hotel where Kaya Laserka was waiting. She recognized him immediately, despite the changes in his appearance since their meeting more than ten years ago. There were some things about the big warrior that were unmistakable. She smiled, sighing with relief, and drained the last of a bottle of soda.

"Been waiting long?" Bolan asked, standing over her at the sofa.

"Not really. I'm just glad you're here. Something strange has popped up."

Bolan sat next to her, and she explained Batroykin's telephone call to her, and how he seemed to be acting out of character. Bolan mused over the new development. "How soon is the meeting?"

"It's at twelve-thirty, which gives us two hours to get there and scope things out," Laserka said.

"Which gives me time to get some intelligence from you," Bolan replied.

"You mean about…" Laserka looked around, then lowered her voice. "Curved Knife."

"And their Chechen counterparts, Iron Hammer," Bolan added.

Laserka raised an eyebrow. "Oh, my God."

Bolan frowned, but nodded at her reaction. The correlation between the two organizational names was something that very few sane people would even contemplate. Even those aware of the mystery enforcement organization were too in denial of the past to dream that there was a group in the administration of the current government that had the brazenness to emulate the eras of men like Stalin and Khrushchev. "That's their armor, such an unthinkable link to a past that the present wants buried."

Laserka wiped the hair from her brow, sighing deeply. "Curved Knife… They're not supposed to exist."

"Neither am I," Bolan returned.

Laserka looked at him for a long, silent moment. "You should. It would be great to see the scum cringe in their boots."

"They do," Bolan replied. "But their fear is not as focused as it used to be."

"Why?" Laserka asked. "Why can't the world know that there is someone out there hunting to protect them?"

"I tried it in a more open setting. All it did was make everyone associated with me a target. Too many friends died that way," Bolan said. "I make myself a known, highly visible threat, I also make everyone else associated with me a victim. So I'm a ghost. A rumor, just like our bent-bladed friends. But we know each other completely."

"Hopefully not on sight," Laserka replied.

"You knew me, despite the changes," Bolan countered. "And they knew me in London."

"Who knew you in London?" Laserka asked.

"The *organasatya*," Bolan told her. "I asked them about who wanted Alexandronin dead. They gave up the Curved Knife right away. The Russian mob doesn't have any love for them."

"No doubt about that. The Curved Knife are the same as SMERSH, Smyernet Spian," Laserka mused.

"Death to spies," Bolan translated. "They're murderers, where most of the KGB, at least domestically, were simple law enforcement. SMERSH enforced all the laws that the lower ranks weren't willing to engage in."

Laserka looked as if she were going to make a comment, but kept quiet. Bolan was very familiar with the hierarchy of the cold war–era KGB, and the changes implemented after the fall of the Berlin Wall. The old era communism returned in the wake of economic turbulence and widespread rebellion and terrorism. Proved methods were attractive, no matter the end of liberty they signaled

"It's only a few who want to do this," Bolan continued. "Bastards who think that they have been given a mandate of history because of a small, violent group. They suspend human rights, they work to start wars, and they proclaim that their method is the only way to wage war on nothing more than a concept."

"Some people could say the same about the United States," Laserka said.

Bolan narrowed his eyes. "I'm not a lackey for my government. I'm someone trying to take care of real problems. It's not my fault that the alleged leadership goes barking at birds flying by the windows while the vermin spread their disease behind their backs."

"So you're not a proponent of the war on terror?" Laserka asked.

"I've fought perpetrators of terrorism around the world, and while I agree there should be a war against them, it is handled with ham-handed clumsiness and inane overreaction. Trying to sell a vendetta as a response to a terrorist attack that was not fabricated by the nation invaded is an insult to the victims of such an act," Bolan told her. "Curved Knife is trying to make their play exactly like that one, and with bodies littering the ground, the maniacs seeking power will have all the justification they require to achieve whatever violations of human rights they want."

"Then what about…" Laserka began, then stopped, catching the cold glare in the Executioner's eyes. "Except for small aberrations, the U.S. war on terror isn't fought with the tactics Curved Knife uses."

"Correct," Bolan said. "And the people of the nation are correcting the mistakes. The system of checks and balances still works, so my efforts aren't needed."

"But the Commonwealth of Independent States doesn't have that luxury," Laserka replied.

Bolan shrugged. "Vitaly and Catherine and you are taking a stand. And if Batroykin isn't giving you over to Curved Knife, then there's more hope. Russia survives because of the strength of her people, not the corruption of her officials."

Bolan handed her a small, hands-free radio unit. "This will keep us in touch at the meeting. This way, he won't run away if he notices me with you."

Laserka placed the earpiece and undid her ponytail, letting a curtain of auburn hair fall over the ear, concealing it. "Noticeable?"

"Nope. Good work," Bolan told her. "Let's get going, we've got an appointment to keep."

IF BATROYKIN WERE SETTING UP a trap, this place was hardly the best place to do it. At least, that was Bolan's initial impression. Sure, the crowd was thick enough to hide an army of agents, but with the hustle and bustle of the people going through the buffet-style restaurant there was no way that a grim, focused watchman could keep an eye on anything. Bolan scanned the ceiling, reconfirming that there were no hidden video cameras in place.

He'd already determined that the standard buffet restaurant's security consisted only of "hand me down" metal detector wands at each of the doors, and they weren't working properly. Laserka had gone through them with her pistol under her sweater without even causing a raised eyebrow. Bolan followed suit, slipping past the security men and grabbing a tray for himself. For a big meeting place that would make a good target for Chechen terrorists, the protection measures taken by the owners had to have been based more on payoffs and bribes than actual upkeep of training and technology.

Bolan took a tray and took some food for himself, grabbing a cup of coffee that smelled strong enough to curl his nose hairs. He took a sip and was glad that he'd inured himself to Aaron Kurtzman's brew back at Stony Man Farm. He thought of an old saying about the Russian Mosin rifle. "Years of abuse and oppression has made the Mosin Nagant immune to mistreatment."

"The same has to apply to Russian taste buds," Bolan mused softly to himself.

"Oh, you've tried the extra-leaded coffee?" Laserka asked over their hands-free communicator.

"Lead," Bolan said. "Yeah, it tastes like ground paint chips."

"This is the stuff we take with us into the field," Laserka told him. "Nothing better for a stakeout. You won't blink for two weeks."

Bolan smiled and took another sip. "And to think that I was worried about Vitaly's taste in vodka."

"Bitter coffee, bitter vodka, bitter cigarettes," Laserka said. "Those are the things that keep us from feeling complacent when we need to focus."

"Nothing in sight," Bolan said, taking a chair.

"I don't see anyone, either," Laserka added. "We'll be… He's early."

Bolan spotted Batroykin thanks to Laserka's description of him. The little, pudgy man was unmistakable. Bolan had thought that Laserka had been exaggerating about his pasty complexion and his puddinglike softness. He weaved through the crowd, scanning faces.

He stopped, recognizing Laserka. His eyes swept around for more faces, nervously wondering if someone else had accompanied her. Batroykin's eyes passed over Bolan's position, and he froze. Bolan could read his lips, seeing a curse word in Russian form on them. Batroykin's hands went to his pockets, then fell away. Bolan kept the link between their gazes for as long as Batroykin dared to keep his eyes open. The chubby little supervisor blinked and tore his eyes away from the Executioner, continuing on toward Laserka.

"What did you do?" Laserka asked.

"I didn't blink," Bolan answered. "He looks like he's seen a ghost."

"You aren't?" Laserka inquired.

"Touché," Bolan said.

Batroykin sat across from the lady agent, setting a small shopping bag on the table between them. Laserka pulled the bag closer to her, looking into it.

"This is light if it's supposed to be a bomb," Bolan heard her say.

"No bomb," Batroykin said. "I said I needed you for tomorrow night."

"With people trying to murder me?" Laserka asked.

"I see that you picked up a guardian angel," Batroykin said. "I guess you were still close with Alexandronin."

Bolan watched as Laserka stroked her hair to one side, obviously revealing the earpiece to Batroykin. Batroykin took a deep breath. "He's staying back in case I brought some friends, correct?"

"What can I say, sir? Two attempts on my life in a twenty-four-hour time span," Laserka said. "I needed someone who I could trust."

"I thought that when we made this appointment you did retain some trust in me," Batroykin told her. "And

I was counting on you being early. In case someone had been listening to me on my end of the conversation."

"So you're worried about someone being on your case, and you still need me?" Laserka asked. "What the hell is going on?"

"Vitaly Alexandronin wasn't a well-liked man, his wife even less so, but there are those who trust such people," Batroykin told her. "You're not the only one who has been in contact with him for the past fifteen years. I just didn't realize that he'd been in touch with…*him*."

Bolan heard Laserka's groan of irritation. "So you kept me in the dark because you were afraid the Curved Knife was on your case."

"You set things up so that you looked to me like you were working for the Knife," Batroykin confessed. "I wasn't sure I could trust you."

"But two attempts on my life made me look better," Laserka said.

"You mention how many times someone's tried to kill you again, I'm going to make you wear your lunch in your hair," Batroykin said. "Something's brewing, and I still need someone I can trust at the party. I'm sure your guardian angel can find a suit or a tuxedo."

"Can you?" Laserka asked.

"I have something packed in an overnight bag that will work," Bolan admitted over the radio.

"He can dress appropriately," Laserka told Batroykin. "You think that Iron Hammer wants a piece of this bigwig party. So you brought me a designer dress so I could slip in and cover your ass."

"How'd you figure out that Iron Hammer was the Chechen group responsible?" Batroykin asked.

"Because the hammer fits in with the sickle," Laserka noted. "And that's what a curved knife is, right?"

"I knew that you were on the ball," Batroykin said. "Smart enough to look like you were being spoon-fed by those bastards, but keeping your head away from their chopping block. I'm sorry about Vitaly."

"I didn't know that you cared," Laserka returned.

"You were covering your ass. I covered mine," Batroykin said. "And I know you girls talk about me trying to get up your skirts. You think I'm only after one thing, but is anyone in this world that single-minded?"

"I am," Bolan said into Laserka's ear.

"The American." Laserka spoke up for him. "And right now, he's looking to stop the Knife."

"That's a good way to get cut to ribbons," Batroykin said, leaning forward. "The old guard was one thing, but these people are ruthless, heartless. They think nothing of trying to murder thousands of their own people in order to make their position more secure."

Bolan strolled over to their table, taking a seat beside Batroykin. The man's already waxy and wan face seemed to turn to porcelain. "I think nothing of killing thousands of people who intend to murder thousands. It'll be a fair match."

Batroykin swallowed hard. "A pleasure to meet you in person."

Bolan extended a hand. "Special Agent Matt Cooper. Pleasure to meet you."

"Director Vasili Batroykin," the Russian answered. "It is wonderful to be in cooperation with the Federal Bureau of Investigation?"

Bolan nodded.

"The problem we have with terrorism in Moscow is abominable, and this situation is only made worse by the fact that we require assistance from our friends in America," Batroykin lamented with a sigh. His shakiness dissolved as Bolan became friendlier. "So what made you decide to come to the table?"

"Better view of the door, and the fact that this meeting is winding down," Bolan answered. "You've told Laserka everything she needs to know, for now. Plus, it's getting close to the time that a surveillance team would be setting up for your scheduled meeting with her."

Batroykin smiled. "Damn, you *are* good."

"I've gone head-to-head with your people for years, and worked side by side with the Russians almost as many times since our nations warmed up to each other," Bolan said.

Batroykin nodded. "Did…Vitaly say anything about me?"

"He was too concerned with Catherine's murder," Bolan admitted. "He didn't leave anything for me to figure out who was who in this. So, forgive me if I don't trust you completely."

"Another reason to come closer. To get a better impression of me," Batroykin mused.

"You're not so bad yourself," Bolan said. "Right now, you're in the clear. Granted, you need to keep your libido in your pocket, but other than that, there's nothing wrong with you."

Batroykin put a napkin to his damp forehead. "Better get moving, unless you want to see who the Knife does have in the area. Of course, that would cause more problems…"

Bolan nodded. "This restaurant is too crowded for my tastes. Enjoy your meal, sir."

"Good luck, you two," Batroykin said.

Bolan took Laserka by the hand and led her out of the restaurant. His sharp senses scanned the crowd, but no threats or shadows caught his eye. The pair disappeared into Moscow.

LASERKA LOOKED AT HERSELF in the mirror. The dress that Batroykin had provided for her was gorgeous, but there was no way that she could hope to conceal a handgun on her person. Luckily, the supervisor was prescient enough to add a matching red silk purse, one that contained a holster for her Makarov and loops that would carry two spare magazines. Anything more she might need, Laserka knew she'd have to acquire on the scene, preferably from someone she'd shot.

Bolan was in his dress shirt and slacks, his tie not yet knotted around his collar. He sat back in a chair, looking at the monitor of his laptop, scanning building plans of the Moscow Expo Center, a meeting center where the party was being held. On a second window was a list of likely targets for the Iron Hammer to hit. It had been supplied by Aaron Kurtzman and the Stony Man cybernetics crew. As soon as Bolan had mentioned Batroykin's "invitation," the computer staff already knew the event.

"A lot of moderate and pro-Chechen individuals are going to be there," Kurtzman explained. "If anyone wants to hurt the Chechnya Independence Movement and alienate the few friends they have in Moscow, this is the best place to hit."

"What will security be like?" Bolan asked.

"We're looking at… Shit," Kurtzman muttered. "We're looking at standard beat cops and fresh-from-battle troops."

"How fresh?" Bolan asked.

"Just out of the region. The units assigned had been pulled from their shift there, and they're running low," Kurtzman said. "They sound good on paper…"

"But they're all wrong for security," Bolan concluded. He was looking at the data transmitted over. "They're jumpy from the field, so if they do open fire, it'll be madness minutes, not controlled fire. They haven't had a chance to decompress and adjust to regular society."

"Good luck heading this off," Kurtzman said. "You're going to need it."

Bolan had spent an hour scanning every possible entrance and access panel on the blueprints, applying his vast experience to the task of penetrating the overworked security force and protection measures. He came up with half a dozen plans that would all result in widespread bloodshed. There were two plans that would insure the survival of the Iron Hammer raiders, or at least provide the illusion that there would be success and retreat for the "valiant" freedom fighters. The one with the perfect getaway was discarded.

The Curved Knife needed too many bodies and undeniable proof of violence on the part of the Chechen insurgents operating deep in the heart of Moscow. Bolan instead focused on the exit strategy that would only work if the enemy had no idea of it.

Bolan picked out four spots along that plan's egress where Curved Knife forces could set up a brutal ambush that left no one alive, but only if they were aware of the plot and the exact plan. The other escape option didn't have such certain kill points available to ambushers on the part of Curved Knife.

Laserka leaned over and began to knot Bolan's tie, her slender, strong fingers folding and tucking the black fabric with uncanny deftness. Bolan looked up into her green eyes and smiled. "I'd have gotten to it eventually."

"Let me just do something nice for you," Laserka told him. "You don't know how much it meant to me to have a friend. Now I understand what they mean about spies out in the cold."

Bolan cupped her cheek and gave her a warm smile. "Don't worry about it."

"Do you really think that Batroykin wasn't trying to screw me?" Laserka asked.

Bolan grinned as Laserka tightened the tie, adjusting it so that it sat straight at his collar. "Not the way you're intending. You have seen the dress, right?"

Laserka mussed Bolan's hair in playful reproach. "Funny, Cooper."

"I don't get much of a chance to toss out punch lines," Bolan confessed. "Let me have my moment."

Laserka winked. "That suit looks too well fitted to hide anything of note. Want to carry my purse?"

"Let me introduce you to the wonders of excellent tailoring," Bolan said with flourish. He slid into his double-shoulder-holster harness, which balanced the Beretta 93R under one armpit and the flat, sleek Storm under the other. Securing the belt hooks to his waist-band, Bolan shrugged under his jacket, which settled over the harness. "Loose along the sides, enough to provide room for the gun and its mirror, or a double-magazine holder."

Bolan turned, and Laserka nodded in approval. Bolan bent and slid two 20-round magazines into calf harnesses.

"That's 120 shots before you have to grab another weapon," Laserka stated. "Think that will be enough?"

Bolan shrugged. "I'm only carrying 120 shots because I can't carry 150 before the pockets bulge. We'll go in through the kitchen-service entrance. That's the one that won't have a metal detector."

"How do you know that?" Laserka asked.

"No way to get proper, consistent power, and if they did, it'd have to come in through an extension cord," Bolan told her. "We pass through there, we've got a better chance of being ignored."

"And if not?" Laserka asked.

Bolan rapped on his thigh, producing a metallic rapping sound. He spoke in Russian. "I do not think you should be harassing a veteran of the Afghanistan Expeditionary Force who gave up his leg for mother Russia."

Laserka's eyes widened.

"A metal band I wrapped around my thigh for the situation," Bolan explained. "Metallic prosthesis make smuggling weapons so much easier."

"Not too easy," Laserka said. "I'd hate to face AKs with only handguns."

Bolan nodded, and the pair left for the party.

## CHAPTER TEN

Vasili Batroykin eyed the glass in front of him, wishing the crystal-clear mineral water were a double shot of the hardest vodka he'd ever tasted, but knew that he had to keep his wits sharp. Looking around, he could tell that the men who were on duty were trying their best to watch over the group of people whose biggest concern was peace in Chechnya, not their personal safety. Speeches had been made, and debating sides voiced. Though there was disagreement among the smaller individual issues, the primary push of the entire group was that the Chechen people not receive the same kind of en masse punishment as Romania or Hungary had received at the beginning of the cold war.

Batroykin threw back the mineral water as if it were hard liquor and set the glass down.

The guardians of this conference were good and honest men, policemen and soldiers drawn from a pool of experienced and determined warriors whose goal was the protection of Russia and the Commonwealth of Independent States. Unfortunately, Batroykin could see the dullness in the faces of the soldiers, exhaustion of the physical and mental kind apparent as they performed their ordinary tasks. The policemen were fresher and more alert, but they were uncertain in these surroundings, constantly patting their sides to be reminded of the presence of their sidearms, and occasionally bumping into partygoers as their attention was turned elsewhere. Either too inexperienced or too worn from battle, the amassed defenders were assembled by a madman in order to facilitate a wave of murder and mayhem that would galvanize Moscow into punitive action.

Batroykin grimaced and poured another glass of water from the carafe, but let it sit in front of him. If he knocked back too many, he'd have to run to the bathroom, and while in there, the small Heckler & Koch pistol in his hip holster would be useless to Cooper and Laserka. He saw the pair come into the party, and while they didn't appear to be armed, he could tell from Cooper's confidence and alertness that the man had to have some ace hidden up his sleeve, or more precisely, under his armpit.

Batroykin sighed and mopped his brow with a napkin. Tonight was a juicy target for anyone wanting to continue the war and the breakdown of civil rights in Russia, spurring a return to the bad old days of the KGB. Though Batroykin had been a benefactor of the old guard's rule, it wasn't something that he had been able to sleep with. Batroykin had learned the art of selling his soul and dreams for the sake of survival, knowing that if he'd spoken up, he'd be one of those who had disappeared in the night, carted off to a camp where he'd be the subject of medical experimentation

or pushed into mining radioactive ore without the bene-
fit of radiation protection. Fear of slow, cruel murder
had kept him silent, and only exacerbated his guilt over
his tacit allowance of evil to be done while he said
nothing.

Now, he had a chance to change things, and it all
hinged on the young woman he'd convinced for years
that he was an enemy of her closest friend.

Laserka and the American were a thin advantage
that he'd have over the Iron Hammer assault team.

He scratched that thought. Batroykin wasn't going
to be the front-line back breaker of the terrorist assault.
He'd be able to help with his little HK P2000, but there
was one human being in this building who could turn
a massacre into a massive failure for the pawns of the
Curved Knife. The American.

If only things could go easily tonight. Batroykin
took a small sip of the water to spare his bladder, resting his hand on the thigh of a pretty young woman he'd
hired from an escort service. She giggled at his touch,
and it sounded almost genuine enough to be worth the
rubles he was pouring into the blonde's paycheck. He
winked to her, continuing to worry about the potential
for violence. Dread hung in the air like a noxious cloud.

He hated being so distracted by work that he
couldn't enjoy the softness of a woman's bare thigh
kneaded between his fingers.

He gave the hired girl another grope almost ab-
sently, his eyes scanning for danger.


THE EXECUTIONER LET the drink in his hand swirl
around, making it look as if he were an active part of

the party, laughing when others laughed, and moving from conversation to conversation, saying only a few words. He hadn't touched the tumbler to his lips except to give his breath a hint of alcohol, and he weaved through the gala event with the grace and ease of a dilettante. Laserka sat at a table, keeping to her own business, occasionally throwing a baleful glare in Bolan's direction, playing the role of jilted girlfriend. She was good at that, and her static position allowed her the chance to keep an eye on four areas where the Iron Hammer attackers could strike from.

Sitting there, with a scowl on her face, also allowed her to deflect the amorous attention of anyone daring to try to chat with her. Her glower kept suitors at bay easily, and Bolan appreciated the willingness of the pretty Russian agent to deglamorize herself to continue the mission. Then again, when they had met that morning, she was free of makeup and jewelry, burying her good looks under a veneer of plainness that she seemed entirely comfortable in.

Given the rumors and stories about Batroykin, there was little doubt that she had cultivated her unenhanced look to grant her more comfort under the notorious self-evident ladies' man. Batroykin was sitting in another corner, and Bolan could make out that the man was armed, and his round, pale face was darkened with concern. The Russian had a reputation that didn't match the assessment that Bolan had made. Batroykin's alleged lechery was just another shield, just like the impressions that had placed Laserka and him on opposite sides of a fence that didn't exist. The veteran intelligence officer had developed layers of subterfuge and armor to keep him shielded from intense scrutiny.

Bolan knew he could trust the man, but he also realized that Batroykin was a desk jockey. His physique was indicative that he would not stand up for more than a few minutes in the stress of combat, no matter how good a shot he was at the range.

"Cooper," he heard Laserka say. "Quadrant three."

Bolan immediately locked on to the position that Laserka pointed out. On the move, he could cover two or three of the enemies likely points of entry, but not an entire wing of them at once, as Laserka could from her vantage point. Bolan spotted the gunmen, three waiters setting up. Their trolley with its covered dishes was, to the Executioner, obviously not filled with hot food or even cold salad. There was no condensation on the metal dome lid indicating freshly chilled lettuce and salad, nor was there steam rising from the top.

When the lid was to be raised, there was only going to be deadly steel weapons within.

"Have them marked," Bolan answered. He looked around. If he intercepted the group, there was a good chance that he could cause a firefight to erupt then and there. With all the bystanders, that would mean a slaughter as war-worn soldiers tried to deal with armed opponents using human shields, resulting in an all too familiar recipe for disaster. The tactics of cowardice were well developed, and against fighting men who had been pushed to the edge of reason by unrelenting violence, it often scored the exact thing that the terrorists wanted—making good men gun down innocent noncombatants.

Fortunately the lone warrior had his own means of dealing with such situations. When he and Laserka had first entered the building, the Executioner had excused himself and, using the blueprints provided by Kurtzman and the Stony Man cybergeniuses, made it to one of the central power junction boxes. Wrapping a worm of plastic explosives around the wiring leading into the juncture, then secreting a small radio detonator in the shadow of the protective pipe around the power conduit, he had the means to cause an immediate blackout.

With wraithlike grace, Bolan slid closer to the gunmen who were speaking softly into their wrist cuffs where radio microphones put them in contact with their partners.

"I've spotted two tertiary groups beginning their setup," Laserka told him. "Groups Gamma and Delta. No sign of group Beta, however."

"They must be running slow," Bolan said. "Get ready, it's about to get dark in here."

"Good luck, Cooper," Laserka said. "Heading to intercept group Beta in case they do show up."

"Same to you," Bolan told her.

He pressed the thumb stud. In the distance, there was a sharp crackle, and suddenly the lights in the party hall went dark. The Russians in attendance, used to power outages due to the harsh Moscow winters and the run-down state of technology in their nation, mostly voiced groans of disdain and disgust as battery-powered lights over the exits came on. Soldiers and cops pulled out their flashlights, as well.

"What the hell is going on? Who killed the power?"

one of the Iron Hammer gunmen asked, visible in bled-off light as he lifted the dome on his tray to retrieve a Bizon submachine gun.

"I did," Bolan answered in Russian.

The Iron Hammer terrorist paused, squinting in the darkness at the Executioner. "And who are you?"

Bolan shrugged, letting his fighting knife drop to his palm from its forearm sheath. "I am your judgment."

The Chechen's face went slack, panic freezing him in place, his fingertips resting on the grip of the SMG that was under the lid. He started to grab the gun, but Bolan punched the double-bladed knife up and under the would-be killer's chin, steel cleaving through the hollow under his jaw. The hard, reinforced point smashed through the roof of his mouth, puncturing the Iron Hammerman's brain right where the spine swelled and expanded into the brain. As the deadly metal tore through the trunk of neural connections, the Chechen's hand flopped slackly on the Bizon, his legs folding as if the bones had turned to rubber.

A second Iron Hammer thug was looking both ways. "Did they know we were coming?"

"Yes, we did," Bolan answered the hapless shooter, ripping his knife from the corpse's throat and digging his fingers into the second faux waiter's collar. With a hard twist, the fabric of the man's jacket and shirt was drawn garrote tight across his windpipe, giving the Executioner all the handle he needed to wrench the doomed thug away from his assault weapon. Bolan didn't have the time to reverse the knife in his grasp, but the hard, reinforced glass-breaker on the butt of the handle sufficed for killing purposes. The extrahard metal striker rammed into the Chechen's kidney with more than sufficient force to rupture blood vessels in the vital organ. With the violent impact pulverizing the kidney, the man's blood supply became poisonous almost instantly. Renal shock paralyzed him with agony, allowing the Executioner to give the collar another hard twist as he swung the pain-racked terrorist face-first into the wall with a sickening crunch of collapsing face bones and grinding neck vertebrae.

With two dead in less than ten seconds, with hardly a sound, the last two members of the Iron Hammer strike team looked toward the big man in the suit with a dripping blade in his hand.

"We've been made!" one of them shouted, slapping the lid of his tray to the floor with a metallic ring.

The other Chechen threw himself at Bolan, whipping up a large butcher's knife from his trolley to deal with the tall, dark wraith. Bolan sidestepped the knife man's initial swing as the ribbon of metal whistled through the air perilously close to his ear. The Executioner lifted his leg, driving his knee into the blade fighter's sternum with rib-cracking force. The Iron Hammer brawler stumbled back, wheezing in agony as broken shards of bone stabbed into his lower lungs. Bolan lunged in close, driving the point of his deadly, sleek knife into the juncture of the Chechen's neck and shoulder in one quick up-and-down stab.

The brutal stroke opened a gash four inches long and six inches deep, the razor-sharp edge severing muscle, artery and nerve clusters in its savage passage. The enemy knife man's eyes glazed over as the blood pressure to his brain suddenly dropped off. He moved his lips, limp right arm flopping and letting the butcher knife clatter to the tile at his feet. Bolan shouldered the mortally wounded raider and rushed toward the last of the gunmen.

The panicked Chechen managed to grasp the Bizon securely in both hands and he swung it around, the stubby barrel clipping Bolan across the jaw. In the darkness, with panic fueling the gunman's reactions, it was just one of those instances where the law of averages had turned in the Executioner's favor. The pistol-whipping blow rocked Bolan on his heels, and his stumble saved his life as the muzzle of the Bizon snarled, bullets searing the air just inches from his head.

With the first gunshots, the situation spiraled out of control as the harried and confused security force noticed the barrel lick out with a tongue of flame in the darkened hall.

"Gun!" several security men shouted, spinning in unison toward the Iron Hammer shooter. Bolan twisted and threw himself flat to the floor as the Chechen was caught in the glare of a half dozen flashlights. A heart-beat later, the air was filled with the roar of handguns and assault rifles, the fake waiter's torso and face exploding under a blazing storm of assault-weapon bullets.

Bolan scurried along the floor as the Iron Hammer gunman was pinned to the wall, nailed there by dozens of rounds of lead that turned his white server's jacket into a crimson death shroud. Had the shooter not staggered the Executioner with a lucky blow, it could have been Bolan falling under the rain of doom.

Given a reprieve from the law of averages, the canny warrior got to his feet far from where the four lifeless infiltrators lay.

The gunfight had started, but thanks to the blackout, the Iron Hammer gunmen were caught off guard, and the guests at the party and their protectors had already filed away from the main floor. The cops and soldiers had a clear line of fire on the Chechen terrorist that Bolan had engaged, no innocents in position to be caught in the cross fire.

Cops herded the Russian partygoers more quickly toward the exits as the rifle-armed soldiers standing guard swept the area, looking for more trouble. Bolan faded into the shadows between their searching flashlights.

In the distance, he heard Laserka shout.

"Police! Drop your weapons!"

Bolan saw the missing team of gunmen burst from the kitchen, assault rifles in hand. Two of the Iron Hammer thugs at the front had their forearms barred across the throats of staff members, using them as human shields.

The Russian soldiers paused, seeing that the enemy had noncombatants at stake. While the fighting men would be trained shooters, in the confusion and darkness, there was no way that the riflemen would have a chance to get accurate shots past the bodies of the kitchen workers, especially not with the flexing barrels of the Kalashnikov rifles they carried.

It would be up to the Executioner to save their lives.

Bolan drew the Beretta 93R from its shoulder holster, melting into the darkness.

LASERKA WAS PREPARED when the lights cut out, although the nosy young politician who was standing beside her gave a girlish yelp of surprise. The Russian diplomat had been trying to soothe her anger and open her up to the possibilities of courtship with the deep, manly tones of his voice. Laserka rose to her feet and grabbed his wrist.

"Quiet," she told him. She pointed toward the exit of the meeting hall where policemen with flashlights and emergency exit beacons cut through the darkness. "Just move that way and everything will be all right."

"What about you?" the politician whimpered, his blue eyes wide with fear.

Laserka brandished the Makarov pistol from her purse. "I've got work to do, protecting you."

The politician swallowed audibly, then nodded nervously. He turned and hightailed it toward the armed security men who were beckoning partygoers toward a safe egress.

Laserka caught a flash of swift, violent movement out of the corner of her eye, and she knew that it was Cooper in action, beginning his cull of the Iron Hammer terrorists before they could initiate a wave of violence and terror that would lead to bystander-chewing cross fire. The big American moved with the speed and grace of a jungle cat, so she could imagine the lightning-quick efficiency with which he could eliminate an opponent with only a knife as his weapon. Laserka sighed, knowing that she was not going to be the same human wrecking machine that could tear through enemy gunmen with silent, brutal skill.

The Makarov in her hand, and the spare magazines in the handbag, were going to have to do her work for her as she vectored in on the team of Chechens that Cooper had labeled Group Gamma. He had divided up the enemy into four squads, three of them who would act as instigators, and the fourth dedicated to cutting off the avenue of escape from the party floor. He had been specific in telling Laserka that it was her job to take down Group Gamma to minimize the potential of slaughter that was vital to Iron Hammer's plan.

Flashlights strobed around the room, reminding Laserka of a quieter version of the smoke- and body-filled raves she'd attended, both as a dancer and as an official investigator. All that was missing was the smell of marijuana and the rhythmic electronic pump and hum of mix music spun by a DJ that would throw the crowd into a trance.

From the looks of the Gamma Group, the four Chechen infiltrators were already getting out their instruments of percussion, the deadly compact Bizon submachine guns with their tube-shaped 64-round magazines. Four men could sweep the crowd with over two hundred and fifty 9 mm bullets before needing to reload. In the tightly packed quarters of the exits, those bullets could slice through the soft viscera of dozens of bodies without being stopped by impact on bone, increasing the horrific wounding potential of the brutal snipers.

"Police!" Laserka challenged, positively identifying herself to her fellow Russian lawmen and soldiers, and anchoring the attention of the four Iron Hammer gunmen on her and away from the evacuating bystanders. "Drop your weapons!"

Laserka didn't wait for a response from the quartet of Chechen killers, pulling the trigger on her Makarov even as her challenge finished leaving her lips. The lady cop's first two rounds punched into the face and throat of one Iron Hammer gunner as he tried to pivot his Bizon toward her, the 9 mm rounds crashing through fragile facial bones and his windpipe. Brain punctured by a drilling Makarov pill, neck bone snapped out of alignment by its fellow traveler, the gunman collapsed instantly, his body crashing across the front of one of his partners.

The dead man's bulk swatted his friend's Bizon toward the floor even as the Chechen triggered his weapon, bullets shattering the tile impotently. A Russian policeman whipped his Grozny sidearm toward the triggerman, firing the big plastic cop gun at the man before he could recover and adjust his aim to cause more harm. The Moscow cop's intentions were good, but in his rush and panic, only one bullet came close to the insurgent's vital organs, a 9 mm slug slicing deep into his shoulder.

Laserka pivoted her weapon toward the stunned and distracted Iron Hammer gunner and cranked the trigger on the compact Makarov. Experience and cool under fire helped her to score a trio of center mass hits where her comrade had failed. The wounded terrorist was now a dead man, tumbling to the floor in a lifeless heap atop his lifeless partner.

"Bitch!" snarled one of the two remaining Gamma group members as he shouldered his Bizon, aiming at her. Laserka knew that she couldn't dive out of the way in time to avoid catching at least a couple deadly bullets, but the roar and snarl of a Kalashnikov flared off to her right.

The Iron Hammer gunman shuddered under a storm of 5.45 mm rifle rounds that shredded through his torso like a chain saw, ripping his rib cage open in a growling staccato of death. Another of the Russian military protectors followed his comrade's example with a brutal burst that punched into the skull of the surviving Gamma sniper, turning the Chechen's head into a gory mist of free-floating blood and brain matter.

Laserka gave the two soldiers a thumbs-up, and they nodded in gratitude for her assistance. She stuffed the Makarov into her handbag and rushed forward to scoop up a fallen Bizon. The Moscow cop who had distracted the second Gamma gunman looked at the handgun in his grasp, then to her.

"Inspector Laserka?" he asked numbly.

"Just keep directing traffic," Laserka ordered the officer. She remembered him as a sweet young man named Petrovik. The brown-eyed Moscow cop nodded, looking guilty for not being the same caliber of warrior as the Russian soldiers and his superior officer. "Get the people to safety. We've got enough shooters here to handle any problems. Good work, Petrovik."

The Moscow cop nodded, a weak smile on his lips before he turned and started grabbing partygoers and directing them toward an orderly exit.

Laserka turned, noting that Cooper was gone, and there was a hostage situation in front of the kitchen.

"We'll kill them!" one Iron Hammer terrorist snarled. "And nothing can stop us!"

That's when Laserka spotted the shadowy form of Matt Cooper coming up on their blind side.

"That's what you think," Laserka whispered, a cruel grin on her lips.

## CHAPTER ELEVEN

The Executioner was a ghost in the darkness behind the team he'd designated Beta Group, the Chechen strike force that had been mysteriously delayed before the blackout interrupted the plans of their partners. The war computer inside of Bolan's skull quickly surmised that the Iron Hammer team's delay had been the result of taking hostages. The lack of gunfire before their rushed exit meant that the gunmen hadn't done more than cuff kitchen staff with rifle stocks, especially due to the lack of blood on their clothing. However, the fact that they hadn't killed *yet* was no consolation due to the fact that the Iron Hammer death squad was here to wreak bloody havoc to facilitate the sparrow hawks in the administration ordering a violent, bloody reprisal against the Chechen people.

As it was, just the appearance of the terrorists at a major political function in Moscow had done enormous damage to whatever peace process was under way at the international level. The two independent states were going to have to soothe a lot of offended egos no matter if only one innocent died or if dozens of Chechen extremists were lit on fire and hung from the railing as decorations.

The Executioner, however, could not tolerate harm befalling innocent noncombatants, and that meant the warrior would have to utilize every ounce of his skill and combat ability to rescue the pair of hostages before one side of the deadly tableau opened fire. The conflagration that would result would bring only death and suffering to those caught in the middle, and the kitchen doors would be no protection for the cowed staff behind them.

Bolan's free hand snaked under his jacket to retrieve the flat and sleek Px4 Storm from its holster. While the use of a pistol in each hand was contraindicated by every combat trainer in the known world, there was a time and place for every technique in the Executioner's repertoire. Right now, he'd be engaging opponents at only an arm's length, and in such conditions, any loss of precision aim by the use of a single hand on each weapon would be mitigated by the fact that he'd have visual confirmation of the direction of his bullets. Also, in such close quarters, it was wholly possible that one of his gun hands would be snagged and restrained by an opponent, so having both fists stuffed and ready to belch fire and lead would give him an advantage.

Moving like lightning, Bolan pistol-whipped one Chechen raider across the back of his head using the blunt nose of the Px4, the impact splitting the man's scalp and creating a crimson mist that spattered in the eyes of one of his partners. The second Iron Hammer man stepped back, touching his face at the sudden sting of blood. As the first gunman collapsed with an agonizing pain in the back of his skull, Bolan whirled and speared his foot between the thighs of the momentarily surprised terrorist. The spritz of blood had left the man flat-footed enough for a jarring bolt of searing pain that cut through his body as Bolan's sharp-pointed dress shoe and its reinforced steel toe mashed his testicles into a paste against his pelvis. The Chechen's voice rose several octaves, going as high and shrill as a human could get without being audible only to dogs.

The crotch-kicked gunman dropped his assault rifle, his face reddening like a stoplight. Bolan turned the Beretta 93R sideways and chopped the butt of the handgun hard against the Iron Hammer infiltrator's face, the steel frame crushing cheekbone and nose cartilage with one shattering stroke that laid him out on the floor.

"What was…" one of the Chechens with a hostage had asked, turning his head at the sound of the unconscious man's squeal a moment too late to help him.

Bolan whirled the 93R around and the end of the 6.5-inch barrel touched the hostage taker's forehead before a 9 mm round drilled through bone into his central nervous system, whipping the doomed gunner's brain into froth with its passage. The Chechen died so quickly, his mind erased by the rapid entry of a 115-grain hollowpoint round, that even with his finger on the trigger, there was no impulse down the spine that impelled his lifeless hand to fire the AK in his fist. Instead, the seemingly boneless corpse dropped his hostage and rifle, pouring to the tiled floor as if he were dumped out of a large soup pot.

The last of the Beta group hostage takers heard the sudden sharp crack of Bolan's 93R and twisted in reaction, trying to haul an apron-wearing kitchen worker around as a living shield. Bolan's other hand and its Px4 was up and in his face immediately, the polymer combat pistol barking a solitary Parabellum pill that took him on the point of his chin, splitting his lower mandible. The flattened ball round, deformed by its hard interaction with solid bone, whirled and slashed through muscle and windpipe before stopping cold at the top of his spinal column.

Though the Iron Hammer rifleman's brain wasn't completely shut down like his fellow hostage taker's, it didn't matter because the destruction of his jaw and the jolting of his spine occurred with such force that reflex yanked the AKM in his fist away from his victim's head an instant before the weapon spit a storm of lead into the ceiling. Bolan fired a second and third shot into the dying man's upper chest, the 9 mm rounds splitting his breastbone and boring into his aorta.

Bolan lowered his pistols, looking at the two stunned hostages who, until a second before, had been at the gates of hell with guns to their heads.

"Get to the cops, hurry," Bolan told them in fluent Russian.

One of the chefs pointed at the doors. "We have injured in the kitchen. No one shot or stabbed—"

"Let me clear the area," Bolan cut him off. "Any other threats in the kitchen?"

"They left two men at the loading dock," the chef said.

Russian soldiers and Moscow cops hurried toward the Executioner and the man he'd rescued.

"Sir?" the lead cop asked. "Who—"

"Special Agent Matt Cooper, here on the invitation of Director Vasili Batroykin," Bolan said in Russian. "International cooperative investigation."

The assembled Russian men looked at one another, then examined the tall, powerful figure. Bolan had worn a dark blue, fine silk suit and tie, and Laserka had joked that he looked a lot like a debonair secret agent. Of course, that was before the cuffs of his powder-blue dress shirt were stained with the spilled blood of the Iron Hammer terrorists on the receiving end of his combat knife.

There was a soft, suppressed whisper among the soldiers as they knew that Bolan was no more an FBI agent than they were a roving troupe of troubadours. Bolan was certain that these men, who walked in the light of public service, knew nothing about the shadowy predator who stalked the back alleys of the old Soviet Union and the shadows of the laboring post–cold war Russia. Still, there was no doubt that the Executioner was a godsend who had come specifically to intervene in what would have been a massacre and political nightmare.

"What do you need us to do, sir?" the cop in charge inquired.

"Continue getting the partygoers to safety. Keep the kitchen and those exits contained, as well. There's a chance that there might be more trouble coming through those doors," Bolan ordered. "Anyone have a radio?"

"We're in contact with the street in front," the Moscow officer said. "Nobody's been allowed out the front doors, and we have Sergei's unit and my people scanning for possible snipers out front."

Bolan nodded. He pulled a folded piece of paper from his pocket. On it was printed a popular search engine's map of Moscow, blown up to show the meeting hall and the buildings across the street. "Concentrate your attention on these two buildings, and get helicopters up. Just knowing about where they could try to engage you will help, but a couple of birds in the air will keep their heads down. Maintain hard cover and alternating fields of fire if they do attempt something, but the confusion caused by that blackout might have thrown them off."

The policeman took the sheet of paper, scanning the markings on it. He looked up at Bolan as Laserka joined him at his side. "Just here on Batroykin's invitation?"

"Entertaining a fellow lawman from across the waters," Laserka lied. "Give him a break, Dmitri."

Dmitri sighed. "Don't you have enough headaches of your own after your apartment got tossed, Kaya?"

The lady cop shrugged, her lean, freckled shoulders rising and falling, drawing an appreciative look from her coworker. "Call this proactive intervention."

"We've got a back door to close down," Bolan told her. "Keep the front clear, Dmitri."

The Moscow cop saluted Bolan. The Russian soldiers looked disappointed that they hadn't been asked to accompany the man into further battle, but they settled into position, forming a rear guard for the precious cargo of citizens and leaders who were still vulnerable to danger. Laserka stuffed a Bizon into Bolan's hands.

"I went shopping," she told the big American.

"Just my size, too," Bolan returned before they went through the kitchen doors. The pair paused, and Laserka peeked through the porthole in the center of the door on her side.

"I'm pretty sure you could take down a tank with a .22, Cooper," Laserka said. "I never saw someone move as quickly as you did."

"You weren't too slow yourself," Bolan countered. "Two men are back there, according to the chef, but they're by the loading dock. They won't have hostages because their purpose is to keep the back way open. There's most likely at least one vehicle on the dock, but if I hedged my bets correctly, there are two trucks."

"And you're putting money on the fact that there'll be someone from the Knife ready to blow up the trucks," Laserka said.

"Not at the back of the building," Bolan explained. "The snipers will be farther along the way. It'll look like the Knife is a part of the Moscow counterterrorism police, and they'll cut off the fleeing Iron Hammers with rocket launchers, maybe a heavy machine gun or two."

"No survivors." Laserka spoke up, remembering their earlier discussion. "Not that these guys are doing well at living."

Bolan nodded, then burst through the door. "Moscow police! Get moving, but stay low!"

Cowering kitchen staff, nursing bruised faces and heads, looked up at the big man in the suit. Because he gestured at the ceiling with his Bizon submachine gun and tossed orders out in booming Russian, they listened to him, crawling on the cold tiled floor for the exit. Being on all fours, the staff would enter the view of the Russian soldiers in a passive manner, a means that insulated them from nervous and itchy trigger fingers. Bolan and Laserka moved through the kitchen, the American leading the way utilizing his memorized directions of the building's layout to give them a swift and efficient path to the loading dock where the remaining two Iron Hammer gunmen were in wait. Their route took them along a path of least resistance and even less exposure to danger.

"Moscow police?" he heard one of the rear guard say. "My ass. They made a lot of noise, but those rental cops are too scared to come at us."

"Shut up! What do you want to do, bring down hell on us?" the other asked.

"Superstitious ninny," the first speaker snarled. "I thought you were a freedom fighter…"

"We're dead if we don't pay attention. I mean, except for a few short bursts, there hasn't been anything," the "ninny" replied.

Bolan whipped around the corner as soon as the superstitious guard spoke, the stock of his Bizon lashing out hard and striking him in the base of his neck with a stunning stroke that threw him to the floor. The first speaker yelped in surprise, stepping back at the sudden appearance of the tall, grim man in their midst. Before he could bring his weapon down and fire at the Executioner, Laserka was in the open, her machine pistol stuttering out a short death note that ripped the man from navel to heart.

Bolan grabbed the dazed gunman he'd struck, pulling him up to a standing position.

"The short spurts of automatic fire you heard were the sounds of your brethren being destroyed," he explained in Russian. "This operation is doomed, son of the Iron Hammer."

"Wait!" the prisoner muttered, his words mushy. "Please, don't kill me."

"I won't have to. On the other side of the kitchen doors are a dozen Russian soldiers who would love nothing more than to kill you by inches," Bolan pushed. "Besides, what worth are you?"

The Chechen terrorist fumbled into his pocket for keys before pressing them into Bolan's hand. "My motorcycle... Georgi has one, too. We couldn't fit in the truck, and Anatoly said that they needed scouts anyway."

Bolan tilted his head. "Motorcycles..."

Laserka's SMG stuttered as a shape appeared in his peripheral vision. "Missed him!"

Bolan grabbed Laserka by the wrist immediately, dragging her to the floor instants ahead of the bellow of a heavy machine gun. The access door that the two Iron Hammer terrorists had been guarding suddenly exploded as 12.7 mm slugs ripped through the heavy metal construction of the panels. The stunned guard's torso disintegrated as the massive antiarmor slugs pulverized flesh and bone, reducing everything between his head and pelvis to pulp and splinters as the 12.7 mm cannon swept the loading dock.

Outside, heavy diesel engines snorted and snarled to life. The Iron Hammer death squad was about to make its getaway, and as much as Bolan wouldn't have minded seeing the Chechen extremists taken down by their phantom masters, his goal was to intercept the Curved Knife assassins and get a prisoner or two.

Of course, the sudden appearance of two sets of motorcycle keys gave the Executioner everything he needed to insure that he could shadow the Iron Hammer trucks. He glanced at Laserka, who had been covered in blood spatter from the devastated guard.

"Are you okay?" Bolan asked.

"I need something to wear," Laserka said. "No way this dress was designed for high-speed pursuit on motorcycle."

Bolan pointed to the man she'd just shot. "Cinch his belt tight. And wear his jacket, you'll need it."

The trucks pulled out, and in the reflection of a stainless-steel refrigerator, Bolan could make out a machine gunner on watch in the bed of one of the vehicles. The two transports were moving slowly, as was the nature of their ancient mechanisms, which gave the Executioner and Laserka time to peel off the dead guard's jacket and pants. She'd kicked off her shoes minutes ago, and had been running around barefoot.

Bolan spared a millisecond to punch a hole in the dead man's belt with his combat knife to enable Laserka to cinch the waist tight over the tops of her hips. There would be no way that her pants would fall down now.

"Come on," Bolan said as she plucked the motorcycle keys from her pocket. As the pair ran out into the loading dock, the two trucks were turning into the street.

A quick glance revealed the two Ural Wolf motorcycles. Bolan gave a low whistle. The bikes were massive 551-pound road machines that had been designed by the Ural company and the Black Wolf Russian motorcycle club to make a comparable machine to the American Harley-Davidson. Their huge 749 cc four-stroke, air-cooled, flat twin-cylinder engines were powerful enough to propel the quarter-ton road machine and its 200-pound riders along at well over 81 mph, according to the factory, but the Ural designers had low-balled the total speed of the machine for safety purposes. David McCarter had taken one up to 150 mph, but the British Phoenix Force commander was a madman on the road who terrified any person who'd ever driven with him.

"You strong enough to handle six hundred pounds of motorcycle, Kaya?" Bolan asked.

She jumped into the seat of her bike and tried the key in the ignition. "Trade!"

Bolan tossed her his keys and caught the set lobbed to him. "I'll take that as a yes."

Laserka kicked the starter on the machine. "On these things, you let their weight do your work for you. Ever ridden a Wolf?"

Bolan kicked his machine to life. "Just keep up, Kaya."

"Sure thing, Cooper," Laserka replied.

The two warriors on their roaring motorcycle tore off into the street to pursue the Iron Hammer to their rendezvous with the Curved Knife.

The pair hoped that they wouldn't lose this tenuous thread on the violent conspiracy.

ANATOLY SIYAAD BELLOWED, ordering the drivers onward, knowing that sticking around once someone had reached the kitchen, would be suicide for the Iron Hammer death squad. The machine gunner on the back of his truck cut loose, spraying the loading dock with a scythe of armor-piercing bullets that tore ruthlessly into the building. A splash of gore exploding onto a wall visible through the loading doors was evidence enough that the gunner had done the job.

"Get moving!" Siyaad snarled.

"These things aren't sports cars, Anatoly! They need time to pick up speed!" the driver complained. "Give us a minute here!"

"We don't have a minute!" Siyaad said. He called up the gunner in the back of the truck with his walkie-talkie. "Any movement or return fire?"

"Negative. I think I got everyone in the loading dock," the gunner replied.

"Stay focused on the door. I don't need someone on our tails as we're getting the hell out of here," Siyaad said.

Watching out the passenger window, Siyaad kept his pistol ready in his lap. It didn't seem to make sense that a center full of soldiers and cops on security duty would have sent only a handful of people into a compromised kitchen area. Something felt wrong, and his instincts were warning him that it was possibly due to the fact that someone other than the Moscow police and the Russian military were on hand, interfering with the Iron Hammer's operation.

There were rumors that the organization had some guardian angels in the form of administration agencies that saw the Chechen rebellion as a means of making their country strong again. Siyaad doubted that they were truly interested in the freedom of Chechnya from outside rule, but apparently the work that they were doing had smashed the Russian government hard enough to show where the foundation was crumbling.

Siyaad hated the possibility that he might be a pawn. He knew that such patsies, once their usefulness had ended, suffered the fate of a bullet in the gut and a burial in a potter's field. The Iron Hammer was meant to be a force to end oppression from Moscow's puppet government. Of course, he was slowly becoming aware that the current administration of Russia actually enjoyed having an enemy to put down, as in the old days. It had allowed them to unleash the secret policemen again, to draw out the old assassins and kidnappers who tormented their people.

Siyaad wondered if that was an intentional thing. That they had been given the information and gear they received, had been honed to deadly efficiency above all other Chechen insurgence groups, to make a hard-line government seem the best of all possible worlds, a regime that would make the people safe by any means necessary.

"Anatoly! Our escort bikes are behind us!" the gunner shouted.

Siyaad cursed himself for getting lost in thought. He leaned out the window and saw two people on bikes. He bit his upper lip when he saw the long hair of one of the riders blowing in the wind as the Ural Wolf raced along the Moscow streets.

Neither of their guards had such long locks.

"Gun them down! They're not our people!" Siyaad bellowed, aiming his pistol at the pair.

The truck in front of them suddenly jolted, struck by a thunderbolt. With the explosion's flash, Siyaad flinched, realizing that his people had been set up.

## CHAPTER TWELVE

Mack Bolan watched as the smoky trail of the rocket-propelled grenade arced from the intersection—the fat, teardrop-shaped warhead spiraling and striking the cab of the second Iron Hammer truck. He lowered his head and accelerated the powerful motorcycle down the asphalt, realizing that he'd found his shot at the Curved Knife. The road machine pushed 90 mph, the fat, knobby tires gripping the road as he swerved around the Iron Hammer truck. Behind him, Kaya Laserka was hot on his tail, maneuvering her big 550-pound machine with a similar deftness.

In the cab of the second truck, the Chechen watched them with confusion and dismay as they whipped past. He had a gun in hand, obviously in response to their pursuit of the Iron Hammer convoy. The insurgent, however, was confused by the fact that Bolan and his ally were no longer interested in the Chechen insurgent team, and were instead accelerating toward the Russian team that had blown up half of their retreating number. The Executioner had to make the most of this mo-

NO POSTAGE
NECESSARY
IF MAILED
IN THE
UNITED STATES

# BUSINESS REPLY MAIL
FIRST-CLASS MAIL   PERMIT NO. 717   BUFFALO, NY

POSTAGE WILL BE PAID BY ADDRESSEE

**GOLD EAGLE READER SERVICE**
**3010 WALDEN AVE**
**PO BOX 1867**
**BUFFALO NY 14240-9952**

# Get FREE BOOKS and a FREE GIFT when you play the...

# LAS VEGAS

## GAME

*Just scratch off the gold box with a coin. Then check below to see the gifts you get!* →

## YES! I have scratched off the gold box. Please send me my **2 FREE BOOKS** and **FREE GIFT** for which I qualify. I understand that I am under no obligation to purchase any books as explained on the back of this card.

**366 ADL EVMJ**

**166 ADL EVMU**
(GE-LV-09)

| | |
|---|---|
| FIRST NAME | LAST NAME |

ADDRESS

| | |
|---|---|
| APT.# | CITY |

| | |
|---|---|
| STATE/PROV. | ZIP/POSTAL CODE |

| | | | |
|---|---|---|---|
| 7 | 7 | 7 | **Worth TWO FREE BOOKS plus a FREE Gift!** |
| 🍒 | 🍒 | 🍒 | **Worth TWO FREE BOOKS!** |
| ♣ | ♣ | ♣ | **TRY AGAIN!** |

Offer limited to one per household and not valid to current subscribers of Gold Eagle® books. All orders subject to approval. Please allow 4 to 6 weeks for delivery.

**Your Privacy -** Worldwide Library is committed to protecting your privacy. Our privacy policy is available online at www.eHarlequin.com or upon request from the Gold Eagle Reader Service. From time to time we make our lists of customers available to reputable third parties who may have a product or service of interest to you. If you would prefer for us not to share your name and address, please check here. □

mentary uncertainty, because caught between the two hostile forces was a bad place to be. While the cross fire would likely bring down damnation and punishment on both antagonistic squads, Bolan and Laserka would be the main focus of their combined fire. The faster that the Executioner and his partner were among the Curved Knife ambush team, the better their chances at getting hold of one of the conspirators. Bolan leveled the Bizon across the handlebars and milked the trigger, spraying a hose of 9 mm rounds out of the 64-round helical magazine, the line of bullets whipping at the armored fender of the enemy jeep and throwing sparks.

The extended magazine would give the Executioner ample firepower and enough time to lay down suppression fire while Laserka swung her bike around their flank and found cover. Steering one-handed and firing with the other wasn't a tactic that Bolan would have considered safe in an urban situation, but the initial shock of the rocket-propelled grenade had produced a signal to the civilians on the street to get out of the way and seek cover. It was only moments after the initial blast, but citizens rushed wildly, racing behind parked cars or diving into still-open storefronts to avoid the wild cross fire. Bolan tossed away the empty Bizon and used his weight and the sudden application of brakes to spin the motorcycle into a sideways skid that hurled wheels first into the side of the Curved Knife ambush jeep. The impact of over 750 pounds of man and machine jolted the parked vehicle, tossing men to the ground.

Bolan had managed to swing his leg out of the way

in time to protect it from being crushed between the two bulks of the bike and the jeep, and he tumbled away from the fused mass of steel before the gunners in the wreckage could recover their senses. He spun and drew his Berettas when he noticed that the men in the jeep were too young. Something was off and the Executioner holstered his weapons.

"Cooper!" Laserka shouted.

"Stand down!" Bolan ordered, reaching out to snatch the barrel of one young soldier's AK-47. He twisted the rifle from the youth's grasp and pinned him to the ground with a sideways kick that knocked the breath out of his lungs. A second of the interception team stirred, going for a sidearm, but the warrior used the metal folding stock of the captured assault weapon as a hammer to swat the pistol from numbed fingers.

The last of them saw that the warrior had easily disarmed them without resorting to lethal force and remained sprawled in his seat, nursing three gunshot wounds that had torn up his right arm. "You're not with Iron Hammer!"

Bolan looked back toward the surviving terrorist vehicle as it whipped through the intersection, taking off. "Laserka, keep on that truck!"

Bolan grasped the wounded officer by his good shoulder and used the grip as leverage to tear the bullet-ripped sleeve off of the bloody arm. "Are you all right? How much blood did you lose?"

"Not enough to be a factor, sir," the young officer replied. "Who are you with?"

"Russian Intelligence, under Director Batroykin. I didn't mean to hurt our own men," Bolan lied. He'd have to arrange with the pudgy little supervisor a solid cover so that the screwup didn't affect their operation. "Who ordered you to this intersection?"

The young officer gave a name, and Bolan memorized it. "You were expecting someone else, weren't you?"

"Stay here and recover," Bolan said. He ran up to an automobile which had paused to gawk at the situation.

"I need your car," Bolan said, pulling open the door, his big, strong hand touching the driver's shoulder. The Executioner took a quick look around the interior, relieved to find that the driver was the only person in the vehicle. He'd have hated to drive off and discover a child in the car.

"What's going on?" the man asked, stumbling away from the car, getting out of the way before Bolan slammed the door shut.

"Police emergency. Hot pursuit," Bolan said. "Check with those men."

Stomping the gas, Bolan peeled out, racing in the direction that he'd seen Laserka and the Iron Hammer truck escape toward. "Kaya, I had to commandeer a car. Where are you?"

"Six blocks up from where the Chechens turned off. They're going full speed now, and they're not going to be able to stop until they hit a brick wall," Laserka replied. "Catch up if you can."

"I'm on it," Bolan said. He had the pedal to the metal, but the engine on the car he had taken was only a little four-cylinder, and the warrior couldn't expect as much pep from the compact as he could from even the big, clumsy diesel truck. "The Curved Knife had regular cops on hand to cut off the Iron Hammer. They didn't want a chance that we'd get hold of their people."

"So what now?" Laserka asked.

"I have a name. I'll run it past Batroykin when we capture the terrorists," Bolan explained.

"Capture them?" Laserka asked.

"We need bait," Bolan said. "There'll be a good chance that the Knife will send in cleaners after any prisoners we gain control of."

"Cleaners like the situation you described in London?" Laserka asked. "Turn east after nine blocks!"

"Got it," Bolan returned. "Yes. They won't be able to trust the elimination of their hand-picked terrorist pawns to anyone other than one of their inside men. We catch that guy, we will have a better handle."

"What about the men you left alive back at the convention center?" Laserka asked. "The Knife might want them…"

"They're not the men in charge," Bolan said. "The leader is the guy in the second truck who was waving a handgun around."

"He'd be the one who could give us the next piece of the puzzle?" Laserka asked.

"I hope so. Because the Knife isn't going to send someone after some inexperienced, gun-crazy malcontents hired off the street," the Executioner returned, whipping the little compact car around the corner at Laserka's directions. The engine was pumping out ninety kilometers an hour, and he could see that the tachometer was revving high and hot. The engine temperature was crawling up into the red, but he could ease off on the pure acceleration, spotting the taillight of Laserka's motorbike, her long, flowing dark hair confirming his identification of the lady cop.

"That you in that little shitbox?" Laserka asked.

"None other," Bolan said.

"I'm surprised you're gaining on us," Laserka noted.

"It's a stick shift," Bolan replied. "Working the gearbox is easing some of the strain on this little number, but it sure as hell is taking a beating from the effort."

He pulled up neck and neck with the Russian operative, and caught his first glimpse of the Iron Hammer escapees in several minutes. The truck was roaring along at its best speed of only 50 mph, and Bolan was able to ease off on the gas, giving the compact he drove some much needed respite. A heavy machine gun was mounted on the back of the trasnport, easily visible, but something had to have happened to have turned off the gunner.

"I managed to wing the man with the machine gun with a lucky shot," Laserka said, noting the Executioner's attention. "Of course it took a whole sixty shots from my Bizon, so I'm back to just a handgun."

"We took their partners out with less," Bolan noted over their communications link. "Sooner or later they're going to try to get someone back on that chopper."

"What's your plan?" Laserka asked.

Bolan tromped on the gas pedal again, accelerating toward the truck, sending the tach into the red. The little four-cylinder vehicle wheezed and whined as it shot forward, cutting the distance between them by half.

With a hard twist of the wheel, Bolan impacted the back wheel of the larger vehicle with the car's fender. He hoped that he'd have enough mass in the small car to perform a pit maneuver, but the axle of the big truck weighed as much as the little vehicle. This wasn't like ramming a quarter-ton motorcycle into a jeep. The blow forced Bolan to swerve, but the diesel snorted and continued growling along unhindered by the impact.

The Iron Hammer leader pushed out of the driver's window, his handgun barking and spitting bullets through the windshield. Bolan jerked the wheel in an effort to avoid the hail of 9 mm. The truck was swerving wildly now, however, and Bolan could guess why.

The shooter had shoved the driver aside to get a shot at the pair in pursuit. Now, with the guy jammed into the driver's face, interfering with his view of the road, the big diesel truck swayed, bouncing off parked cars.

The row of automobiles off to the passenger side kept the truck from jamming up onto the sidewalk, but the Executioner knew that it would only be a matter of time before they reached another intersection, and the big two-and-a-half-ton missile would plow into the cars head-on. The line of automobiles would knife into one another and be strewed across the sidewalk, any civilians in their path crushed mercilessly in the on-coming onslaught of mechanized mayhem. Bolan yanked the little compact into the truck's path and bailed out of the driver's seat, scurrying into the road instants before the front grille hammered into its small frame.

Two-and-a-half tons rammed into three-quarters of a ton of automobile, collapsing it beneath the front fender. Chunks of the car's body was squashed into the front wheel wells, jamming up the axle, even though the rear tires continued to pour force into the road. The back end of the compact came to within an inch of pulverizing Bolan's feet as he leaped for cover. A heart-beat slower, and the Executioner would have been smashed, squeezed out like a tube of toothpaste. The truck and the mangled blob of deformed metal crushed under its fender swerved hard, plowing into the row of parked cars. The added mass of the sacrificed compact had put on the brakes, with only two cars knocked up onto the sidewalk, not a domino effect of dozens of vehicles spilling into the walkway. Bolan took a quick scan to see if any civilians had been in the way, but the parked vehicles had only bumped halfway onto the sidewalk. A couple of walkers had raced away from the sudden intrusion of dented metal into their path, but everyone looked healthy.

The shooter grunted and opened fire with his pistol. The Executioner sprinted, swerving as the off-balance terrorist made an effort to catch the warrior in his charge. With three long strides and a leap, Bolan seized the guy's gun hand and yanked down hard, ripping the man out of the cab and spilling him onto the street. The Chechen was stunned by the sudden lunge, the pistol flying from his nerveless fingers. A hard punch under the chin put the field commander out like a light, and Bolan drew the Beretta in case the driver had any ideas.

The Chechen man raised his hands, his eyes wide at the sight of the machine pistol leveled at him.

"Get out of the cab," Bolan ordered.

The driver did as he was told, keeping his hands

where the big American could see them. Laserka pulled to a halt behind the truck and got off the motorcycle. She tracked the scene with her handgun, but saw that Bolan had everything under control. A man lay in the street, a large dent on his chin, his eyes staring glassily into the Moscow evening.

"This your big man?" Laserka asked, walking over to the dazed man.

"He's big enough," Bolan returned. "Watch the driver, I'm going to check the bed of the truck."

Laserka moved around to the cab and saw that the driver had already leaned against the fender, resting on his hands, his legs spread so that he could be frisked. Laskera gave him a quick pat down, looking for hidden knives or pocket pistols, but didn't find anything under his clothes or in his pockets. "Keep standing like that."

Bolan swung around to the back. Two big trucks was a lot for transportation, but one of the trucks had much of its room taken up by a swivel-mounted 12.7 mm machine gun to discourage pursuit. Eighteen Iron Hammer raiders had been left behind at the convention center. The Executioner didn't want to take a chance. His mental calculations allowed for six men to turn the front of the convention center into a death trap via sniper action, and two trucks could handle thirty men. He had to factor in guards for each of the vehicles, as well as the two dozen allotted gunmen who were assigned to positions of slaughter.

The bed was empty except for two men, one slumped over the 12.7 mm, a second Chechen sprawled out on the floor. It might have taken a whole magazine to get the machine gunner, but Laserka's extended burst from her Bizon had also taken out a remaining guard. Bolan figured that there would be about four men in the truck who had been torn asunder by the RPG warhead at the intersection. Bolan climbed into the bed and confirmed that both men were dead, not lying in wait for a potential ambush. Sure enough, he found no life signs.

The warrior hopped back down to the street and confronted Laserka, who was patting down the unconscious Chechen leader.

"Anything?" Bolan asked.

"Found a tiny little Walther PPK in his back pocket," Laserka said, holding up the pistol.

"Keep it. It's got a lot in common with your Makarov," Bolan noted.

"I'll be fine with my Glock…" Laserka began.

"Which is back at your hotel room," Bolan countered. "As you can tell, I'm a big believer in backup weapons."

Laserka tucked the Walther into a pocket, frowning as she looked down at the unconscious prisoner. "So we wait for the Moscow police to arrive?"

"With the ruckus we've made, they'll be here shortly," Bolan said. He pulled out his cell phone and made a call to Director Batroykin.

"Cooper?" the supervisor answered, sounding confused and nervous.

"It's me," Bolan said. "How are things back at the party?"

"Under control," Batroykin said. "Russian army teams cleaned out the nest of snipers you informed them of. Everything's been cleared out, and we have five prisoners."

"You found the fourth group?" Bolan asked. "We left before they had made their move, but I was sure that your men could take care of things."

"It's all right," Batroykin replied. "I've got word about your encounter with some patrolmen not far from the center."

"It seems that our opposition tried to strike a moral blow against me," Bolan stated. "I almost ended up shooting a lawman in the commission of his duties."

"You did put three bullets into one," Batroykin said. "But he's still able to walk."

"Is there a team on its way here?" Bolan asked.

"Yes. Will you be accompanying any prisoners back to the station?" Batroykin asked.

"Absolutely," Bolan answered. "And don't be stingy on information about where you've sent them."

"Trying to draw more trouble with your newfound lightning rod," Batroykin mused. "It's a good plan to get more information. I just hope no one gets hurt in the process."

"I'll do my best to make certain that the men who wear badges under your command will remain un-harmed," Bolan promised.

The paddy wagon and two squad cars pulled around the corner, their sirens bleating as they came closer.

"That could be your men," Bolan noted.

"Judging by my estimate, you're right," Batroykin said. "Are you going to accompany your prisoner here?"

"I'm not going to separate from him," Bolan answered. "I've spent too much time and receive too little information to let such a succulent piece of bait get away from me."

"Good luck, Cooper," Batroykin said. "I'll attempt to conduct some damage control here."

"Great idea," Bolan said. "If we let this incident harm the peace process, everything we've risked and everyone who died tonight did so in futility."

"I know just which egos to massage, Cooper," Batroykin stated. "We're not letting our sharp friends get away with this affront."

Bolan smiled. "Thank you."

"Call it even, Cooper." Batroykin signed off.

The squad cars and paddy wagon pulled to a halt. It was time to take Bolan's prize back to the police station.

BENNORIN LISTENED to the reports on the radio, his face twisting into a sneer as the announcer spoke.

"Seven members of the Iron Hammer had been captured alive due to an unexpected blackout at the Russian Expo Center throwing the terrorists off balance," the accentless voice droned in Russian. "The security forces on hand, alerted to trouble in advance of their violent actions, contained the violence in a display of interagency cooperation that carried the day against the forces of anarchy."

Bennorin thought about putting a silenced bullet through the radio, but he didn't want to waste the ammunition. Still, it took every ounce of self-control not to punch the radio across the room.

Efim Berdysh entered the room, carrying a bottle of

water, frowning at the news. "Did someone betray our plans to the enemy?"

Bennorin shook his head. "It was an obvious situation. The Russian Expo Center was a juicy target, and the party to promote cooler heads was perfect for us to make a move against. It took someone who actually gave a shit about the damn Chechens and the peace process to be aware of the situation and call the American in."

Berdysh's frown deepened. "And how the hell would anyone know to summon that particular interloper, let alone know about our interference?"

"I can only think of one particular person who would be aware of us, as well as have a tenuous lead to the man," Bennorin mused. "It must be Vasili Batroykin. He can't know too much, because the American tried to intercept our assassination group."

"But since we were dispatching a team of SWAT police to deal with the Iron Hammer, he held his fire," Berdysh noted. "Why would he do that?"

"From what I have heard, he is a man driven by ideals, not political fanaticism, nor pragmatism," Bennorin replied. "He has been willing to be shot rather than defend himself from police officers or soldiers doing their 'job,' especially if he perceives them as being on his side."

"Foolishness. It's simply a good way to end up murdered," Berdysh said.

"You would think, but he left the policemen he encountered with minor injuries, not dead," Bennorin replied. "I thought perhaps that my stratagem would have forced him into an untenable situation."

"It didn't, and now he has the leader of the Iron

Hammer strike team in custody," Berdysh said. "Would he have information that could compromise us?"

"Given that the American took him captive, that appears to be the case," Bennorin stated. "I did my best to sanitize all contacts with the man, but it's possible that something might be shaken loose."

"Either way, leaving him alive will only give the Chechen people the impression that the administration tolerates their existence, in that they have legal rights," Berdysh replied. "He'll need to die anyway, in order to make a martyr."

Bennorin smiled. "That thought did cross my mind. Don't get caught."

Berdysh nodded.

"And try to do it with a minimum of Knife operatives," Bennorin said. "I would like to see you as far from the scene as possible. He made an extraordinary effort to capture our operatives in London."

"Yes, I know," Berdysh said. "I'll stay well back. I know just the people to call in."

Bennorin smiled. "I figured you would."

The conspirator left the office, and Bennorin lit a cigarette. As the smoke rose from the burning ash, he wondered if his plans would be as transient as the wisps that spiraled upward.

## CHAPTER THIRTEEN

"Enough beating around the bush," Siyaad muttered. "You take me prisoner, you put me in an interrogation cell, and for what? There aren't any cops in the building."

Bolan stood silently in the corner, having changed out of his suit coat and dress shirt to expose the skin-tight blacksuit. He donned the battle harness he knew he would need. "Anatoly, you're just the worm on the hook. I'm after some real prey."

Siyaad looked at the handguns, knives and spare magazines bristling on the warrior's battle load. A VEPR rifle leaned. The high-tech update of the AK-47 was actually built from the frame of a Romanian light machine gun, making an already tough and reliable weapon even more invulnerable to the elements and far more accurate. Black fiberglass-injected Kevlar stocks and forearm guards rounded out the futuristic rifle's visible improvements over the classic design, except for a holographic scope and a three-point sling. A half dozen 30-round magazines rode on the warrior's harness, and Siyaad frowned.

"What kind of fish? Land-walking sharks?" Siyaad asked.

"That'd be an insult to sharks. Ever hear of the Curved Knife?"

Siyaad's eyes narrowed. "I thought you were one of their operatives."

"If I were, you wouldn't be sitting here," Bolan countered. "I'm not even Russian."

"Pardon me for being behind the learning curve here," the Chechen complained. "I was unconscious until a few moments ago, and when I wake up, you tell me we're alone in a Moscow police station, and yet you look like you have enough firepower to retake Afghanistan by yourself."

"An exaggeration," Bolan commented, looking over at the rifle.

"I exaggerated? No kidding!" Siyaad muttered. "You're insipid enough to be a Russ—"

Bolan leaned forward, holding his finger up.

The Iron Hammer prisoner held his tongue, eyes widening. The Curved Knife had a reputation of carving men into their constituent body parts, mailing organs to families in alphabetical order. If this mystery man in black were lying about being one of their number, his taunting might have pushed the psychopath over the edge into further violence. "Sorry…"

"Quiet," Bolan requested softly. He touched a bud in his ear, a thin wire resting against his jaw picking up the vibrations from his mandible bone. "Kaya, what's up?"

"There's no movement that we can tell," Laserka answered. "But since your superhero costume seems to defeat our infrared cameras, there's no doubt that our opponents might have similar options in dress."

"Just as long as no one's launching antiaircraft rockets at you, just keep a high orbit over the building," Bolan replied. "If there's trouble, you'll see heat sources soon enough. Nothing can kill the thermal signature of a firearm."

"Truth spoken," Laserka said. "I just wish…"

"On the ground here, my only advantage is that I'm alone and can outmaneuver anyone they send after me," Bolan told her. "You're fine against cold-blooded murderers like Siyaad's ilk, but when it comes to out-of-control commandos with the best gear…"

Bolan went silent. Something moved in the hall outside. He slipped down his night-vision goggles and looked through the window. Sure enough, the fuzzy green haze of the Starlight goggles were cut by the beams of nonvisible illuminators, designed to assist in the operation of the NVGs in areas without ambient light. "They're in, and they're using alternate frequency illumination."

Bolan clicked off the lamp on the interview-room table and scooped up his VEPR. He looked toward Siyaad, then pulled a Beretta Storm pistol from the small of his back, handing it to the man butt-first. "There's a round in the chamber, and a 20-round magazine in the handle."

Siyaad took the sidearm, then looked toward the sound of Bolan's voice, unable to see a thing in the oppressive blackness of the darkened police station. "Why?"

Siyaad heard the sound of something being slipped

out of a pouch in the warrior's battle harness. "I don't want you to be murdered. I'm giving you a chance to survive. However, it's best if you sit tight in this room and don't venture into the open. Now close your eyes until you hear the pop."

"What pop?" Siyaad whispered.

Bolan tossed a small cube-shaped device through the door of the interrogation room, then clenched his eyes shut. Even through them and the night-vision goggles, he could register a harsh green glare accompanying the hiss-pop of the flash-unit strobing on the other side of the door. Screams of pain and dismay filled the air as the Curved Knife death squad's light amplification gear turned a simple flash bulb unit with a powerful capacitor battery into an eyeball-burning antipersonnel bomb.

With the speed and grace of a living shadow, Bolan was out into the detective's offices, entering the rows of cubicles where he spotted four men clutching their pained faces. Through the NVGs, he could tell that one of the Russians had peeled off his own glasses, his eyes showing up as black, soulless holes in the cast-off illumination of their ultraviolet lamps. Bolan swept the blind man's feet out from under him and threw a nerve-jarring punch that struck behind his ear. The stealth-cloaked marauder grunted in pain and went still.

A second gunman squeezed the trigger on his rifle, sweeping the room with a hose of 5.45 mm rounds at the sound of the scuffle. "It was a trap!"

"Check fire!" another of the attackers called out, throwing himself against the wall. He clutched his chest, scarred by glancing hits from the panicked shooter's rifle. "You're hitting me!"

The gunman didn't care, squeezing the trigger for wild three- and four-shot bursts that lit up the detectives' meeting room like lightning. Bolan had set his NVGs to a limiter that filtered out light sources stronger than the minimum visible frequency the human eye could see comfortably, so while the rifle's muzzle flashed white, it wasn't a painful searing like the powerful capacitor-charged strobe he'd used to render the gunmen useless in a stand-up fight. Bolan rushed the rifleman and slammed the fiberglass stock of his VEPR against the man's neck. The blow produced a sickening crunch that signaled the end of his panic fire and his life in the same bone-grinding crackle.

"Two down, and you can't even see yet," Bolan called out in Russian before he jammed his forearm under the chin of the wounded assassin. With a hard surge, Bolan bounced the man's head off the wall, the blow stunning him. A gunshot rang out, forcing the Executioner to duck, dragging the gunshot Russian with him instinctively as a shield. It wasn't one of the AKs, so that meant Bolan's anti-night-vision strobe had forced the fourth gunman to lose his rifle. The wounded marauder lifted a knee to try to catch the warrior off guard, but Bolan blocked it with a palm before it could reach his stomach. A follow-up punch put the would-be assassin on the floor and would leave him there for at least half an hour. That left one still to account for, and that guy was stumbling toward the stairs.

The last of the assassination team turned on a flashlight, but his footing was unsteady as he walked toward the steps. Bolan figured that the man had been shielded by his partners, but once the blind fire cut loose, he took the cue to exit, stage left. With three long strides, Bolan was on him, snaking an arm around the guy's throat and pulling back hard enough to lift the Russian's feet off the ground. The murderer swung his Grach auto-loader toward Bolan's face, but the soldier pivoted on one foot, driving the Russian hard into the wall. With his forearm sandwiched between his body and the wall, the impact knocked the pistol from the attacker's grasp.

"Going somewhere?" Bolan asked, keeping the man in a tight choke hold.

"Fuck you and die!" the gunman grunted. He reached for a knife on his belt, but Bolan punched him just over the kidney, not hard enough to induce renal shock, as he had done earlier with the hardened pommel of his knife, but more than enough to deposit the stunned man into a pool of agony at his feet.

"I've got too many questions for you or me to die yet," Bolan told him.

Wheezing and red-faced, the assassin looked up at the Executioner. "What kind…of an…idiot…"

Bolan stepped closer, then heard the tinkle of a pin on the floor. He whirled and dived, his face turned away from the downed gunman. The sound was unmistakable for all the times that the Executioner had pulled the pin of a grenade and let it clatter to a tile floor. With a somersault, he tucked himself behind a desk as the minibomb went off, an overpressure sheet of 145-decibel sound shattering the frosted glass between cubicles.

The grenade had only been a flash-bang, but that

didn't make the so-called stun grenade any less dangerous. Bolan had personally seen men whose skulls had been crushed by the detonator core of the "distraction device," which had the power to hurl one and a half ounces of solid metal over 150 yards. He glanced up and saw that the detonator had penetrated a metal desk drawer, and counted himself lucky to have been aware of the impending blast. He looked around and saw that the last of the gunmen had slithered down the stairs. Bolan rushed to the steps and spotted a dark shadow lying in the well. A sharp crack illuminated the final gunman, the bullet creasing Bolan's rib cage, high-tech polymer fibers deflecting some of the impact, but it still felt as if he'd been punched in the chest. He lurched to one side and grabbed the railing, pivoting on his arm to swing both feet around in a wicked arc.

Bolan's boots connected with the assassin's hand and with all of his momentum and speed thrown into the kick, it pulverized finger bones and jammed the Grach so hard that it burst through drywall and stuck there. Bolan let go and came down on the landing between levels. The stunned and broken-handed killer struggled to turn, but the big American grabbed the mangled paw and twisted hard.

Blinding agony sliced through the hapless killer, and he passed out.

Bolan heard Laserka's voice over the radio. "Cooper! Get down!"

Bolan didn't look for the problem. He simply hurled himself down the steps as the stairwell detonated in a crack of thunder. An antiarmor RPG round had struck the building right where the stairs were, a gap ten feet wide blown through brick and mortar as if it were a sheet of paper. Even at the bottom of the steps, the shock wave had disoriented the warrior, his back a mass of bruises from even the impact of the stairs and chunks of flying brick. He'd managed to protect his head with his arms, but they ached, as well.

"Backup outside?" Bolan asked over his headset.

"Not anymore. The car's taking off," Laserka said. "I'm ordering the helicopter into pursuit."

"Stay out of range!" the Executioner ordered. He rushed to the landing and saw that the man he'd endeavored to capture was a greasy smear of sagging skin and pulped flesh on the stairs. With a deep breath, Bolan launched himself through the blast crater in the wall, landing with a roll to slow down his descent from the second-floor drop. "That RPG will tear your chopper out of the sky with no problem! Make certain Siyaad doesn't get away! And I gave him a gun for his own protection."

"Damn it, Cooper," Laserka cursed, but the warrior had his Desert Eagle out. Whoever the first four members of the team were, they must have been hired muscle. They had been extremely well-trained and well-equipped, and only the Executioner's vast experience and superior technology had allowed him to get the drop on them so easily. The fight with the last of the attackers proved that they were hardened, skilled mercenaries.

Bolan tore open the door of a cop car, a Volkswagen Passat import, and slid behind the wheel. He reached into his battle harness and pulled out his lock gun, inserting it into the ignition. The Executioner had spent enough time trying to hot-wire a variety of cars that he realized that the best means was to utilize the multikey tool, shaped like a small gun, for quick-starting vehicles. He had the engine grumbling to life as Laserka continued to appraise him of the location of the escaping rocketeer from her aerial vantage point. "Siyaad hasn't moved, has he?"

"No," Laserka answered. "Eight blocks west already."

Jamming the squad car into Reverse, he peeled away from the station, spinning the ride out into a 180-degree pivot with a tap of the brakes. Working the gearshift and the clutch, he slid the automobile through the first four gears before he was up to 70 mph, the winds whipping through the cracked driver's side window. A chunk of brick had lodged in the glass, part of the obliterated wall that had been blown up only moments ago.

The streets of Moscow were empty tonight, and this time, Bolan had eight cylinders of power propelling his ride, allowing him to swallow the distance between himself and the escaping rocket man and his driver.

"Police are moving in to secure the building," Laserka explained. "We're going to maintain your overwatch, Cooper."

"He pops a rocket grenade at you, you break off the pursuit and head back to base," Bolan ordered.

"I'm a big girl, Cooper," Laserka challenged.

"No one's bigger than a 77 mm antiarmor warhead, Kaya," Bolan said. "Keep at least four hundred meters away from their car."

"You'll be getting closer," Laserka said.

"This car's not as big a target, either," Bolan stated.

He pushed the squad car into fifth gear, his masterful manipulation of the stick shift buying him another few seconds, cutting closer to the Russian assassination team.

The RPG gunner had to have had only one shell on hand, or he was not certain of his ability to hit a speeding automobile on a bumpy Moscow road. The assassin had transitioned to an automatic rifle, and its muzzle flash preceded a series of stars punched into the windshield of Bolan's racing VW Passat. Using the mighty Desert Eagle as his hammer, he smashed the glass out and triggered the massive weapon at the rifleman hanging out of the window of his car. Bolan's initial two shots missed due to the uneven street and their relative velocity causing jumps and jolts. Keeping up with the enemy was not going to be a problem, thanks to the 2.8 liter V6 turbocharged engine under the hood. The vehicle had sufficient horsepower to do whatever the Executioner asked it to, despite being a model from the turn of the century.

It didn't concern the Executioner, as the night was quiet. No civilians were walking the street, and they wouldn't catch a .44 Magnum slug or a wildly skidding automobile for their worries. The enemy car swerved around a corner, and Bolan downshifted and braked, skidding into the turn. Though the warrior hadn't been part of the drift-racing scene in any capacity, he still took updated defensive driving courses that taught him the art of using momentum and the car's weight to grind through a turn with a minimum of disruption in speed. Using the drift method, Bolan managed to close another twenty feet on the fleeing conspirator before he upshifted, rocketing to make up another ten feet of distance between them. The enemy driver turned another corner, and he was wide-eyed as he saw Bolan drift the Passat, a rooster tail of white smoke flying as the tires squealed on the pavement.

"Faster! Go faster!" the rifleman in the window bellowed.

"I'm going as fast as this can go!" Bolan heard the driver complain.

It was too late. Bolan downshifted and whipped the tail of his car around, rear bumper smashing into the enemy's driver's door. The impact rocked the escaping car and sent it into an out-of-control skid up onto the sidewalk. The passenger-side fender exploded in sparks as it ground on the front of a building.

The rifleman had dropped back into the car, but his weapon cartwheeled off the roof. Another second slower and the assassin would have been bloody spray paint on a Moscow residence. The driver somehow managed to recover control of his ride, but the Executioner swerved again, hitting the brakes and spiraling the police car around. The back of the squad car chopped across the grille of the conspirators' vehicle like a hammer.

The collision was only glancing on Bolan's ride, but the hood flew up into the windshield of the other car. The twisted panel of metal wrenched off the front of the car, skidding into the street as the driver accelerated. He tried to hammer the Volkswagen, but Bolan broke, downshifting and dropping away from the enemy's line of sight with deft agility. It may have seemed as if the Executioner were a cat toying with a mouse, but Bolan wanted prisoners alive to give him answers. So far, across the width of a continent, he had been chasing the solution to a mystery and only ended up with corpses for his troubles. Now the warrior was using every ounce of skill at his command to insure that he had something to put questions to.

That meant utilizing his Passat in a ballet of black-top martial arts that left the enemy driver and his passenger shouting in rage and frustration. Once more, Bolan cut off the assassin's car, a whirling near hit that threw them up onto the sidewalk, bouncing off another brick wall, sheet metal screeching like a wounded dinosaur. The Russian yanked his car back onto the street, only to catch the fender of the cop machine in his rear axle.

It was a brutal knockout blow that spun the enemy in a 360-degree spiral. One of the wheels had snapped off, torn loose by centrifugal force after the shaft holding the tire and wheelbase in place had splintered under the enormous force. The police vehicle had only taken mangling blows to the corners of its frame, but the escaping Russians' had been struck in vital spots, a blow to stun the driver in his seat, a wallop to shatter the radiator and cooling fan, and finally the destruction of its rear axle.

The back of the fleeing car spit sparks as its undercarriage ground on the asphalt. Bolan hit the brakes and came to a halt, nose to nose with the assassins. He had the Desert Eagle up and leveled at the driver and his passenger, the fat, trapezoidal barrel of the monstrous handgun an unmistakable shape in his fist.

"Throw your weapons out the window!" Bolan ordered.

The driver screamed and folded under the dashboard as the other man in the wrecked car tore at his jacket, reaching for a handgun. Bolan fired the Desert Eagle, the big .44 belching a fireball that propelled a 240-grain jacketed hollowpoint round that obliterated the right shoulder of the passenger. An explosion of blood sprayed across his face, and the limb flopped uselessly at his side.

"Try to reach that pistol with your other hand, and you won't have an arm to speak of," Bolan warned. "Open the door and keep your hand above your head."

"Bastard," the passenger growled, looking down at the cowering driver.

"Don't look at him, do as I say!" Bolan ordered.

The gunman glowered at the Executioner, but self-preservation kicked in. He didn't make a move for his weapon again, but he still wheezed in defiance. "You're not going to get anything from us."

Bolan slid out from behind the wheel. "Why's that?"

A muzzle flash flared from the dashboard of the shattered escape car, and Bolan jerked violently back onto the hood of his police vehicle. The hammer shock of a heavy slug slamming into his chest knocked the wind from his lungs, and his head spun under the impact with the squad's front end.

"Bastard!" he heard the driver snarl. "Who do you think you're dealing with?"

Bolan winced, gritting his teeth against the pain of a newly forming bruise on his chest beneath the trauma plates. He blinked and looked down the barrel of a monstrous revolver. Dazedly, he gauged that the cannon in the driver's hand to be at least .50 caliber, and he recalled that the Russian defense industry had been developing heavy-duty revolvers in that size. He'd never come under fire by one of them before, but it was not an experience he'd wish to repeat. The driver took Bolan's Desert Eagle and the Beretta in his thigh holster.

The wounded gunman squirmed out of the passenger seat. He was red-faced, not only with blood spatter, but the agony of a destroyed shoulder joint. Through squinted eyes, the Executioner could tell that the man was going into shock. "We have to get out of…"

The big half-inch revolver barrel swung toward the crippled assassin and bellowed, a football-sized muzzle flash illuminating the death of the driver's remaining liability. He turned back to Bolan and pushed the hot muzzle under his chin. Skin sizzled on contact with the hot barrel, and Bolan winced, trying to turn his head away from the weapon.

"Oh no, you're not squirming anywhere, American," the driver snarled. "You're getting back behind the wheel and driving me out of here."

"Can barely move…" Bolan replied.

The muzzle cracked across Bolan's jaw.

"Deny me again, and I'll make sure your little bitch partner ends up the main ingredient in dog food!" the driver growled. "Get behind the wheel!"

Bolan slid off the hood and limped to the driver's seat. The gunman watched him warily, slipping into the back of the squad car, putting the backs of the seats between him and an effort at a gun grab. Whoever this man was, he was a rock-solid professional, and knew how to limit his vulnerability. The massive hogleg would have no difficulty putting a round through Bolan's head through the rest behind his neck.

"Quit pretending," the captor snarled. "I know you're wearing some form of body armor."

Bolan coughed, still playing the role, but given the amount of pain he was in, it wasn't too much of a charade. "Sure, *you* wear a vest and take a hit from that bazooka."

The man snorted in derision. "Drive. And lose the helicopter!"

Bolan nodded. The gunman's hand whipped out, plucking the bud and microphone from the side of his head. The wire connected to the communicator snapped and he tossed the assembly out of the window.

Bolan put the squad car into gear. He wasn't a man who smiled much, so suppressing his pleasure at encountering a Curved Knife professional was easy. Playing the role of captive, choosing the role on the fly, he accelerated away. It took only a few minutes to lose Laserka and her high-flying bird. There'd be time to pick her back up when he dealt with the man in the backseat. "So what do I call you?"

"Your death, but Berdysh sounds less pretentious," the gunman said. "And don't delude yourself that you'll get to make use of that information."

Disappearing into the Moscow night, Bolan knew that he was in the middle of a mental chess game. The Executioner was playing a gambit, though. He'd been in this position before, and allowing himself to be captured brought him closer to the end of the line in this hellfire mission.

## CHAPTER FOURTEEN

Kaya Laserka looked for Agent Matt Cooper, and knew that there was no way she'd be able to find him. The man had stopped the two Curved Knife assassins in their car with some of the most incredible martial-arts driving she'd ever seen in her life. If there was a human being who could use an automobile the same way that a Hong Kong action star could wield a pair of nun-chaku, it was the American. Utilizing emergency brakes, a clutch and the momentum of the car at the expense of its tires, he had whirled the police vehicle around at breakneck speed, pounding the other driver into submission.

There were three gunshots on her infrared camera, one the bellowing flare of the American's Desert Eagle hip cannon, but then there came two more monstrous thunderbolts from the stopped vehicle, one that threw Cooper back onto his hood. The third round had killed one of the other stealth-clad men down there.

She could hear Cooper's conversation about how he was injured, and thus slowed by the enemy's bullet.

There was a snatch of static, and the radio had gone dead. The hiss of static was more ominous than any rattle of gunfire

The infrared camera tried to follow the battered and dented squad car as the American raced off. Even with all the speed and agility that the Moscow police pilot could squeeze out of the helicopter, there was no comparison between the pilot's ability and Cooper's phenomenal skill. Using buildings and side streets as cover, he swiftly dropped out of camera range, whipping the squad car out of sight. Laserka sighed, resigning herself to the fact that if her partner didn't want to be found, there was no way a moderately experienced pilot and even a veteran Moscow branch RIS investigator could hope to locate him in the hundreds of square miles of city sprawled beneath them.

She was about to pluck the earpiece from her ear when she heard Barbara's voice on the bud.

"He activated the fail-safe locater beacon in his transmitter when the radio was removed," Price said. "Can you read me?"

"Yes. You've been on this line all this time?" she asked.

"Constant monitoring," Price confessed. "Hope that doesn't embarrass you."

"Well, it's a good thing we didn't have the communicators in while we were having animal sex before, but I'll keep that in mind," Laserka snarled.

"Sarcasm will get you nowhere," Price said, obviously trying to keep her annoyance out of her voice. She cleared her throat, regaining a little more composure. "I'm trying to keep the trace running on Cooper.

Hopefully he won't be trying to evade our satellite coverage."

"If he can do that, then he's a better driver than I thought," Laserka stated. "I was impressed with him ditching our helicopter."

"It's easier having…eyes in the sky," Price said, catching herself before she stated the limits. "If Cooper manages to escape that particular perimeter, that means Volkswagen's been holding out on transonic Passats on this side of the Atlantic."

"If you can make out the model…" Laserka began. "Good eyes in the sky."

"That's so we can keep up with our man in the field," Price responded. "And even then, technology goes only so far in helping us find him."

"Even Superman has his Fortress of Solitude," Laserka noted.

"Except Cooper doesn't have an allergy to green rocks or bicycle locks, as far as we can tell," Price said with a nervous chuckle.

"Though bullets can give him a bad day," Laserka replied, returning to somber reality. "And the man who kidnapped him had a bazooka for a sidearm. From the sound over the radio, it made his Desert Eagle sound like a cap gun."

"We heard," Price said. "If Cooper hadn't had trauma plates in his battle harness, he'd be a dead man."

"You'll tell me if he stops, right?" Laserka asked.

"The moment he does, but that doesn't mean to swoop in right away," Price admonished. "The noise your helicopter kicks up might distract him from whatever endgame he has in mind."

Laserka took a deep breath. "It's hard working with a man like him. You just don't want to let him down."

"No," Price returned. "He inspires that in a lot of people."

"I hope he continues to." Laserka sighed.

Price hung up on the line and Laserka returned to speaking Russian to the confused pilot. The helicopter continued to circle in the sky, waiting for the signal to rush to Mack Bolan's aid.

BERDYSH KEPT the .480 Ruger Redhawk Alaskan aimed at the driver's seat, level with the Executioner's kidney. The power of the massive 350-grain slug out of the three-inch barrel of the fat little revolver would be sufficient to slice through the back of the seat and smash Bolan's kidney, even through the ballistic armor he wore under his blacksuit. The warrior knew that, too, and seemed to be going along for the ride. He had to have been hedging his bets that when they got to a new location, there would be the opportunity to effect an escape.

Berdysh didn't need Bolan to stay alive for long, just enough to get him back to his hideout, so the moment the car stopped, he'd pull the trigger. While the bullet induced renal shock through Bolan's protective sheath, the Russian would maneuver into position to blow his head off at contact range.

It was a simple plan, and he tried to keep the smile off his face as he gave directions to the Executioner.

"How much farther?" Bolan asked.

"Not long now," Berdysh promised. "Once you drop me off, you can go where you want."

"I doubt that," Bolan said.

"You don't trust me?" Berdysh asked, putting on airs of mock disappointment.

"It's simply not logical for you to give me such a chance," Bolan said. "I know my race will have been run the moment I stop this car."

"Disarmed, you really have no choice," Berdysh told him.

"I also have managed to figure that you won't bring me any closer to the real head of this operation," Bolan added. "We're stopping at a place where you stashed some clean vehicles."

"You are as brilliant as your reputation, American," Berdysh said. "It'll be a shame to dispose of you."

"Wouldn't it?" Bolan asked. He worked the clutch and stick shift, accelerating up through fifth gear, speeding onto a straightaway. Berdysh glanced out the window as the Passat zoomed past 90 mph, buildings along the street melting into a blur.

"What the hell are you doing?" Berdysh asked.

"Since we're not going to meet anyone I can bring in for more answers, I'm just going to have to deal with you," Bolan told him.

He wrenched up the emergency brake and let go of the steering wheel. Those two acts turned the Volkswagen into a hurtling missile that spun out of control. Berdysh howled in impotent rage, pulling the trigger on the Ruger. Unfortunately for the Russian, centrifugal force wrenched his aim off, the fat .480-caliber slug tearing through the Passat's back door. The back end of the spinning car crunched against a parked vehicle, and the VW's uncontrolled spiral came to a gut-wrenching halt.

Berdysh was slammed against the passenger seat and he rebounded upward. His head bounced into the roof with stunning force. The Ruger dropped to the floorboards, and he blinked hard in a hope that he could clear the cobwebs out of his head. A slashing hand swooped into the backseat, Bolan's karate chop slamming into Berdysh's shoulder and deflecting him from his grab attempt.

The Russian winced and kicked at Bolan's head, but his foot glanced off the Passat's headrest and most of the force of his blow went into the roof of the car. Bolan had ducked the rest of the kick and slithered with the speed and power of a python into the backseat. A powerful fist crashed hard into Berdysh's breastbone, the impact on his xiphoid process freezing the breath in his lungs for several unbearable seconds. Berdysh tried to punch back, but the combined effects of the car crash trauma and Bolan's sudden assault had taken far too much fight out of him to allow Berdysh anything more than a couple of impotent slaps that distracted the warrior.

The Executioner punched Berdysh in the stomach again, and the second shock to his lungs expelled breath from his nose and mouth. As the Russian folded, Bolan wrapped his hand around the back of his head and yanked him face-first into the passenger-side headrest. Blood gushed from the man's crushed nose and split lip, and Berdysh rebounded deeper into the backseat, hands flying to his crimson-splashed features. Bolan twisted the rest of the way into the backseat and brought his knee down hard into the Russian's groin.

A roar of agony split the Passat's interior. As

Berdysh's hands dropped in reaction to his battered genitals, Bolan brought his left hand down hard on his jaw. The left cross, a knockout blow, overloaded Berdysh's overwhelmed central nervous system. He collapsed into unconsciousness, and Bolan leaned back. He rummaged into the pockets of his battle harness and plucked out a replacement for the lost earphone and jawbone microphone.

"Laserka, you still listening?" Bolan asked.

"It's only been a few minutes," the lady cop said. "I didn't have anything better to tune into."

Bolan smiled at the retort. "I have a man named Berdysh in custody. He killed at least two of his accomplices."

"We have three more in holding back at the police station. And something funny happened," Laserka said.

"Siyaad handed over the sidearm I lent him for self-defense?" Bolan asked.

"How did you know?" Laserka asked.

"He's more frightened of me than the Curved Knife," Bolan answered. "He knew that if he tried to break loose, I'd be on him."

"You're one scary man, Cooper," Laserka said. "Whereabouts are you?"

Bolan relayed the closest intersection. "Unfortunately, I wrecked the police car I was in. I tried to minimize things so that it was only cosmetic damage that could be fixed in a body shop, but Berdysh forced my hand."

"We'll chalk it up to Curved Knife," Laserka told him. "After all, they punched a hole in a police station trying to kill you."

Bolan opened Berdysh's jaw and shone his compact

LED flash into the unconscious man's mouth. Under the harsh blue-white glow of the lens, finding the false tooth and its hidden pill compartment was easy. When Bolan pried the cap off, he found out that it was empty. He sighed and checked Berdysh's pulse to make certain the man hadn't inadvertently swallowed the poison pill, but he was alive, strong and breathing. Bolan gave him a gentle tap on the cheek and crawled out of the back of the Passat.

He finally had his prisoner. Now to find out why Catherine Alexandronin had to be brutally beaten to death.

BENNORIN HAD BEEN monitoring the helicopter that was overseeing the bait operation and he sighed. Berdysh was one of his best men, but had a streak of self-preservation that would make his silence a problematic issue. He got on the phone and arranged for a flight to Grozny, Chechnya. Moscow was going to become too hot for his tastes once Berdysh gave up the answers that the grim American wanted.

The American was not someone Bennorin wanted to underestimate. He destroyed the phone that he used to call for a taxi and make the airline reservations to Chechnya, then grabbed his luggage. Inside an insulated compartment, he put in his favored 9 mm Heckler & Koch P10 and two magazines, as well as his securely encrypted Web-capable smartphone. The hidden compartment would resist metal detectors and X-rays, as it was designed to penetrate U.S. airport security, so the more primitive Third World technology of Chechnya would present no difficulties for him.

He took out another disposable cell phone and slid it into his pocket after securing the suitcase's compartment. Bennorin thought about calling Batroykin, but then he'd have to sacrifice another short-use cell phone. Someday, though, Bennorin was going to have to deal with the two-faced traitor who dared to turn the clock to an era of incompetence and failure for the great Russian nation.

When that time came, a bullet in the head would be welcomed as a mercy, not a final punishment.

Bennorin smiled, feeling relaxed at the plans of torture and murder ahead of him. For now, he had an appointment to keep with Kroz.

DIMA DAGROYCH, the liaison between the Curved Knife and the Grozny Iron Hammer, was an ugly, hairy man with a face that looked like it had been torn from the south end of a northbound yak and glued to his skull, but Kroz was glad that the man's efficiency and abilities made up for the unpleasantness of his looks and smell. The man's beard and long, shaggy mop of hair had trapped a seeming lifetime of cigarette smoke and cabbage stink.

Kroz wasn't doing much to better the smell of the dirty little hovel that they were in by smoking another cigarette and drinking rancid coffee, but there wasn't much to do as he awaited the safehouse. His cell phone warbled in his pocket and he plucked it out. It was Bennorin.

"What's wrong?" Kroz asked.

"Moscow has become too much of a compromise so I've decided to relocate," Bennorin said.

Kroz took a deep breath and let it out slowly.

"Been a while since you last encountered the American, hasn't it?" Kroz asked.

"I've never encountered him, and I do not plan to," Bennorin replied. "However, an operative I have personally been in contact with has been captured."

"So it's time to take a quick trip," Kroz said.

"Astute as ever, Kroz," Bennorin replied.

"What can I say except welcome to the club," Kroz told him.

"I don't like being part of large groups, Curved Knife included," Bennorin replied. "I'm at the airport, and I'll be in Grozny by noon tomorrow."

"We'll have someone pick you up, unless you want to keep a low profile," Kroz said.

"I'll make my own arrangements. I trust you, but I know the man we are in conflict with," Bennorin replied. "There is a good chance that your third encounter with him will not go well, and…"

Kroz sighed. "Yeah. Not exactly the news I wanted to hear, but at least you're not telling me everything's going to be all right."

"This is the most not right that I've ever encountered," Bennorin replied. "If you have a chance to avoid contact with him, then do so. Otherwise—"

"You're certain that he'll come here?" Kroz cut him off, not wanting to think about eating a bullet.

"Berdysh is aware of our focus on turning Grozny into a hell zone," Bennorin told him. "As it is, we have the advantage of a terrorist act in Moscow. Two of them actually, since a police station took a hit while we were attempting to shut things down."

Kroz's eyes narrowed. Bennorin was a master of the espionage game, and he realized that any operation depended on almost paranoid levels of operational security. Right now, the Russian spy lord had violated communications discipline on multiple occasions, and there was only one reason for such sloppiness.

"You're not using a secure line, are you?" Kroz asked.

"My apologies, Kroz, but no," Bennorin said. "However, it will be incomplete bait, since your telephone is disposable, as well."

"But enough to scatter his focus should he come to town, correct?" Kroz asked. "He'll be looking for me, looking for you, and trying to root out the operation we've assembled."

"That's my goal, at least," Bennorin said.

"Pardon my saying this, boss, but your planning alarms me," Kroz told him. "You spring all kinds of shit on me at the last minute, and you blab my name and position to the people who are listening to cell phone conversations for him."

"I know you can handle it," Bennorin replied. "You are the best operative I have."

"That's because everyone better than me died in London or just got caught in Moscow," Kroz snarled. "Anyone ever inform you that you can be a true bastard at times?"

"I've also given you the quiver of information necessary to beat him, or at least escape with your life," Bennorin replied.

"Well, that's the thing. You've given me something with a lifetime guarantee that, if it fails, can't be cashed in upon," Kroz told him.

"Think of it this way," Bennorin said. "You'll have the satisfaction of being able to expose me if he does find you. A little revenge from beyond the grave."

"Won't matter to me by then, but I'll take you up on that offer," Kroz said.

He hung up and looked at Dagroych.

"So, the American is on his way to Grozny?" Dagroych asked.

"Yes," Kroz answered. "My boss just painted a big arrow in neon paint to let him know about us and our operation."

Dagroych nodded, taking a sip of coffee. "In order to cover for himself."

"That's the plan," Kroz said. "I figure we have only a few options."

"We don't have any," Dagroych said. "The Iron Hammer has come to expect our support. If we fail them, we end up a target of an international manhunt, as they will no doubt expose our complicity in the murders they have committed."

"So it won't just be the American, but all of RIS," Kroz said.

"And Interpol, and most likely the American CIA," Dagroych added.

Kroz squeezed his forehead, wincing at the thought. "So instead of having one man after us, it'll be the whole world against us."

"We continue operations, and at the same time, prepare our escape plans just in case," Dagroych told him. "Otherwise, nothing can help us."

"Escape plans?" Kroz asked.

"I have something set up for myself," Dagroych admitted. "And no, you can't know about my trip."

Kroz smirked. "I'll work something up."

"Good," Dagroych replied. "Don't let me know about your plans."

"I won't," Kroz said.

"This is the start of a beautiful friendship, Kroz," Dagroych told him.

Kroz remembered the movie that line came from. He seemed to remember a moment of betrayal in that very same scene, one where friend murdered friend. He didn't say anything.

He just knew that he'd have to watch his back from now on. Grozny had all the earmarks of becoming his burial site if he wasn't careful.

## CHAPTER FIFTEEN

Berdysh opened his eyes, finding himself dangling upside down in a blackened room. He was naked, except for his underwear, and his wrists were bound tightly behind his back. A strong length of rope was cinched tightly around his ankles, and his feet felt as if they were falling asleep. He noticed the American standing in the room, pacing back and forth like an impatient lion awaiting his next meal.

"I figured that the blood rushing to your head would wake you up," Bolan said, stopping his pacing. Berdysh swallowed hard, knowing that his life was going to become very hard and painful over the next few hours. If only he hadn't disposed of his cyanide capsule years ago, he'd have been able to spare himself some agony. He debated whether to swallow his own tongue and choke himself to death, but in his position, it would be easy to coax the tongue out of his airway.

Bolan knelt in front of the Russian prisoner and laid out a set of stainless-steel surgical utensils on a white strap of fabric next to him. The gleaming reflective polish of the tools belied the cruelty with which they could be forced into nerves and muscle groups, or pry apart bones at the cartilage junctions between them. Berdysh could see the small boxy frame of an automobile battery with bright yellow jumper cables attached to it.

"You could just try chemical interrogation techniques," Berdysh said. "Sodium pentothal?"

"I had a medic run an EKG on you," Bolan confessed. "You have an irregular heart rhythm, so if we used scopolamine, a much superior interrogation drug, there would be a good chance that you would die before you provided any information of use."

Berdysh sighed. "And physical pain is your preferred means of prying that out of me?"

Bolan looked down at the utensils. He slipped a long, angle-tipped metal probe from its cloth sleeve. It glimmered like a ribbon of silver in the light of the room.

"Actually, it isn't," Bolan said. "I don't like torturing people, but the thing is, you're a trained professional. You had been provided with a suicide pill, but you seem to have misplaced it. I've dealt with your kind before, and I know the kind of mental conditioning that the KGB gave to its agents. I've dealt with dozens of you, and it's all but impossible to stay completely bloodless while interrogating you."

Berdysh wrinkled his nose, looking around. He was scanning for possible escape routes, but tied up so securely, there was no way that he could hope to get from his inverted position and down before the madman in front of him inflicted all manner of ungodly harm upon him. "You should also realize that we aren't supermen. Have you considered asking questions?"

Bolan tilted his head. "Are you trying to make me believe that you'll tell me what I want to know to save your skin?"

"It doesn't hurt to ask," Berdysh stated.

Bolan traced the needle-sharp tip of the probe down Berdysh's abdomen, the fine point raising a welt in the wake of its scratch. Berdysh flinched at the minuscule cut.

"I barely applied any pressure," Bolan said. "And someone who could handle that monster little snubby you were packing earlier surely has the strength and endurance to deal with a scrape like that."

"That's a sensitive area," Berdysh explained. "To tell the truth, it tickled."

Bolan sat back, putting the probe on the cloth. "So you want to make me think that you're a human being. Someone with normal emotions, fears, foibles... I'm too desensitized to the violence I've inflicted over the decades to see you as a person."

"My birth name was—" Berdysh began.

Bolan shook his head. "No."

"My name is—"

"You are Berdysh. A faceless, identity-deprived minion of a monstrous conspiracy that I have to exterminate," Bolan told him. "You know the drill. You've given up your humanity, so now any straws grasped at are only the panicked gyrations of a doomed man."

"This isn't fair," Berdysh replied.

"Putting a bullet in the back of my head would have been?" Bolan asked.

"It was self—" Berdysh stopped. Even he couldn't buy that kind of a lie.

"Self-preservation or self-defense?" Bolan asked. "Either way, you come out on a losing end of an equation. Thousands of lives for yours? That's a trade I'd be willing to make any day of the year."

"I'm unarmed. I've heard that you do not murder helpless men!" Berdysh complained.

"Wrong."

Berdysh squirmed, trying to loosen the noose around his ankles. Bolan grabbed his waistband, pulling out a pair of surgical scissors. He snipped the underwear off, leaving the Russian naked and vulnerable.

"Wait!" Berdysh said.

Bolan rapped the scissors on his hip bone, interrupting the man's thought. "Greb Strakhov. That's a name I haven't heard spoken aloud for a while. And you were under him?"

"The lowest initiate in his division," Berdysh replied.

Bolan stepped back and walked toward a darkened part of the room, disappearing. There was a long, uncomfortable silence as Berdysh hung upside down, only a dim wattage bulb providing any form of illumination. He looked up toward the surgical implements on the roll pad, his stomach churning at the concept of all the damage that they could wreak on his vulnerable flesh. A cool breeze washed over his genitals from a cracked window, and Berdysh looked to see where it was coming from, but realized that the gentle wind was a reminder of his dangling manhood.

Bolan stepped back into the open, in sight of the bulb. Berdysh swallowed, looking at the grim glower on the man's face. He knew it would be impossible, with all the blood resting in his head, but he could have sworn that he felt his face blanch with terror at the glare of anger burning in Bolan's eyes. The scissors opened and closed with the ominous, cold grind of metal on metal.

Bolan stepped closer to him, his face revealing Berdysh's impending doom. He thought of a biblical prophecy. "And they will seek the covering of mountains, not monuments, to escape his wrath." The big American reached out for Berdysh's manhood.

"My boss is named Bennorin!" Berdysh cried. "I don't know his real name, but that is the identity he was given under the Smyernet Consortium!"

Bolan paused. "I thought you worked for an organization called Curved Knife."

"That's the name of our action arm, but the Smyernet Consortium is an overarching organization," Berdysh confessed. "It's a conglomeration of public officials and private businessmen who long for the days when Russia was a world power, worthy of respect."

"There you go, pissing me off again," Bolan said. He started forward with the scissors.

"Their words! Not mine!" Berdysh shouted so hard that his voice cracked.

Bolan lowered the scissors, glowering at the naked, helpless insurgent. "If they weren't your ideals, you wouldn't have allowed them to remove your name from the book of the living and transform you from Aloise Mieckovic into Berdysh."

Berdysh froze, eyes wide with horror. "You…"

"Give me a break," Bolan said, tossing the scissors aside. They clattered on the concrete floor as punctuation to his level of frustration. Urine splashed down Berdysh's stomach and chest, as his bladder emptied itself all over him.

Berdysh coughed, spitting out the foul liquid. Bolan glared at the man as he messed himself, shaking his head in disgust. "I asked you to give me a break, not to make this sloppier."

"I'm sorry," Berdysh said, sobbing. His breath caught in his throat as he swung back and forth helplessly. "I'm so sorry."

"What about Vitaly and Catherine?" Bolan snapped angrily.

Berdysh took a moment to figure out who the man was talking about, then choked back another sob. "The Alexandronins!"

Bolan stepped closer and scooped up a scalpel. "Thanks for reminding me the price I have to exact from your sorry flesh. I almost was feeling sorry for you for a moment there."

Berdysh whimpered. "That was all Bennorin's plan. She was investigating rumors of a hard government crackdown in Grozny. Some of the refugees we let get away were given the message to convey to the rest of the expatriates in London, but she intercepted it, and she knew the old ways. She was putting facts together faster than we could cover up our operation."

"So that was a reason to crush every bone in her body and leave her in a coma?" Bolan asked.

"Bennorin didn't get to be the head of the Smyernet Consortium by being sloppy," Berdysh said. "I would have been all for the threats we made to make the international news. Better to be feared than respected, right? You know all about that."

Bolan flicked back the protective plastic sheath on the disposable scalpel's tip with the sound of plastic ratcheting on plastic. This wasn't one of the pristine instruments that had been laid out on display. Of course, those tools had been splattered with urine in the midst of Berdysh's panic. "Don't make this about me. You're a party to mass murder, and you and I have a form of history together. There's nothing left that you could tell me that will keep me from removing ten feet of your intestines, then strangling you with them. How long do you think you could last with a cauterized gut injury and multiple asphyxiation attempts? I'll be willing to bet seven hours, but that's not my record…"

"You don't have a record for torture! You're the American! You're not a torture fiend!" Berdysh complained. "You kill quickly and cleanly!"

"That's old news, my friend. You heard that back when there was a KGB. Things have gotten progressively worse in this world since then. We've had our nation bloodied by terrorism, thousands of our citizens murdered by fanatics who have no concern for human life or the decency and dignity of humanity," Bolan told him. "I tried to use the same honorable methods I used on your old guard on those crazies, and all it got me was more dead friends. Times change, and a man has to adapt with them."

Berdysh's eyes widened with horror. "You're not kidding."

Bolan knelt, holding the surgical blade right by his eye. "Do I look as if I'm trying to amuse you?"

"You look as if you're going to dissect me," Berdysh admitted.

"Now that we have that disambiguation out of the way, are you left or right-handed?" Bolan asked.

"What does that matter?" Berdysh asked.

"It allows me to determine which side of your brain has more sensitivity to pain," Bolan said. "You see, the reason why I don't enjoy torture is because I can hardly afford the time I waste. I could easily lose myself for weeks while carving a man into his components."

"If you waste time with me, though, it only means that Chechens will die as you're having your sick fun."

"They're not Americans," Bolan said.

"You're not who we know as the crusader," Berdysh snapped back. "If there was one thing we knew about him, it was that he cared about people. It didn't matter what color they were, or what language they spoke, or even if they were Communist or capitalist! If they were not the enemy, then he broke his back to rescue them, to preserve them from the cross fire of our games of cloak and dagger. You are a fraud! I knew it. What happened? Did the real hero die? They assigned some psychopath to the job, a replacement crusader?"

"You wound me, Aloise," Bolan taunted. "I'll have to return the favor."

"Go ahead. Go ahead and do it!" Berdysh challenged. "I told you everything! Bennorin is probably already on his way to Grozny to oversee the massacres. All you'll find out is what color my liver is."

Bolan lowered the scalpel. "Did you get that, Kaya?"

A woman's voice cut through the darkness. "Every word of it."

"Lower him down," Bolan ordered.

"You are him," Berdysh whispered in awe. "You got me to spill… You barely touched me, and I broke. What is going to happen to me?"

"That all depends on whether the Russian Intelligence Service is as merciful as I am," Bolan noted.

"Few are," Berdysh said.

Laserka brought a blanket that Bolan used to cover the naked Curved Knife agent. "Do you have anything else that could help us?"

"No doubt you've already cracked my smartphone's password protection," Berdysh said. "If you know my real name…"

Bolan nodded. "There's a few files we're still having trouble opening, but my team is hard at work on it."

"I'd expect nothing less of you," Berdysh said. He sighed. "I presume I'll spend the rest of my life in a cell, at least until I take a long fall off of a short rope."

"You're a murderer," Bolan told him. "At least you're getting off with all your parts still attached to you."

"You are a man with a Russian soul, seeing the best in the worst," Berdysh said.

"It comes from seeing the truly worst," Bolan replied. "Whichever fate you feel is the most merciful, I'll put you in for."

Berdysh looked to Laserka. "I've always wanted to stand before a firing squad."

Laserka shook her head. "Insane romantics."

"But romantics nonetheless," Berdysh replied.

Bolan rose and he and Laserka left the conspirator alone in the empty cell.

PRICE WAS ON THE LINE, talking to both Bolan and La-serka at once over the laptop's teleconferencing programming. High-speed wireless Internet was one of the technologies of the twentieth century that had made it into the former Soviet Union, if only because enforcement laws made it harder to trace renegade ISPs that catered to various pornographic fetishes, or provided more secure communication between illicit organizations.

Either way, the bonuses of twenty-first century instant communications made it much easier for Bolan and his partner to remain up to speed on the case.

"Berdysh's smartphone had more than enough information for us to get the Russian Intelligence Service to release Laserka to our 'joint strike force,'" Price explained. "He had plans to travel to Grozny, Chechnya. We also picked up a cell phone number off Igor Rastolev's smartphone, and we ran a trace on it. Your friend Kroz was talking to someone. Guess where he was?"

"All roads lead to Grozny. Have you got any data on someone named Bennorin?" Bolan asked.

"We've got a few hints here and there. Lev Bennorin is one of those legends in the community," Price said.

"With Bennorin, you're definitely going into bogeyman territory," Laserka noted.

"So we're going to Chechnya?" Bolan asked.

"Yes," Price said. "Aaron picked up fragments of erased files off of Catherine Alexandronin's computer, and we managed to get some text out of them, thanks to data reconstruction."

"What did she have?" Laserka asked.

"The typical tales of fear and torture and messages

forwarded to those who are under the delusion that they have escaped the sphere of influence of the true masters of the Soviet Union," Price noted.

"Soviet Union?" Bolan asked. "That's a direct quote?"

"Written in black pixels on a white background," Price said. "Nothing about Russia or the Commonwealth of Independent States."

"So they are intending to turn back the clock." Laserka sighed. "Berdysh said something that Bennorin was intending to unleash a massacre in Chechnya. What's going on there that would be a good target?"

"We have our team working on it, but there's nothing that screams 'drop bombs here,' unfortunately," Price replied. "We're still working on the smartphone flash memories, as well as keeping a close eye on current-event calenders, which could give us a direction to look in. We aren't lucking out like Batroykin's party."

"Berdysh only knew generalities. Do you have any data on the Smyernet Consortium?" Bolan asked.

"Drawing blanks there. It's the same kind of RUMINT as Bennorin himself," Price said.

"What is RUMINT?" Laserka asked.

"Rumor-based intelligence," Bolan said. "The same kind of whispers you need to listen to in order to keep up with my activities in the field."

"You know, you have a lot of thinking and digging around to do to get to the next shooting," Laserka complained. "I thought things went by faster for you."

"I forgot, you've only been in one gunfight tonight," Bolan replied. "I'll try to make things more exciting for you in the next city."

Laserka rolled her eyes. "I'm not complaining. I'd come too damn close to catching a bullet in my face."

"And if Berdysh had still had shells for his RPG, then you'd have crashed in flames," Bolan said.

"Only if I hadn't taken your sage advice," Laserka said.

"Reluctantly," Bolan interjected.

"Reluctantly, but I'm still here," Laserka told him.

Bolan nodded. "We have our plane ready?"

"I've got a flight to Grozny," Price said. "Private charter so that you can slip your extra luggage past customs."

"How much luggage do we need?" Laserka asked.

"If you don't want a Kalashnikov, just say so," Bolan answered.

"Oh, *luggage!* I thought you were talking about something useless like shoes," Laserka said.

"That all for now, Barb?"

"We'll update you in the air if necessary," Price replied.

Bolan closed the laptop. "Come on, Kaya. We've got air to burn."

The Executioner and Laserka left for the airport, heading for their appointment with the Curved Knife, Iron Hammer and the mysterious Smyernet Consortium.

## CHAPTER SIXTEEN

It had taken Kroz the better part of the night to complete his escape plan to get out of Chechnya, but it was worth the loss of sleep. When he took a look at the Iron Hammer gunmen that he was supposed to be assisting, a wave of nausea and regret filled his chest like pleurisy.

Dagroych saw the discomfort on Kroz's face and chuckled. "Something wrong, friend?"

"I thought you said that we were supposed to have a crack strike team working with us," Kroz said.

"These are the best," Dagroych told him.

Kroz winced. "Every single one of them is standing with their fingers on the triggers, and who knows what their concept of muzzle discipline is, because they keep crossing each other with their rifles. How did these morons happen to survive firearms training?"

"Empty weapons until it was a moment before live fire," Dagroych said. "Don't worry. At least half of them have their safeties on."

"And the ones that don't?" Kroz asked.

"They have one of their partners in the way of the muzzle. If an AK discharges, we lose a sack of cement with manure for brains," Dagroych said.

Kroz shook his head. "You're not filling me with confidence here, Dag."

"When it comes time to make the snatch, we'll be out of the way," Dagroych told him. "It doesn't matter if we grab the big glowing prize. And it's better if we leave a few bodies behind for the authorities to recognize."

"We're nobodies, Dag. If we end up dead—"

"We won't." Dagroych cut him off. "You've let the American steal your spine, man."

Kroz frowned. "No. He hasn't gutted my courage. I'm still ready for combat."

"Good to know," Dagroych returned. "I sympathize with you, but these are just cannon fodder. Throwaway bodies, but they're still better trained than the lame morons who are at the plant."

Kroz looked at the group of Iron Hammer troopers and sighed. "You've just given me whole new layers of despair."

"Think of it this way, their incompetence will inspire a return to the glory days of Russia," Dagroych said.

The two Curved Knife operatives stepped out to confer with their men. It didn't escape Kroz's sense of irony that the majority of the gunmen on hand were Muslims by religion, similar to the French ruffians who had been on hand to delay the American's sweep through their London operation. If anything, these men were older and harder than the thuggish youths recruited by Rastolev.

Maybe a layer of experience would give them a slightly better chance. But considering that three of the four Spetsnaz-trained warriors had also been eliminated by the superior skills that the American had possessed, Kroz held no illusion that any force he assembled would be able to stand up to a one-man army who struck like lightning and had the reflexes of a cobra. Kroz dismissed those thoughts, and tried to restrain the urge to rip the rifles out of the hands of men who accidentally crossed him with the muzzle.

He remembered that the more radically violent Muslim men were of the delusion that God had granted them the ability to kill with any weapon, and things such as firearms safety and the basics of simple marksmanship were meant for nonbelievers. It was their faith that directed their poorly aimed streams of automatic fire at targets. That wasn't to say that all their brethren were so mentally feeble. Kroz remembered that mujahideen armed with single-shot muskets had been able to harrow the Soviet military from hundreds of yards away, behind cover. Their colorfully ornate rifles were works of art and archaic simplicity, and accuracy out to 800 meters was possible in their hands. It was the younger men who, having discovered the joys of the Avtomat Kalashnikov, discarded the ways of their fathers for the hip-fired, high-capacity chatterboxes captured from dead Russians.

Kroz didn't blame them. Most of the Soviet military had received similar training and that had crossed over to the simple peasant folk who ended up with the assault rifles. The AK-47 and its descendant AK-74 were designed to produce long ranks of men laying down suppressive fire that could break any enemy defenses. The flexible barrel and frame of the rifle, which bent and warped wildly in response to full-automatic fire to spare the mechanism, was meant to spread strings of fire even with a single point of aim. It was the Spetsnaz that received sturdier versions of the rifle cobbled from light machine gun frames with reinforced barrels who utilized short precision bursts when it came time to kill.

Such tactics, however, entailed long hours of marksmanship training, something the Red Army and its CIS successor force didn't have the material and logistics to encourage. Only the best of the best were allowed to burn through ammunition in quantities enough to make the most of the world's most durable and reliable assault rifle. Still, in the hands of the lesser-trained terrorists, it would prove more than sufficient for the task at hand.

"Are your men ready to go down in history?" Dagroych asked.

The Chechens saluted as one.

Kroz looked at their nominal display of discipline and nodded.

Maybe this could work. If the American swept through and eliminated all of them, it didn't matter. The battle with the Iron Hammer would be another incident of mass slaughter in the war-shattered city of Grozny, and would be sufficient impetus for Moscow to declare a return to the days of harder, iron-fisted rule. The new Russian order, the failed experiment of democracy and capitalism, would be ground beneath the government that had worked at keeping the peace, even if it meant a sacrifice of thousands of lives.

Kroz didn't intend to turn in his ticket to the relative safety of Siberia just yet, however.

The American had missed two chances to take him out of circulation, and Kroz wasn't about to allow the third time to be the charm.

TRAVEL BY ROAD was difficult through Grozny, since the Russian army and the Chechen rebel forces had done their best to tear the city of 200,000 souls to pieces. Residential and business neighborhoods looked as if an angry god had cast down an entire quiver of thunderbolts at an unfaithful congregation. Houses and buildings were battered if they stood, pockmarked with thousands of rifle rounds from fearsome house-to-house fighting.

The hardest hit neighborhoods were the ones closest to the oil pipelines that ran from the Caspian to the Black Sea. The Russian army had come in for one reason—to protect its economic interests, and the rebellious Chechens made every effort to destroy the flow of life-giving oil to the Russian people. Two massive wars had been waged, and even today, minor skirmishes broke out on a regular basis. If it hadn't been for their trucks' all-wheel drive, traversing the battered city would have been impossible.

The whole situation reminded Kroz of the city of Beirut during the height of the conflict between Israel and Lebanon. Kroz had been assigned to an operation behind their lines, thanks to his facility with the Arab language and Muslim culture. Like Beirut, Grozny held glimpses of what had been, displays of architecture betraying a long, storied history, but the scars of senseless war had worn them down to rubble.

Kroz could understand how the American people, protesting the war in Iraq, could say that the folly of war for oil was insane. How many Russian soldiers had died to protect the massive steel pipes carrying the black blood of the earth? How many Chechens threw their lives away to wrest control of the Russian government from their soil? The administration, however, wanted its oil, and didn't want to pay a transport tax through some other nation.

Kroz dismissed the argument. Chechnya, as part of the Chechen-Ingush Republic, was part of the great empire that had been known as the Soviet Union. While the European nations had been simple buffers, sacrificial cushions of land and people between the greedy, overbearing United States and their NATO lackeys, the Chechen-Ingush Republic was part of the Union.

"This land is my land," Kroz thought, repeating the words of a radical American song. The signs in another language meant nothing, like that tune had proclaimed. This land was made for me.

Kroz chuckled at his mangling of the classic chorus. In a way, the Chechen conflict had been a place that he was at his most comfortable within. With the Spetsnaz, he had come here to deal with the rebellious Islamicists who insisted that they could no longer recognize the authority of Moscow in their affairs. They no longer had wanted the hand-holding from the men in the Kremlin, and when they rose up in violence, Kroz had met them fire for fire, blood for blood. It was a glorious warrior's baptism and he reveled in the clash. As his skills grew, he was handpicked for the Curved Knife, the Smyernet Consortium's special operations action branch. Under their aegis, Kroz had traveled the globe, not only advancing the cause of the return to the old ways in Chechnya, but across all of Europe and in northern Africa.

He courted old allies who had been bolstered during the cold war, and sought out new friends among the various factions that arose. And while those covert diplomatic sorties among the stalkers in the shadows were enjoyable, where he'd truly come into his own was when he had been sent to kill people and destroy facilities that had gotten in the way. Surveillance operations disappeared, nosy reporters were found at the bottom of ditches, and radio stations that broadcast slander against the old times were rendered into twisted wreckage by applications of high explosives.

Kroz only wished that he had been able to see the death of the traitorous slug, Alexandronin, on the night he had first encountered the American. Watching the old man bleed to death on a dock far from his home would have made the bruises and split lip he'd suffered salve enough to warrant the beating. At least he'd escaped from the American's clutches. He checked his watch and did a little mental math. Bennorin had phoned him just after the American had captured Berdysh, which meant that the man had to have had Bendysh in custody for at least three hours.

Given the legendary interloper's skills at psychology and intimidation, Kroz could assume that Berdysh could have broken by now. Even if an airplane had been made instantly ready at the American's beck and call, there was still a window of six to eight hours where the

Iron Hammer could acquire what it needed from the hospital and begin to sow panic among the Chechen people and the Russian forces on hand for "peacekeeping" purposes.

Looking through the windshield, he could see how the road had smoothed out, signs of reconstruction taking hold around the major Grozny hospital. The ride became more comfortable without bomb-blasted potholes and chunks of rubble bouncing the truck for every inch of movement. For a moment Kroz entertained the simile of a light at the end of the tunnel, but that light would only last for a few more hours, despite the arrival of dawn coming in only an hour. He picked up the AK-74 assault rifle from between his knees as the truck slowed, swinging around toward the Radiological Medicine wing of the complex. There they would have access to high-energy radioactive waste that was earmarked for a delivery to a distant, remote landfill that had only limited and army-controlled access.

Kroz's truck rolled to a halt at the back of the building near the unloading docks. Four armed guards stood under a single lamp, sharing company and a pack of cigarettes. One of the men noticed the transports and looked at his watch. The Muslim guard rested his hand on the butt of his handgun, then hopped off the dock to jog up to the truck.

"You're an hour early," the Chechen said.

Kroz smirked, and his Russian features confused the rent-a-cop. "No. We're just on time."

Kroz whipped the muzzle of his rifle over the window and pulled the trigger. A trio of 5.45 mm bullets erased his face, spraying brains into the loading dock. The other three men jolted to alertness at the sound of autofire, but the Iron Hammer gunmen in the back of the truck had dropped out of the bed, their rifles stuttering loudly in the night. Where Kroz had achieved his goals with only three bullets, the four men emptied over 140 rounds into the direction of the Chechen sentries. Kroz turned his head away in embarrassment as the guards managed to pull their handguns before the waves of assault rifle bullets finally tracked into them.

The quartet seemed pleased with their sloppy marksmanship as Kroz exited the truck. Dagroych jogged over from his vehicle.

"Impressive display," Kroz said.

"You think?" Dagroych asked, not certain what to make of Kroz's compliment.

"I've never seen someone need so much ammo to take out three men standing in the open," Kroz continued. "It has to be some sort of record."

"Not so loud, the boys might hear you," Dagroych admonished.

"Speaking of being heard, half the city must know something is up by now," Kroz said. "Short bursts don't call down this kind of attention. Those four idiots, however, made enough noise to indicate a massacre."

"That's the point, isn't it?" Dagroych asked. "Inspiring more fear and loathing here in Grozny?"

The Iron Hammer gunmen kicked open the door, and one of the Chechen insurgents jerked violently as a security guard with a handgun shot him. The rent-a-cop's accuracy laid out the self-assured pawn, his body slumped over the rail on the loading dock. The other

Hammer shooters opened fire, their assault rifles blazing violently in the confines of the office.

"Oh look, there's the first proof of our operation flopped over the railing," Kroz quipped.

Dagroych gave Kroz a bump on the shoulder with his fist. "Everything according to plan. Bring enough men, and it goes that much more smoothly."

"Please." Kroz sighed.

More gunfire, this time the single-sided rattle of AKs, erupted deeper in the building. Kroz wrinkled his nose. "They do know that shooting the barrels full of radioactive isotope waste will make things very bad for us, right?"

"You're a prince," Dagroych commented. However, he did reach into his pocket for a compact Geiger counter, reading the ambient radiation. "It's hot, but not enough to indicate a breached container."

"How hot is hot?" Kroz asked.

"The equivalent of an airline flight or a couple of X-rays," Dagroych explained.

"Which is precisely what we're taking. The radioactive isotopes which release the X-ray radiation that makes those pictures possible," Kroz said.

"As well as ingestible high-energy metals for endoscopy and a few other things," Dagroych added. "Sorry, I've been doing a lot of research for this operation, so that we know what to take to make our dirty bombs."

"I was just as bad with my Muslim cultural studies," Kroz confessed. "Don't worry about it. A little knowledge is still something to crow about. So, do we head in and see what they're doing?"

"Stay out here," Dagroych said. "They just opened

the storage container for the radioactive waste. We're safe here, but inside, those men are receiving lethal dosages of radiation."

"Will they last long enough to load the trucks?" Kroz asked.

Dagroych nodded. "They'll have a day or two left of usefulness before their bodies begin their break-down. It's not like entering a full-on nuclear reactor."

"Good. I have another way to broadcast our posses-sion of deadly materials," Kroz said. "Once they're finished here, we'll drop them off at the airport as a welcoming committee."

"For the American?" Dagroych asked. "Sounds like a good plan."

"He's working inside the system with RIS," Kroz said. "Once they look at the bodies, their irradiated corpses will help inspire a greater panic."

"We'll have to phone in an anonymous tip to make sure they notice the radiation levels," Dagroych sug-gested. "Which, of course might limit their willingness to release such information."

"We'll also contact the press in multiple nations. A gunfight at Grozny Airport will be big news," Kroz said. "Especially since it's a mixed-use airport."

"The military presence will be an issue," Dagroych mused. "But then again, you thought that the security here would be a problem, as well."

"They're dead men. Whether they die from soldier bullets or are put down by the American, it's all cake," Kroz continued. "And, if by some stroke of luck they actually take him down, we've caused a crisis and eliminated a problem."

Dagroych chuckled. "If they only knew we were talking about them like this—"

"Shut up," Kroz cut him off. "Here they come with the barrels."

Dagroych popped a radiation sickness pill, glad for the added bulk of lead-lined underwear to protect his organs from the radiation. Kroz still shifted uncomfortably in his clothes, but assisted the Iron Hammer gunmen in loading the drums of waste into the back of the second truck. Both of the Russian advisers took seats in the first vehicle, leaving only a few to guard the drums and a single driver. The excuse was given that they didn't have room, but from the look on the guards' faces, Kroz could tell that they suspected the worst.

Kroz made sure to point out the glory of the airport attack to those particularly glum gunmen.

Maybe the fear of catching a bullet would make their martyrdom a little easier.

MACK BOLAN LOOKED OUT the window of the airplane as the jet swung toward the south of Grozny to approach the airport nine kilometers north of the war-torn city. It was an opportunity to get a better look at the shattered metropolis. Though the fighting had died down since the end of the Second Chechen War, it still bore the horrible scars of conflict.

He remembered the cost in homes—sixty thousand apartment buildings and homes destroyed in the conflict. In the years since the end of the hostilities, only nine hundred of those structures had been restored by reconstruction efforts, meaning that fifty-nine thousand families had nowhere to lay their heads. It was no surprise that refugees had scattered across Europe.

Neither side had covered themselves in glory during the battle. Where suicide bombers and hostage takers murdered large groups of people, the Russian military had destroyed entire communities in angry reprisal. It wasn't just the housing that had been wrecked in the angry fits of warring factions. Several dozen industrial enterprises had been demolished as forces clashed. According to the records, only three of those businesses had rebuilt their factories and offices, the others were in the middle of reconstruction. Unfortunately, funding to replace what was lost just didn't exist, and many of the businesses were doubting whether to continue operating in a region that had been ground zero for a devastating conflict. The investment in new buildings could easily be washed away by more suicide bombers and Russian air strikes when the hostilities bubbled to the surface again.

The bombings and skirmishes between Russian and Chechen forces weren't the only issues at stake. Political murders continued against both the Chechen federal government and the separatists. At one point, in 2001, ethnic Russian civilians were found in Leninsky, the victims of unknown murderers who killed for no reason other than their race. Since no one had claimed the responsibility for those crimes, it was unknown whether it had been the work of a serial killer or an organized effort on the part of the insurgents to lash out at anyone who wasn't a Chechen Muslim.

"How many factions are down there?" Bolan asked.

"Including pro-Russian vigilantes and the splintered

separatist movements?" Laserka asked. "According to RIS records, it fluctuates between four and nine active forces operating in this region. And that's only Grozny and the surrounding area. There are more troublemakers closer to the border of Ingushetia, since the Ingush liked the idea of having a piece of the Chechen republic. There, Russians and Chechens work side by side holding off their incursions during the day, and at night return to trying to murder each other."

Bolan closed his eyes, trying to quell the anger in him. "I remember in 2003 that the United Nations called Grozny the most-destroyed city on the Earth."

He looked down, seeing the fields of oil tankers just north of the Sunzha River. A little farther northeast, he could see the rail hub, which had been restored by Russian army engineers in an effort to keep the oil fields and their precious lifeline in operation. Unfortunately for the citizens of Grozny, the rebuilding there had been limited to keeping the oil flowing, not restoring a shattered infrastructure. A hundred thousand people huddled in apartments and still-standing homes, deprived of running water and electrical power. Compared to the misinformation spread about the destroyed infrastructure of Iraq, this was the real deal, but American activists didn't have an interest in a real city of two hundred thousand deprived of heat and comfortable shelter. The Herculean efforts of American engineers in the Gulf had given cities like Baghdad a chance to rebuild, and the teeming Iraqi population were glad for their restoration of infrastructure.

In the meantime, Grozny sat, the victim of drive-by politics and apathy.

Bolan's PDA warbled, and he took it off of hibernation mode. A news article had been forwarded to him by Kurtzman.

"What's wrong?" Laserka asked.

"A ton and a half of radioactive waste was taken from one of Grozny's remaining hospitals last night," Bolan said. He frowned. "That's not good news at all."

Laserka tilted her head. "They can't make a nuclear weapon out of that stuff."

"No. But they can create a dirty bomb, making entire sections of the city even more useless," Bolan said. "And there are plenty of oil fields down there that can be denied with the fallout."

Laserka's eyes widened with horror. "Russia and Chechnya need that oil. The only reason there's any reconstruction down there is because of the pipeline and the rail hub."

"What better way to convince the Russian people that their leadership is right in pulling out all the stops to secure their republic?" Bolan asked.

Laserka shuddered. "God help us."

Bolan looked down at the most destroyed city on Earth, realizing that the horrors of war were not over for its poor citizens. "Until we get that kind of backup, we're on our own for now."

The plane lowered for its approach, leaving behind the aerial view of hell on Earth.

## CHAPTER SEVENTEEN

Thanks to their credentials and the fact that they were on a charter flight, Bolan and Laserka were able to have their handguns with them and holstered the moment they disembarked from the plane. The sky was a shade of gray that reminded Laserka of the pregnant pause before the heavens opened up in tears.

Laserka looked at Bolan, who threw his duffel bag over his shoulder with an ease that belied its remarkable weight. For all his lean muscle and perfect proportions, the man possessed power that surprised her, but considering that the man lived in a state of combat on a regular basis, his endurance and strength were prodigious. The breeze blew and she flinched, tugging her jacket tighter around her body.

"Kaya," Bolan said softly, drawing her attention to him as he pointed toward the distance. "Company."

Laserka turned to see what he was referring to and saw two jeeps loaded with men rolling toward the airplane. "We didn't ask for someone to meet us here."

"I know," Bolan said.

"I was just kidding about not getting enough action." Laserka sighed.

"I know that, too, Kaya," Bolan said softly, swinging the duffel bag from his shoulder and unzipping it. "Grab a rifle."

Laserka plucked the long gun from its place in the bag, unsnapping the Velcro fasteners that made the weapon one of the structural supports of the war bag. Two magazines had been taped into place and she worked the bolt of the assault rifle. Bolan handed her another pair of taped magazines.

"The VEPR's in 7.62 mm ammo," Bolan told her. "It might have a little more oomph than you're used to."

Laserka stuffed the taped magazines into her jacket pocket, frowning as she did so. "This is heavier than the usual AK-74 we use, and the stock feels a little better. I can handle the extra recoil."

"Get into the cabin and tell the crew to hit the deck, preferably behind the seats. I'll need you to give me cover fire," Bolan continued.

Laserka nodded, running up the steps. The men in the jeep, if they noticed the hardware that the Executioner and his ally were pulling out, didn't appear dissuaded by the presence of the extra firepower. One jeep peeled away, though, and Laserka could see that one of the men had shouldered an RPG.

"Get behind cover!" she shouted to the crew, shouldering her VEPR. The holographic sight didn't magnify the image of the distant jeep gunner, but thanks to the hovering red dot, she was able to gauge where to aim to hit the man with the rocket launcher.

She pulled the trigger at the same time as Bolan, their two rifles chugging out heavy-caliber rounds at the target.

Someone had to have hit the rocket grenadier, because he jerked violently, spilling from the jeep and tumbling in a bloody mess of twisting arms and legs. The RPG's body snapped as it bounced on the hard tarmac. That was their last free shot as the second jeepload of gunmen opened fire. Laserka ducked through the doorway as rifle bullets punched into the fuselage of the charter jet, perforations appearing in the pressurized shell just over her head and shoulders. The supersonic passage of the slugs caused her hair to fly and whip around her face as she dived even tighter to the floor, automatic mayhem chattering outside.

Laserka twisted and writhed back to where she could aim her assault rifle out of the doorway, triggering the weapon even without a target as she got a view of the outside. The initial burst was a waste of ammunition, but it caused one of the speeding enemy vehicles to swerve violently.

That's when the Russian lady cop spotted her partner on the move. He was running toward the two vehicles, charging faster than they could adjust their aim.

He didn't have an inch of cover out there, relying on his speed and maneuverability to avoid being hit by the gunmen in their vehicles. One lucky shot, and Cooper's brains would be sprayed on the tarmac, leaving her alone to face a hostile conspiracy. Laserka wanted to scream his name, to warn him about the suicidal nature of his charge, but she knew that he couldn't afford the distraction.

The big American was alone as he blitzed toward the enemy force, and all she could do was what he'd asked.

Laserka milked the trigger, pouring on suppressive fire to cover him.

THE SPUTTER OF LASERKA'S VEPR reassured Mack Bolan as he charged toward the swerving jeeps. His own assault rifle was at his waist, doing what it had been designed to, keeping the head of the enemy down as it bellowed out its 7.62 mm death song. The grille of one of the jeeps exploded in a spray of sparks as Bolan's steel-cored rounds tore through the engine with vicious abandon, forcing the vehicle into an out-of-control skid. The driver cranked on the steering wheel and the jeep jerked to one side. It was a small victory to keep the two jeeps full of gunmen off his case, but the Iron Hammer attackers were hardly slowed as one of the vehicles zipped past at 60 mph, cutting so close to the Executioner that he felt the rush of wind past him.

Of course, the attackers' speed made it harder for them to track him. If Bolan had been standing still, then there would have been a target to lock on to, but the warrior's movements, his broken field running and serpentine adjustments of course kept the enemy from anticipating. Already he noticed one jeep full of riflemen reloading their weapons, having wasted ammunition trying to gun down his elusive form. Bolan couldn't count on his luck holding out forever, and his only saving grace was that there was only one rifleman in one jeep and two in the other. In the distance, he heard the chatter of other automatic weapons, meaning that this was more than an ambush meant solely for him and La-serka, and from the sounds of things, the besieged air-port security would need support.

The partially unmanned jeep rushed toward him, the driver intending to use his vehicle's front bumper to erase the Executioner from the face of the world once and for all, but Bolan spun at the hip, tracking the VEPR assault rifle with a familiarity borne of a hun-dred battles. The rifle chugged its payload at a rate of 650 rounds per minute, the powerful slugs going through the windshield as if it were a soap bubble. A row of full-auto rounds walked up the driver's chest and cored his face in a volcanic eruption that left a decapitated corpse at the control of the speeding all-wheel-drive vehicle. The lifeless hands tugged the wheel to the right as the body behind them slumped, so Bolan leaped to the left, barely avoiding having his legs crushed by a half ton of hurtling machinery. The rifleman riding in the vehicle roared in rage as his rifle flew from his fingers.

The Chechen had let go of the weapon to gain con-trol of the steering wheel, but the driver's death spasm had jammed his foot on the gas. The jeep had turned into an out-of-control rocket and though the gunman had stabilized the steering wheel, he was off balance and unable to reach either the hand brake or the floor pedals. The terrorist screamed in horror as the vehicle smashed through a chain-link fence and speared into a marshy wallow just off the tarmac. His squeal of dis-may ended as the jeep flipped onto his back, one thou-sand pounds of metal grinding him into soft, wet mud. Bolan hoped that the force of the vehicle landing on him had killed him instantly, because drowning in mud was an ugly, terrifying way to go.

The Executioner didn't have time to concern himself with whether the terrorist's demise was swift or slow, as the other vehicle full of gunmen was trying to take him out. This crew had learned the lethal lesson of their compatriots. Attempting to gore the warrior was to tempt the evasive skills of a true matador who could take a dance of death and be the chooser of the slain. Bolan discarded his empty VEPR, realizing that he wouldn't have time, even with Laserka's cover fire, to reverse the taped magazines in the rifle. He pulled the Desert Eagle in a rapid movement, the big gun slicing out of its quick-draw leather. The driver ducked his head as Bolan's first .44 Magnum man-stopper cut the distance between them, but the heavy slugs had managed to connect with one of the two riflemen.

A 240-grain widemouthed hollowpoint round tore massive wound channels through the gunman, and pain-induced reflex caused the dying man to kick out of his seat. The centrifugal force of the jeep's sudden turn tore him off the vehicle and spilled him onto the tarmac. The bullets had smashed the Chechen's rib cage, but he landed face-first on the unyielding graded stone. Cheekbones and jaw collapsed under the powerful impact, vertebrae fusing as his whole body's weight came down on his neck. Swathes of skin shredded off the cracked and broken skull, depositing a bloody trail in his wake.

The jeep's remaining passengers looked back in shock at the gory smear that used to be their companion, the driver's attention distracted for long enough that both Bolan and Laserka were able to track him. No longer concentrating on his evasive maneuvers, the driver had doomed himself and his companion as a relentless torrent of Magnum and ComBloc rounds ripped into the jeep as it took the straightaway. The gunman in the back absorbed the first wave of killer rounds, his head and chest chopped apart. As he died, he slumped across the driver's shoulders, but the steel-cored AK rounds and Bolan's thundering .44 turned the human shield into a sieve as they continued to empty their weapons into the wheelman.

Head and back peppered with bullets, the dying Iron Hammer driver collapsed behind the wheel, his foot skidding off the accelerator.

"Kaya, everything okay on the plane?" Bolan called out.

"No casualties among the flight crew," Laserka answered.

Since Bolan and Laserka had been the only passengers, that was good news. The Iron Hammer ambush had not been a deadly situation that had brought harm to innocent bystanders. However, there were still the sounds of battle rising from the airport itself. Bolan took a moment to retrieve his fallen rifle, then rushed up to the idling jeep and pulled the two corpses from the front seat. Laserka didn't need a summons to race to his side.

"Ready for round two?" Bolan asked, slipping behind the wheel.

"No, but when has that ever stopped things?" Laserka asked. "It's not like the bad guys ask, are you ready?"

Bolan threw the jeep into Drive and rocketed toward the main terminal.

KROZ LOWERED his binoculars after watching the deadly exchange on the tarmac. In the space of thirty seconds, Bolan and his companion had eliminated the gunmen sent to head them off at their plane. Kroz cursed himself because he hadn't taken into account the possibility that the American would have brought a small arsenal with him to Grozny airport. Well, they had planned on that contingency, but actually seeing the man pull two fully ready assault rifles from his war bag had been a slap in the face. He'd been expecting the compact little P-90 machine pistol from London, backed up by his regular two handguns.

The assault rifles, modified Kalashnikov designs by the look of them, had put him on an equal footing with the similarly armed Chechen insurgents. Still, he was outnumbered three to one, even with Laserka on his side, and there was no way that a man on foot could have had the speed and maneuverability to deal with two speeding vehicles. Kroz cursed himself for making that assumption.

Kroz followed the jeep's rocketing progression toward the Aeroflat terminal where the rest of the irradiated Chechens had been storming the building. Granted confidence from the inevitability of their martyrdom, the Muslims had fought like lions, fearless in the face of security guards with their handguns. Their assault rifles chewed the hapless defenders of the airport to pieces. Obviously the prospect of a glorious death had also improved their aim, as it didn't take nearly as much ammunition to eliminate the security force.

Passengers waiting to board planes and travelers

having disembarked from their flights cowered in terror as the purpose-driven Chechen insurgents walked through the terminal, looking for likely targets. Kroz pulled the walkie-talkie to his lips and issued a warning.

"Men, heads up," he said. "The American has acquired a vehicle, and he's on his way to intercept your operation at the terminal."

"A jeep? From whom?" one of the gunmen asked. Kroz could see him through the windows in a terminal, AK in one fist and the portable radio in his other hand.

"Your dead partners," Kroz told him. "The American eliminated them, and he's noticed your actions against civilians. It's your choice whether to stand your ground, or fight your way out of the airport."

"We have been tasked with the duty of destroying an enemy of our nation," the terrorist said. "Let him come, and we shall have a reckoning."

Kroz didn't blame the Iron Hammer team leader. If given the choice between slow death by radiation poisoning or the relative swiftness of a bullet, Kroz would have made the same one. Luckily, the Russian was able to minimize his risk by not personally handling any of the drums, and taking the proper medications to inure his system to the milder exposure effects of the medical waste. He popped another pill just to make sure, observing as the American approached the besieged terminal.

Laserka was with Bolan, riding shotgun, so that gave Kroz some consolation. If the warrior survived this encounter, there was always the likelihood that she would perish. Perhaps her death or injury would distract the American from his relentless pursuit.

"The man is a machine," Dagroych stated. "Six men in half a minute, and he acquired wheels."

"If it weren't real, I'd be sitting back, noshing on popcorn," Kroz admitted. "The man moves better than a Hong Kong action star."

"The transition from rifle to handgun was especially smooth," Dagroych commented. "We should demonstrate that for the new operatives joining the Curved Knife."

"You think we'll live long enough to be teachers?" Kroz asked.

Dagroych raised an eyebrow. "You aren't giving up so easily, are you?"

"I'm being realistic," Kroz said. "This is the second time I've seen him in action."

"What about at the docks?" Dagroych asked.

"I didn't see a thing. He just loomed up and knocked me on my ass," Kroz explained. "The next thing I know, this hammer-hard fist connected with my face and I was out cold. And in the other gunfight, he did his best to keep walls and ceilings between the two of us."

"We'll probably be the rare enemies who've observed him in action," Dagroych said. "Though it's not like just watching him will give us the kind of reaction time we'll need to counter his speed and accuracy."

Kroz shrugged. "Then just enjoy the show. He's in the terminal, with Laserka hot on his heels."

Dagroych raised his field glasses again, focusing on the two figures running through the terminal. "Oh, I can see the anger in his face. They must have come across the first civilian victims."

Hundreds of yards away from the Curved Knife pair, the American looked for a focus for his anger over murdered innocents. Kroz felt a sinking feeling in his stomach as the warrior's face grew emotionless.

BOLAN TURNED AWAY from the body of a bullet-riddled youth, scarcely older than fifteen, the victim of a renegade Chechen gunman in the terminal. The boy had only been one of many, each corpse mutilated by the relentless fury of a fully automatic assault weapon supplied to him by an out-of-control government agency. This wasn't some disgruntled citizen who had gotten control of some cosmetically altered semiauto, these men were whipping scythes of burning lead left and right, unleashing lethal fury.

The Executioner poured on the speed, leaving Laserka behind as he spotted the first of the Iron Hammer mass murderers standing at the end of a concourse. The gunman noticed the grim wraith charging toward him and took a surprised step back. Bolan fired from the hip and on the run, his reflexes and marksmanship putting half a dozen rounds into the Chechen's torso despite the soldier's furious pace. The gunman flopped onto his back, rib cage sawn open by a line of deadly bullets.

Other Chechen insurgents saw their ally collapse under the Executioner's hail of fire and they scrambled, looking for cover. The warrior swung into the intersection and spotted one hapless rifleman as he lurched onto a counter, hoping to fall behind it for cover. The

VEPR in Bolan's hands snarled, stitching the murderous gunman along one thigh, walking the stream of auto fire to the bottom of his pelvis. Steel-cored bullets had been stopped by the thick femur bone in the thigh, but the rounds that entered the man's crotch had plenty of open fluid mass to churn through. Several 7.62 mm rifle rounds seared into the killer's bowels, inspiring a bloody torrent from the dying man's lips before he flopped headfirst to the tiled floor behind the counter. A sickening crack resounded, informing the killing machine that he was dead.

The Executioner spotted two more men who had taken cover behind a row of fiberglass chairs inset on steel railings. They had to have assumed that the seats would have provided a modicum of protection from the warrior's assault rifle, but the killing machine triggered his weapon, disabusing them of that notion. Fiberglass exploded into splinters as the high-velocity, heavyweight penetrators continued on through the seatshells and into the cowards who had hidden behind them. Hearts and lungs obliterated, the Chechen terrorists slumped bonelessly to the carpet, their guts pouring into ever-widening stains beneath their corpses.

The Executioner looked for the next terrorist who grabbed hastily for a young woman, clutching a handful of blond hair in an effort to take her as a shield. The soldier fired his rifle, catching the Chechen hostage-taker at his knees. Bone and muscle disappeared in a storm of steel-cored vengeance, and he collapsed, releasing the young woman. As blood pumped from the stumps of his severed legs, the insurgent begged for mercy from the black wraith walking up to him.

Bolan looked down at the mewling man who had so recently engaged in the slaughter of unarmed innocents. Mercy came in the form of a single round.

"How many more?" Bolan asked the stunned former hostage.

"Three of them," she answered, pointing numbly. "Who…"

The Executioner turned away from her, continuing on. Maybe Mack Bolan would return later to answer the young woman's questions, but that wasn't the issue now. Animal Man was on the rampage here, gunning down unarmed civilians. One of the remaining three snarled, bellowing an incomprehensible challenge to the avenging force that swept through the terminal.

"You want me? Take me!" the Chechen bellowed, thrusting his rifle into the air.

The Executioner shot him through the face with a single round. He ejected the empty banana magazines, letting them clatter to the floor, slowly withdrawing a second taped pair.

The remaining two Iron Hammer killers swung into the open and leveled their autoweapons at him.

"You crazy maniac!" one shouted.

The soldier snapped his magazine into place and pulled the trigger, a round still chambered from the remnants of the older load. The Chechen who had disparaged Bolan's sanity folded over, a hot bullet seared into his intestines. The other man pulled the trigger on his rifle, but panic had loosened his grip on the weapon. The ceiling over the Executioner's head disintegrated.

With a scream of terror, the Iron Hammer survivor

threw down his weapon. His suicidal confidence had evaporated in the fury of the Executioner's cold gaze.

"I surrender! Mercy!" the last gunman called.

Bolan whipped the stock of his rifle across the Chechen's jaw.

"Consider yourself a prisoner," Bolan said. "But don't expect mercy. Not after this."

The Iron Hammer prisoner whimpered, his chin painted with blood.

"Are there any more?" Bolan asked, as grim as a living embodiment of death.

The Chechen looked out the window. Bolan turned and squinted into the distance. He could see another terminal, seven hundred yards away. He figured that if he had a set of binoculars, he'd be able to see the men who directed this massacre observing from the anonymous safety of sheer distance.

And they had watched him take their gunmen apart.

"Soon," Bolan growled, turning back to his barely conscious prisoner.

## CHAPTER EIGHTEEN

Vlad Mahklov looked at Bolan and his companion as they entered his office. As a local representative of the Russian Intelligence Service, watching over the interests of the whole Commonwealth in Grozny, he had received a phone call from Batroykin about the arrival of the two operatives from Moscow. Mahklov wasn't surprised by Kaya Laserka, who had developed a reputation as a fine investigator for the RIS, but the sight of the big man with jet-black hair and cold blue eyes set off alarms in his head.

Bolan looked at Mahklov, and nodded. "I see that you've been promoted since the last time I saw you."

"You two know each other?" Laserka asked. "And if so, do I have to put a filing cabinet between me and the cross fire?"

"I'm not going to make a move against..." Mahklov made a point to look down at the sheet of paper full of notes on his desk. "Agent Matt Cooper of the American FBI."

Bolan nodded. "And I've been keeping an eye on

his career. He's really turned himself around since Afghanistan."

Mahklov swallowed uncomfortably. "I try not to break too many eggs here in Chechnya."

"You're not the chef I'm looking for, Vlad," Bolan said, calming him. "You're still in my good book."

Mahklov wiped his forehead. "Thank God."

"Sorry about the mess at the airport," Laserka said. "I think that was our fault, since they knew we were coming."

"It wasn't just us they were after," Bolan said. "Whoever is supporting and directing the Curved Knife intended to send a message to Moscow and the Chechen people about how the war is still going on. Plus, the man I hit started developing skin lesions while I was waiting for a police team to pick him up."

"Lesions?" Mahklov asked. "So you think he was involved in the radioactive waste theft last night?"

Bolan nodded.

"How bad was the radiation poisoning?" Laserka asked. "A lot of blood was spread over the terminal."

Mahklov punched a button on his conference phone. "I'll have to dispatch a hazmat team. Right now, we still have crime-scene technicians securing the area and recovering evidence."

"Given that they were slow in developing the first visible symptoms since two in the morning, they only barely received a lethal dosage," Bolan stated. "I don't think there'll be much concern of serious radioactive contamination of the terminal."

Mahklov detected a dull note in the American's speech. He looked tired, but it wasn't physical exhaustion. "Do you want to take some time to recover from this morning?"

"I'll cope," Bolan returned. "I was just thinking about the victims who we won't be examining with a fine-toothed comb. I'm sure the hospital would have discovered the radiation poisoning and determined how severely he was irradiated after their first X-ray turned out to be blanked."

Mahklov nodded. "As it is, we now have some form of time line, especially if the dead men also have evidence of radiation poisoning."

"The conspirators who assigned them to attack the airport must have known about the lethal dosage they'd received, and gave the insurgents the option for a more glorious end than vomiting up their liquefied entrails," Laserka mused.

"And they figured you were on your way here?" Mahklov noted.

"I've been working against them since London," Bolan said. "The Curved Knife has been aware of my investigation for about four days, which is when I first encountered them."

"The battle at the peace conference, back in Moscow," Mahklov pointed out.

"Fortunately, I managed to minimize the violence there, so this group of Iron Hammer terrorists split into two assault groups, one to deal with me, and one to engage in violence to make the Russian government and their representatives and allies here in Chechnya respond in force," Bolan said.

"And it was Batroykin's urging that had me hold off on conducting raids against various insurgent groups," Mahklov replied. "We've managed a cease-fire with the less radical and violent separatists. The Iron Hammer still manages to rally the truly insane thugs to their side. There's a man in charge of the Grozny cell—"

"Dagroych." Bolan cut him off. "Thanks to information gleaned from captured data in London and Moscow, my people have been able to narrow down his potential identity. Boris Rosenberg was born in Israel and defected to the Soviet Union as a teenager. Being a Russian with semetic features, he was used by the Spetsnaz to operate in states with large Muslim populations, like Bosnia and Chechnya. He can look like a local with a minimum of effort and is polylinguistic."

Bolan handed over a printout taken off his laptop. "We figured that Dagroych was Rosenberg because he fit a profile."

"Which profile would that be?" Mahklov asked.

"A dead, Russian, special-forces operator whose homicidal ideations were catered to by the old guard of the Soviet Union," Bolan told him. "Basically the type that I passed you over for."

Mahklov nodded. "I remember. Who's this Kroz?"

"Someone I bumped heads with back in London," Bolan said. "He got away from me twice."

"Third time will be the charm?" Mahklov asked.

"This time I have someone to punt him back into play if he manages to slip past me," Bolan noted, looking to Laserka.

She smiled. "So we have radioactive waste. Are there any reports of missing high explosives or large lots of fertilizer in the wind?"

Mahklov stifled a chuckle. "Nope. Didn't smell anything."

Laserka winced at her unintentional miswording. "Sorry."

Mahklov cleared his throat, regaining his composure. "No, it was an honest verbal flub. But no, we don't have any evidence that the Iron Hammer is assembling a large bomb."

"That doesn't necessarily mean anything," Bolan interjected. "There are probably stockpiles of weaponry on hand. Laserka was on a stakeout for buyers for the Chechen insurgency, but they didn't have a need for grenade launchers or other launched munitions. Plus, there's always the option that they could load drums onto civilian prop-driven aircraft and crash them into the oil fields."

Mahklov's brow furrowed. "Prop planes?"

"We're talking about terrorists. They slip grenades into teddy bears and put dynamite in inflatable rafts to park next to naval combat vessels," Bolan said. "We're so used to high-tech options to put a nail into a board, when they just grab the closest rock handy and pound it into the wood."

"That'd be suicide," Mahklov suggested.

"We have a dozen men who were dying of radiation poisoning and who loaded up for war in an airport," Laserka said. "They could have sought medical attention, or just simply died in their beds with overdoses of morphine to ride into the next life. Instead, they wanted to go out in fire and steel."

"You're not looking at stable people here, Vlad," Bolan added. "They have no concern for rules of engagement, and if there's a chance for them to make a statement with their deaths, then they'll die in the most explosive means possible."

Mahklov looked at his computer, then tapped a few keys, looking for something on the monitor. "We had word of a raid on a farm commune on the border between Chechnya and Ingushta."

"Crop dusters?" Bolan asked.

Mahklov nodded solemnly. "Four of them were stolen."

"So we're talking a double worst-case scenario," Bolan said. "Not only is there the possibility of suicide pilots hammering the oil fields with waste-packed planes, but they could have the insecticide tanks topped up with aerosolized materials."

Mahklov turned the monitor around so that Bolan could look at it. "What you're describing could mean that we have at least an hour or two more."

"Determining how to transform at least part of the waste into a dispensable format," Laserka noted.

"The best-case scenario would be about sixteen hours, which means the aircraft would fly at around midnight," Bolan said. "Counting the time that it took to transport the materials to the location where they'd perform the liquid suspension."

Mahklov rubbed his brow, looking older. "You seem to have a handle on how this would go."

"Only because I've kept an eye on all manner of articles dealing with what the terrorists haven't done yet," Bolan said. "I want to be able to keep ahead of them."

"I know, and trust me, I am very glad that you have

a handle on this. What did those articles say about the lethality of airborne release of high-energy radioactive waste?" Mahklov replied.

"There was an incident a year or so back where a consortium threatened the world with a metallic form of radioactive isotope which they planned to drop from the International Space Station," Bolan pointed out. "Given that it was radioactive metals dropped from orbit, we were looking at an area half the size of Manhattan Island for a single orbitally dropped drum. Radiation sickness from shrapnel and environmental metals emitting gamma rays would have killed ten thousand people within the first twenty-four hours, with genetic damage and cancer as secondary effects for another 200,000."

"One drum of radioactive isotope would affect a city the size of Grozny, causing suffering," Mahklov replied.

"And that was a relatively primitive dispersal format," Bolan said. "Throwing a water balloon from high orbit. With crop dusters, we're looking at higher lethality rates, especially since it was ten drums of waste material stolen."

"Numbers?" Mahklov asked.

"Fifty thousand dead," Bolan answered glumly. "And everyone else in the immediate greater metropolitan area doomed to giving birth to genetic disasters, if they aren't rendered sterile or suffer cancerous effects."

Mahklov winced.

Bolan pulled out his PDA and took the information off Mahklov's screen.

"Your people might have something?" Mahklov asked.

"Letting them know what to look for," Bolan replied. "Every set of eyes we can get on this project will be vital. I hope you don't mind."

"I'm not going to risk thousands dead and hundreds of thousands genetically damaged because of some interagency pissing contest, Cooper," Mahklov replied. "You've got every ounce of cooperation you can get from me."

Bolan nodded, entering the data with his stylus on the miniature keyboard, working the keys with lightning speed. He received a message almost immediately.

"Will start narrowing down airfields within fifteen minutes," Kurtzman wrote back. "We have satellites with radiation detectors moving back into orbit over Russian airspace."

Bolan showed Mahklov the information. "I'll need to take a look at a map of the surrounding area. Also, what would be the fuel capacity of the four stolen crop dusters?"

"You'll calculate the distance they could travel?" Mahklov asked.

Bolan borrowed a pencil and a pad of scratch paper.

"What else will you need?" Mahklov asked. "I have the entire resources of the federal government in Chechnya at my disposal."

"Do you have a fast helicopter on hand?" Bolan inquired.

"Armed or unarmed?" Mahklov asked.

"Armed would be good," Bolan replied. "A decent pilot would also help. I'll need someone on backup."

"Mi-24 Hinds are a dime a dozen in the Chechen air

force," Mahklov admitted. "I'll call someone up and get my son on this. You said you needed a backup pilot?"

Bolan nodded. "I'm checked out on the Hind."

"Not surprised," Mahklov said.

Bolan and Laserka retired to a nearby office to begin their dead reckoning.

DAGROYCH LOOKED at the technicians in their heavy rubber-and-lead radiation suits, manipulating the drums of stolen waste, pouring their contents into a large vat. It would have been technically safer to use a less volatile suspension, but he figured that since his men were already wearing respirators, why not mix the waste with the insecticide. If the people didn't end up sickened by radiation, the lethal chemical concoction used to eliminate locusts and other hungry vermin would help ruin their lives.

He took a puff on his cigarette, watching the operation from a safe distance. He considered it a shame that such a quiet, pastoral farm would be the site of so many dangerous hazards, both chemical and radiological. Dagroych considered the possibility of someday coming to a farm like this to retire, once the idiotic Chechen separatists were exterminated. He sucked in another lungful of smoke, realizing that this particular farm would be a deathtrap unless teams of hazardous-material specialists sterilized it. Such things weren't cheap, and other farms between here and Grozny would be equally contaminated, thanks to the overflight of the four crop dusters.

He flicked the ash from his cigarette with a sigh.

Maybe it was just time to move on and leave this part of the country. There were nicer places to retire to. And with his activities within the separatist community, his return to Chechnya would only serve to be a menace to his life. Besides, if things went according to plan, Grozny would be as inhospitable as Chernobyl, an empty ghost city evacuated when the reactor belched up its wormwood, poisoning the skies and the rivers.

Sure, people now took road tours through the wasteland, but it had been over two decades since that "accident" threatened lives as far away as Moscow. Grozny would heal in about the same time, but Dagroych was no longer a young man, and twenty years to clear the land and air of radioactive waste would find him too old and infirm to care about owning a farm. Maybe the quiet life just wasn't for him, he thought.

Kroz approached him. The Curved Knife operator accepted a cigarette and lit it up. "How are things going?"

"We'll be ready to launch around midnight. And since these planes don't have much metal in them, they'll be hard to keep track of on conventional aviation radar," Dagroych replied.

"Nice touch using insecticide to cut the waste," Kroz noted.

"Figured that if we're going to render a city unlivable and useless, we might as well throw in as many toxins as we can," Dagroych replied. He looked at his cigarette. "Then again, I keep thinking of retiring, and I'm inhaling cyanide and ammonia through these stupid little coffin nails."

Kroz let his cigarette rest stickily on his lower lip,

smirking. "We'll die, but we look and feel fucking cool right now."

Dagroych laughed and took a fresh puff. "You have a point there, friend."

Kroz took a seat on the ground, resting his back against the fence that Dagroych leaned over. "Did Bennorin tell you that he was in the area?"

"No, but if he were, he'd be an idiot to be in Grozny. Especially since this was his plan," Dagroych said. "In less than a day, that place is going to make a gas chamber seem like a health spa."

Kroz nodded. "I just want to have my bases covered."

"If the American comes for us, you want some payback," Dagroych said.

"Yes," Kroz said. "Of course, Bennorin told me that I was free to share that information if I ever got caught. He just wanted to make sure I didn't end up captured."

"So why are you musing about all of this?" Dagroych asked.

"Because I want to be sure that I can get out of this, period," Kroz said. "Wouldn't you like a little insurance to keep the biggest, baddest hunter in the world off our necks?"

"I always have you to cough up," Dagroych countered with a laugh.

"Oh, you're funny."

Dagroych grinned. "Seriously, the American isn't going to get anything out of me. Plus, you didn't even tell me where you were going."

"Thanks, Dag," Kroz answered. "And I'm not going to tell you where I'll be heading."

"Good. That shows you have some survival instincts," Dagroych said. "Then again, you did survive two encounters with the American."

Kroz checked his watch. It was approaching noon, and his stomach rumbled loud enough for Dagroych to hear where he stood.

"Let's get something to eat," Kroz said. "Unless you'd prefer to watch the radiation mix."

Dagroych grimaced. "No fucking way. Let's go."

The conspirators left the technicians to their deadly concoctions.

LASERKA LOOKED UP from her calculations, exhaustion apparent on her face. "I've checked this four times, and right now, I can barely see the numbers straight."

"Take a break," Bolan said, scribbling down more figures. "If you can't read my calculations, then there's no way you can confirm my math."

Laserka sighed. "I'm pretty sure you have it figured out on that map. And your cyberfriends will confirm it with their own simulations."

Bolan looked up from his paperwork. "You're suggesting that I take a break, too?"

Laserka rolled her eyes and grabbed his hand. "Come on."

She pulled him away from the table. "You're just making busywork until the satellites and mathematicians send us their results. And there's only one reason I can tell that you'd want to keep yourself preoccupied."

Bolan flipped his pencil onto the table. "Denial of sexual tension."

Laserka smirked, then caressed his cheek. "What's to deny? I'm a grown woman. And you most definitely are a full-grown man."

"So I've been told."

Laserka pulled him in for a kiss. He tasted good. Once the kiss broke, she took a deep breath, looking into his eyes, searching them.

"What's wrong?" Bolan asked softly, his hands gliding around her trim waist.

"Nothing," she answered. "That was the closest thing to perfect that I've ever had. I'm just waiting for this daydream to be over, and for me to wake up with a damn pencil in my hand, doing math again."

Bolan caressed her back as he slid his hand up to the back of her neck, cupping it gently. He guided her in for another kiss, and she surrendered to it. It was a short, tender one, and when he broke it, he rested his forehead against hers. "No worries. You've been excused from your homework."

She giggled. "I'm sorry… I don't even know if you're free to do something like this."

"For you, I am," Bolan returned, cupping her neck again, feeling the spill of her silken hair over his hand before he moved in for another kiss. His hands ran down her trim, athletic hips and she hung on to his neck tightly, her tongue performing a dance with his. His powerful arms lifted her off her feet so that they were more on the level. In his grasp, she felt like a child's doll being handled by a gentle giant. She slid her knees up so that they rested on his hips, her hands sliding down his cheeks as he supported her, cradling her bottom in his hands.

He pushed her back against the wall, bracing her there as his hands unbuckled the belt that held her jeans to her slender waist. Bolan was able to untuck her blouse and she let go, letting him peel it up and over her head. He tossed the blouse aside, and she dug her fingers under his collar, popping the buttons on his shirt as she exposed his muscular chest. Her fingernails scratched over his broad muscles, tips caressing the lines of his faded scars. Laserka felt a surge of sadness that such a remarkable physique had been violated by guns, knives and fists, but he still looked and felt magnificent.

The two lovers continued disrobing, and Laserka explored every inch of him. Though he bore the reminders of a thousand battlefields, he was still supple and responsive to her touch, and when he returned the favor, Bolan was a man who was as skilled at finding what worked for her.

*Eat, drink and be merry, for tomorrow we die.*

They would be merry, but death would come at midnight, not tomorrow.

## CHAPTER NINETEEN

Wayid Mahklov, at the controls of the Mi-24 Hind, looked back at the big man and the beautiful brunette clad in gray-and-white camouflage in the passenger compartment.

"We're five minutes out from our destination," the younger Mahklov told them. "You certain that I shouldn't soften up the farm with a few volleys of machine-gun fire?"

"It'd be easier for us, but then there would be the likelihood that you'd puncture a waste container," Bolan replied. "I promised your father that I wouldn't put you in jeopardy, and that includes taking the blame for a biohazard contamination breech."

Mahklov looked at the countryside ahead of him. "I appreciate that, but according to the infrared camera on this bird, there's something along the lines of forty people on that land. Enough of them look as if they have rifles to make things very hot for you."

Bolan moved up to the cockpit and looked at the display for the FLIR camera installed on the war bird. He frowned at the numbers, but they didn't represent new information to him. He checked his watch, and double checked the thermal imagery on the camera. Four powered-down aircraft sat inside a hangar, being attended to by men with low-heat signatures. Bolan had seen enough men in hazardous-material handling suits through IR imagery to recognize their lowered-heat signature. The planes were cold and inert on the screen, which meant that his calculations had been correct on the time line for when the materials had arrived at this particular farm and how long it took to filter and reconfigure the deadly cocktail of waste and pesticide into an airborne cloud of unstoppable death.

"Well, the planes aren't close to ready for launch," Laserka said. "But if we make any noise, those things are quick to warm up."

Bolan nodded. "Five minutes by my best estimates, but then I had an ace pilot operating the craft."

"Is there a situation you haven't been in?" Laserka asked.

Bolan frowned as if concentrating on it. "None that I can recall."

"Responsibility for ecological disaster be damned. If one of those birds taxis onto the runway, I'm hosing it down," Mahklov said. "Better to lose one farm than have Grozny catch that shit."

Bolan gave Mahklov's shoulder a squeeze. "If that happens, I'm not going to stop you. But for now, we're going to take this stealthily."

The three kilometer range of the FLIR camera allowed Bolan to observe the Iron Hammer staging ground from relative safety, but the sound of the Hind would eventually give them away. He tapped Mahklov on the shoulder.

"Set us down at the insertion point," Bolan said. "We'll hoof it the rest of the way."

The pilot nodded. "Good luck, you two."

"If we're lucky, we won't need to have you rain fire on that farm," Laserka noted.

THE PHONE WARBLED and Kroz picked it up. It had to be Bennorin.

"What is it?" he answered with a snarl.

"Is that any way to talk to an old friend?" an unfamiliar voice asked.

"Who the fuck is this?" Kroz asked.

"After all the head butts and gunshots we shared, you don't know what I sound like?"

Kroz was never that slow, but when the truth hit him, he felt like kicking himself, that is if he didn't feel as if he were caught in the glacial runoff of chilling realization. "The American."

"It certainly took you long enough, but I suppose that since we never really spoke, you wouldn't have known the difference," Bolan taunted.

"Looking to trace my position?" Kroz asked.

"That would imply that I didn't know where you were in the first place," Bolan said. "Nice farm you picked to die on."

The phone clattered to the floor in numbed fingers and Kroz rushed to the window. His memory took over, and he reminded himself that the American was a master sniper. He ducked behind the wall, wincing at his foolish overreaction. His phone buzzed, and it took a moment for the Curved Knife operative to realize that he hadn't hung up. Kroz dragged his handgun from its holster, in case the enemy somehow had the magical ability to teleport through a wireless phone.

"I think it's nice that you ran to the window to look for me, but I am not that stupid, Kroz," Bolan said. "You have a few options available to you right now."

"You've got to be joking." Kroz groaned. "A deal with you?"

"Your old friend Berdysh informed me that, even in the Knife, I have the reputation as an honorable man," Bolan told him. "You make me happy, and I'll let you walk away with your life."

"What would it take to make you happy?" Kroz asked.

"World peace," Bolan answered.

"You've got the wrong man for granting that wish," Kroz countered.

"You can give me the next rung on the ladder. Bennorin and his Smyernet Consortium are causing a lot of conflict on this part of the planet," Bolan said.

"Give you Bennorin, and you'll let me live?" Kroz asked. He thought about it for a moment. "Trouble is, Bennorin told me that he was already in Grozny."

"Which is a stupid set of travel plans since you and your friend Dagroych are about to turn the city into a radioactive contamination zone in the next few hours," Bolan said.

"That's been nagging me, too," Kroz replied. "But if he's not where he's said—and presumably your people would have picked up his conversation with me—where would he be?"

"You know more about him than I do," Bolan stated. "What do your instincts tell you?"

"Moscow's out of the question," Kroz said.

"I'm not going to be impressed with places he's not," Bolan told him. "My offer of amnesty is starting to dissolve."

Kroz grimaced, looking around his room. He could see Dagroych out the window, heading toward the hangar, wearing his lead-lined rubber protection. If Kroz took too much time on the phone, he'd be late for the inspection. However, there was no way he could be caught on the phone with the enemy.

"Keep stalling, and Dagroych is going to wonder what's keeping you," Bolan said, giving voice to his worries.

"I know that," Kroz answered. "I'm trying to think of where Bennorin would go."

"Then I suppose I'll just have to take action for Catherine Rozuika," Bolan said.

"Wait, what?" Kroz asked.

"The woman that you and your partners beat to death in London," Bolan reminded him.

"Yes, I know. It just reminded me of something," Kroz replied.

"You have my undivided attention," Bolan informed him.

"Rastolev had dealings with one of the Russian mobsters in London. It wasn't related to the reporter and her husband," Kroz explained. "And he kept the information away from the rest of us."

"Who was the Russian?" Bolan asked.

"Yanos Shinkov," Kroz answered.

"I was just talking to him. He only mentioned that Rastolev was bullying him," Bolan said.

"That might be the case. Rastolev was a bastard," Kroz replied. "But a lot of money had changed hands between Rastolev and Shinkov."

"Enough to set up house for a spy on the run?" Bolan asked.

"Five hundred thousand pounds," Kroz answered. "You can hide for three, four years with that kind of money. Twenty if you're on a tight budget."

Bolan gave a rumble of pensive thought. "Shinkov set up lodgings for Bennorin, on Rastolev's behalf. It makes sense now why Shinkov was so quick to shuffle me off to Moscow. Good work, Kroz. You've earned your respite."

"Actually, I had a deal with my boss. If you were to come by, and you were set to kill me, I could give him up to buy myself some time," Kroz admitted. A strange sense of calm washed over him.

"What are you talking about?" Bolan asked.

"I'm talking about the question that's always going to haunt me. Would I have been good enough to take you down," Kroz said.

"You have your chance to walk away," Bolan offered again.

"I don't know how to explain it, but action is the only thing I know," Kroz replied.

Bolan sighed. "So you're going to let Dagroych know I'm aware of your position?"

"I'll give you two minutes to prepare. It's only fair. The two of us can then start cleaning out the extraneous personnel."

"The three of us," Laserka interjected.

"Ah, the lady cop. All right. We don't have any women on the premises, so it'll be easy to avoid shooting you," Kroz replied. "Just stay out of it when the American and I face off."

"You're going to go along with this craziness?" Laserka asked.

"It's one way to even the odds," Bolan admitted. "How can I make certain that you won't let one of the waste-container planes out, though?"

Kroz looked toward the hangar. "Let me take care of things. If I don't, you're in range to finish me off."

"Fine," Bolan said, doubt in his tone.

Kroz hung up the phone and tucked it into his pocket. He thought about it. He had just betrayed Bennorin and was going to emasculate Dagroych's operation, a plan that he'd been working on for a year. Such a betrayal should have gnawed at his conscience, but he realized that there had never been any loyalty to Bennorin or to Dagroych. Bennorin was a man who employed him, and gave him carte blanche to engage in the kind of combat that he'd become addicted to, and travel the world in relative comfort while doing it. Dagroych was a coworker, a man who shared cigarettes with him, but there really hadn't been a hint of friendship. Dagroych simply had a personal army that would have given Kroz an edge over whatever force the American would have brought to bear on him.

But that was not the way that the American had worked. He was the epitome of the one-man army, and Kroz wanted to have his shot at the legend. The man had bested him in hand-to-hand combat once, but that was due to surprise. They had engaged in a vicious fire-fight, but the walls and ceilings of the old flats had kept them from seeing each other most of the time. With the third and deciding battle, Kroz and the American were going to have to do it as a straight-up, face-to-face battle, muscle against muscle.

It would be a fitting and glorious way to die. If the Grozny plan had succeeded, Kroz would have been hunted to the ends of the Earth. Even if he had walked away from the farm, the Curved Knife assassin would have been looking over his shoulder, anticipating the arrival of Russian Intelligence or the CIA or Interpol, ready to snatch him and drag him into a long, tedious trial. If they weren't able to follow him, Kroz would have to lay low. The adrenaline rush of combat would be gone because he couldn't do his lethal work with the kind of impunity that Bennorin had bestowed upon him.

Making a deal with the American devil was the only way for Kroz to have a sense of satisfaction. If he lost to the American, it would be a swift demise, no torture, no rotting in a cell, no interrogation or waiting for the trapdoor to fall from beneath his feet as his neck was circled by a noose. If he won, then Kroz would know that he was one of the finest warriors on the planet, having faced the single most experienced combatant ever to walk the Earth. He would never have to prove himself again against another man.

It was as close to a win-win situation that Kroz could find, and he could still manage to salve his conscience about the despicable nature of Dagroych's mass-murder plans.

Stepping out of the farmhouse, he saw that Dagroych was tapping his wrist.

"Get the fuck into your hazmat suit," the Russian told Kroz.

"Why? It's not as if I have to inspect every rivet myself," Kroz answered.

Behind the glass faceplate, he could see Dagroych's brow furrow in anger and frustration. "Damn it. What is wrong with you?"

"What's wrong with me?" Kroz asked back. "Maybe something is right with me for once. All this time, I've only been acting on the whims of others, and only because I knew that following their lead, I'd actually have a shot at the kind of fight I've always wanted."

"And you're disappointed that we'll be done and gone before the American can drop by for round three in your little pissing contest?" Dagroych asked. "You want a third chance at dying? Because from the looks of the bruises all over your face, you haven't covered yourself in glory."

"What kind of glory is there in shooting unarmed people? Or being part of a team of five men jumping and beating a lone woman to near death?" Kroz mused.

Dagroych clenched his eyes shut. "The American is on his way, isn't he?"

"Yes, he is," Kroz replied. "And for a shot at the crown I've decided to give him a little hand."

Dagroych's brown eyes locked on Kroz. "What?"

Kroz swept his leg across the Curved Knife operator's ankles, knocking his feet out from under him. As Dagroych flopped onto his back, Kroz threw himself forward and jammed his knee under the man's sternum. Breath fogged Dagroych's visor as it exploded from his lungs. A hard shove against the headpiece of the hazmat suit, and Dagroych's head bounced on the hardpacked ground, laying him out stunned. Kroz scooped the rifle out of his former partner's hand and shouldered the weapon, aiming it at the open doors of the hangar.

Iron Hammer technicians saw the weapon come up in the wake of the sudden burst of violence. The unarmed mechanics waved their hands, trying to ward off Kroz. He pulled the trigger on the AK, firing single shots into the propeller turbines and then into the front landing gear of each of the aircraft. Tires popped or the axles broke, forcing the planes to lurch as they were destabilized. Iron Hammer insurgents scattered, drawing their weapons as one of their allies from Moscow had suddenly gone berserk.

Kroz only needed a few seconds to fire the ten shots he needed to make certain that none of the crop dusters were going anywhere. Even on semiautomatic, he was able to crank off the shots so fast that the Chechen insurgent group thought he was cutting loose on full-auto. Right now, he might have been outnumbered, but now that the apocalyptic air force had been grounded, the American and his ally Laserka would swoop in to even the odds.

Then it would be time to finish the fight.

DAGROYCH STRUGGLED to sit up, and spotted Kroz racing away at full speed, reloading his Kalashnikov on the run. He turned his attention toward the hangar and noticed that the planes were sitting wrong on their front landing gear. He figured out why a moment later when his vision focused and he could see that their wheels and support shafts had been blasted apart with rifle fire.

"You idiot," Dagroych gritted, ripping the hood off of his hazmat suit. "Kroz! You're a dead man!"

Rifle fire crackled from one of the overgrown fields, precision rounds whipping through the air and striking armed Iron Hammer gunmen with deadly accuracy. Three Chechens twisted as bullets riddled their chests, then dropped lifelessly into the dirt. Realizing that Kroz had taken his rifle, Dagroych scrambled to his feet and raced toward the farmhouse. There would be more weapons within, and only three of the forty gunmen he had in his employ were down. There were another technicians on hand, and they could arm themselves as well with guns left in the hangar.

"Get on the defensive!" Dagroych bellowed. His Iron Hammer gunmen cut loose with their rifles, sweeping the field where the initial burst of lethal fire had originated. Automatic weapons crackled from a different position, and Dagroych knew that the American had to have had an ally, splitting apart to get the maximum amount of disorder injected into their security force. "Stay behind cover!"

He spotted Kroz pop up with his rifle, triggering a short burst. Dagroych dived through the door of the farmhouse, avoiding the spray of slugs that tore the jamb. He fished his cell phone out of its pocket and hit speed dial.

"Bennorin," a voice stated.

"It's Dagroych. Kroz has gone insane, and he's working with the American now."

"It is of no concern to me," Bennorin replied. "Do you think that I let him know anything that could damage me?"

"He's not stupid," Dagroych told him. "There's going to be something that you thought you'd hidden from him."

"Just make certain that the pipeline through Grozny is rendered useless," Bennorin said.

"With the American here?" Dagroych asked.

"You stole a dozen containers of radioactive waste. The airplanes could only take eight. That leaves you with four and a good-size truck bomb," Bennorin told him. "Of course, you've already factored that into your plan, in case the Chechen federal air force made an effort to intercept your crop dusters."

"Damn you…" Dagroych snarled.

"Put your hazmat suit on and drive the truck. You'll be safe," Bennorin told him.

Dagroych sighed.

"Listen, do you want the money that we're being paid to gut the Commonwealth's oil supply?" Bennorin asked. "We're not going to do that while the pipeline is intact. Once we cut that supply off, Russia is going to spend billions to restore their oil needs. Wear the hazmat suit. I'm not asking you to make a suicide run."

"Middle Eastern petrodollars, eh?" Dagroych asked.

"And official political power for me once the administration realizes that I've been right all of this time," Bennorin said.

Dagroych hung up and rushed to the closet. Inside, he found a Kalashnikov with several loaded magazines. He jammed a full stick into the well of the assault rifle, worked the bolt to chamber a round, and stuffed spare mags into his hazmat suit pockets. He'd retrieve his hood on the way to the truck.

It was time to start earning his million-dollar payday.

THE STACCATO SOUNDS of gunfire rolled across the empty fields and Bennorin sighed. He hoped that he'd given the American's people enough red herrings to draw them away from looking for him in Chechnya. Of course, none of that would mean a thing if the American's interference at the farm initiated a containment breach on the stored materials. Actually, Bennorin had calculated that it would require the detonation of fifty pounds of high explosives to disperse the contents of a canister far enough to reach the farmhouse.

Bennorin held few illusions that the American would not have that kind of firepower on hand. Luckily, Bennorin had a supply of radiation sickness medicine and had slipped into a containment suit for the purposes of riding out the battle. He would have a chance, though the city of Grozny was already rumbling with the leaked information about the mission-contaminated waste containers and the terrorists who were depositories of radiation. Chechen newscasters obligingly shared information about the nature of "gamma bombs," which were simply normal, high-radiation isotopes and cast-off reactor materials dispersed through conventional explosives. As a dirty bomb, the concussion wave would drive particles of the dense metals as fast as bullets, creating a ring of brutal shrapnel that not only would enter bodies at full speed, but embed into the environment and continue to emit deadly waves of electromagnetic energy.

It wasn't a quick killing weapon, except for those people lucky enough to be within the blast radius of the bomb as it detonated, but the poisoning of people and landscape would render a city uninhabitable. And of course, the news emphasized all manner of grotesque, horrible demise thanks to the ravages of radiation poisoning.

Bennorin relished the panic as it grew in Chechnya. If Grozny could receive a brutal blow like that with the content of only a few drums, then the rest of the countryside would be vulnerable due to the mass of materials stolen by the Iron Hammer.

Refugees would flood into neighboring Commonwealth states, causing further political unrest. Ingushta in particular would be put on alert to the possibility of Chechens looking to uphold old feuds or seek out new land for themselves. It would require a strong Russian government to rein in the potential conflicts.

Bennorin would step forward, outlining a plan of law enforcement. The Chechens were only one small faction of violent insurgents who were targeting the motherland. Russia would have a moral imperative and legitimate reason to go to war with rebel states to restore order.

The gleeful politicians in the Kremlin who were part of the Smyernet Consortium would polish a crown for Bennorin's head if he asked for it. It had taken the phenomenal effort of a former cold war spymaster and dozens of disenfranchised agents to get the ball rolling, goading and supplying one particularly vicious faction into such naked hostility that the only sensible response was a scorched earth campaign to eliminate any opposition to the administration in Moscow.

Hunting season would be open for any and all dissidents again. The rallying cry of "we cannot let the terrorists win" would prove to be the justification for kidnapping, imprisonment and murder.

Bennorin listened to the chatter of assault rifles wafting through the window and he poured himself a glass of vodka. The warriors of the shadows made such beautiful music to welcome Armageddon.

## CHAPTER TWENTY

Kroz was as good as his word, crippling the crop dusters, which were still in the process of being loaded with the aerosolized radioactive materials. Now permanently grounded with a few well-placed shots, the aircraft were no longer a factor in the current crisis. However, the dozens of Iron Hammer insurgents were a matter that Bolan had to address because the drums could still be used to secure this particular farm under the threat of environmental sabotage. According to collected geographical studies, the farm was right on top of a large groundwater reservoir that fed multiple wells in the surrounding seventy-five miles. A waste spill could cost hundreds of lives and ruin the terrain for farming as irradiated water was pumped out in irrigation.

The Executioner took out a trio of riflemen who were responding to Kroz's sabotage of airplanes, tapping off 2- and 3-round bursts that brought the Chechen terrorists to heel. Dagroych bellowed out commands in the distance, and the Iron Hammer fighters rushed for cover, a fire team laying down suppressive swathes of full-auto slugs at the copse of gone-to-seed crops he'd initiated his part of the battle within. Fortunately for Bolan, he'd scurried into an irrigation ditch, three-foot earthen berms protecting him from the onslaught of defending separatists.

"Give them something to think about, Kaya," Bolan said softly into his hands-free radio.

From her concealed position, the tough lady cop opened fire. While she'd only tagged one of the fire team, her bullets still managed to force the Hammer gunmen to duck behind heavier cover.

Dagroych waved frantically, pointing out Laserka's position to his defenders, but Bolan cut loose again with two fast bursts that chopped apart two riflemen who were shifting their aim toward her. The gunmen collapsed, one jetting a stream of arterial blood that showered a third member of the fire team. Bolan didn't blame the Chechen gunman for his recoil of horror from the spattering gore. It was a common human reaction to be repelled by the spray of lifeblood in your face. As it was, the third and fourth man of Dagroych's response team didn't know what to do.

The blood-sprayed gunman gave in to his terrors and lurched into the open. Laserka's VEPR chugged from her position, and the crimson-splashed terrorist folded over. Judging from his reaction, Laserka had to have been aiming low as her bullets had hit him in the abdominal muscles, likely causing severe trauma to his pelvic girdle and lower lumbar spine. Given the predominance of major arteries in that part of the body, he would be dead in moments. Bolan turned his attention to Dagroych, and his burst barely missed the Curved Knife holdout as he leaped frantically through a doorway. Kroz's rifle chattered and tore splinters off the doorjamb.

The Executioner and his allies had accounted for seven of forty die-hard Iron Hammer defenders, which meant that they still had an arduous battle ahead of them. Bolan rose from his position and leaped over the berm. His broken-field style of run carried him past rotting crops with a minimum of exposure to enemy fire, though Chechen rifles continued to crackle. His camouflage uniform helped to break up his profile as he rushed past dark green, seven-foot stalks that began to sag. It was similar to a zebra's defensive coloration as it caused the eye not to focus on the blur of the body. Though the zebra's stripes enabled it to confuse the color-blind mega predators of the open savannah, the swathes of gray, dark blue and white made him equally difficult to home in on. The only real improvement would have been if Bolan had raced along with a dozen other men similarly dressed, their bodies blended into one rushing form that made individual targeting impossible. As it was, the deepening gloom of dusk had rendered the Executioner into a phantom that sliced across distances from cover to cover, confounding the Iron Hammer gunmen who didn't have night-vision goggles among them. Things improved for the warrior as emergency lamps clanked to life, bathing the farm's compound with the harsh glow of bright lights that only deepened the gloom in the fields.

Bolan cut hard left to attain the cover of a tractor parked on the edge of the main farm. Its big, rusted iron tires formed massive shields that would only be broken by a rocket-propelled grenade. As well, its massive bulk produced an impenetrable shadow that concealed him from the frantic defenders. He swung around one of the knobby wheels and caught a flanking Chechen out in the open. A short burst zipped the man from crotch to heart and shoved him onto his back in dying reflex. Two men who had fallen a few yards behind him skidded to a halt and triggered their rifles. They were too late to hit Bolan who had ducked behind the three-foot-thick tires. Their bullets sang off the huge metal disks and elicited a cry of pain as one of them took a ricochet in the leg.

The distraction of his comrade's cry left him flat-footed enough for Bolan to pop out again and punch a single 7.62 mm round through the side of his head. Brains excavated through a quarter-size hole in the hapless gunman's head, and he tumbled across his friend. The injured Chechen screamed at the vision of his friend's death. The Executioner allowed that man to live, aware that panic would render him useless for several minutes at minimum. Bolan swung back toward the front of the tractor as he heard Laserka on the line.

"I've got a group on your north," she said. "I don't have the range to hit them as they have the farmhouse between us. You're in range to take them, though."

"Keep to the perimeter. There's a shed forty-five yards from you. I'll keep the enemy busy while you take up an overwatch there," Bolan ordered. "You have enough ambient vegetation to hide you while you make your way."

"Try not to attract too much attention," Laserka admonished as she broke into a run.

Bolan pulled a concussion grenade from his harness. He hadn't wanted to bring any fragmentation bombs to this particular site due to the possibility of shrapnel opening up a canister of radioactive waste. The large detonator core, on the other hand, had less penetration power against metal drums, even though the explosion it incited could hurl it hard enough to break bones out to one hundred yards. A dent in a waste containment drum would be a greatly reduced risk. However, even a stun-shock grenade had the power to turn a small team of gunmen into dazed targets.

With a hard throw, Bolan nailed one of the Iron Hammer gunmen that Laserka had warned him of. The flash-bang grenade detonated as it bounced away from his chest, his eyes burned by thousands of lumens of high-intensity light. Both he and his partners were deafened by the roar of its flash powder's incineration. If Bolan had given the man he'd struck the opportunity to recover his eyesight, it would have been unlikely that his hearing would ever recover from the contact-range exposure to the blast. Rather than allow the Chechen to suffer, Bolan put a burst into him, then walked a figure eight of full-auto withering fire across the other gunners.

Mercy was not going to be on the menu this night for these murderers. The Iron Hammer were not legitimately motivated Chechen separatists who wanted independence. They were hardened, bigoted men who despised legal intrusions by a western government into their rights, and they saw no moral quandaries in the detonation of bombs near schools. Bolan only had to think back to the airport massacre to realize that his enemy required only one response, a swift death. The Executioner believed in clean justice, not the extended suffering of torture or crippling injuries. A quick ticket to the afterlife was as much kindness that Bolan could spare for such low and callous murderers.

Something rattled at the back door of the farmhouse, and Bolan turned his attention toward it. The sound and movement had pulled his attention away from the wounded gunman who had caught his own bullet. Only Bolan's peripheral vision and sharp hearing had given him enough of a warning to throw himself into the dirt as bullets sliced the air over his head. The Executioner rolled onto his side and raked the injured rifleman with a quick burst. Two of Bolan's rounds had missed, but the last four bullets crushed his face and shattered his collarbone. So much for giving the Iron Hammer insurgent the opportunity to sit out the gunfight.

It was one less man to send to jail and possibly be turned into a martyr for the cause of psychotic separatists in Chechnya. Bolan wasn't disturbed by his enemy's failure to take the easy way out. If he had been willing to open fire on the Executioner, then he had proved himself willing to die for his cause. It was simply Bolan's duty to allow a politically motivated murderer the opportunity to do just that.

"Kaya, what's going on?" Bolan asked. "I noticed movement behind the house."

"Looked like a man wearing a hazmat suit," Laserka noted. "He disappeared into one of the fields, and I'm catching too much enemy fire to keep track of him."

"I see your problem," Bolan returned. "Sit tight and I'll free some room for you."

A second concussion grenade lobbed toward a pickup truck that three Iron Hammer riflemen had utilized as a barricade. They had noticed Laserka's muzzle flash in the darkness beyond their island of illumination, and wanted to bring her down. The canister-shaped bomb landed behind a particularly burly gunman who worked to reload his RPK light machine gun. The sound of the bouncing grenade distracted him from the LMG, and he looked at the supernova as it flared between his legs.

One of his allies dived into the open to escape the effects of the grenade. While he had escaped blindness and deafness, he ran right into a stream of bullets fired by Laserka. The unlucky Chechen crumpled like discarded paper under the onslaught of autofire from Bolan's ally. The Executioner triggered his VEPR again and raked the remaining two enemy shooters with ruthless efficiency.

The phone in Bolan's pocket chirped, and he pulled it out, paying attention to his surroundings as he heard Kroz's voice. "American, I spotted Dagroych. He ducked out the back, and he's working his way around toward the transport truck."

"I was afraid of that," Bolan answered. "There's still drums in there, right?"

"Backup plan was to have plastic explosives on the vehicles. We drop the transport off at the oil fields and let the whole thing go sky high. When the waste burns, it turns to radioactive ash and with prevailing winds—"

"I'm familiar with the concept," Bolan cut him off. "You have a shot at him?"

"No. I was hoping that he'd come around to where you could hit him," Kroz replied.

"Movement by the truck!" Laserka interjected.

"Check fire!" Bolan shouted. "You put a bullet into the transport."

Bolan didn't have to finish his statement, which was a good thing as he caught movement to his right. He let the phone drop from his hand and swung up his rifle. A wrench arced around and batted the barrel aside and vibrations from the impact jolted up his forearm. It was one of the lead-suited technicians. He'd armed himself with a three-foot wrench that would have crushed the Executioner's skull if not for the VEPR's length deflecting the blow. Bolan didn't dwell on his good fortune and whipped around behind the swing of the tool. He powered his fist into the tech's gut with enough force to lift him a foot off the ground. Bile burst from his lips, and if it hadn't been for the technician's foresight to remove his hood, it was likely that he would have drowned in his own puke. Bolan pivoted and drove his elbow hard into the Iron Hammer tech's neck, feeling the sickening pop of dislocating neck bones. Paralyzed or dead, the technician crumpled to the ground.

Bolan was about to scoop up his rifle when more insurgents popped into the open. They only possessed handguns, but Bolan was not as bulletproof as he'd liked to have been. His dive for his rifle transformed into a lunge under the tractor as enemy rounds chased him.

The Iron Hammer gunmen paused, looking at the rifle that Bolan had left behind. They turned to each other with grins of premature victory, but the Executioner rose from behind the tractor, his Desert Eagle drawn. Magnum bullets obliterated the heart of the leader of the impromptu ambush, leaving behind a fist-size cavity in his ribs. The man to his right jolted backward from the grisly wound that opened up in his friend's chest, but his disgust at the gore blast disappeared along with the rest of his brain.

The other two gunmen froze in horror at the sudden return of Bolan, his Desert Eagle blazing. One whirled and broke into a terrified run while the other sprawled on his rear, dropping his pistol. Bolan leaped down from the seat of the tractor and landed on the sprawled technician with both feet. He used the fallen Iron Hammer tech as a springboard to reach the running man with a shoulder block. The frightened Chechen was knocked from his feet, and sprawled face-first into the dirt.

More of the terrorists had noticed that the Executioner had been disarmed of his rifle and opened fire on the lithe, agile warrior. Their autofire cut only into empty air and Bolan rebounded from the stunned tech to roll prone. One of the riflemen realized that the enemy had dropped below their line of sight, but the soldier's cannon speared a Magnum-powered rocket through his face before he could track down on him.

"Cooper? The truck's in motion!" Laserka spoke up. Even as she appraised him of the situation, Bolan saw that she gave him fire support. Her VEPR snarled out strings of full-auto that tore into the other gunmen who had tried to get the drop on him.

Bolan rose to his feet and retrieved the improved

Kalashnikov. "Mahklov, get the helicopter into the air now!"

On the other end of the radio signal, the young pilot responded instantly. "I saw movement. You want me to open fire on the truck?"

"Belay that! Swing by and retrieve me!" Bolan ordered. "That vehicle is packed with high explosives and radioactive waste. You put anything on that bird into the bed, this part of Chechnya becomes a contaminated zone."

"You're not seriously suggesting that I drop you on a truck full of irradiated waste," Mahklov said.

"Can the debate and get over here now!" Bolan snapped.

The warrior looked back toward one of the lead-suited technicians who still had a head after he gave them a piece of his mind with the .44 Magnum. Bolan was able to retrieve a hood from one of them and slipped it over his head. He also took a pair of heavy rubberized gloves. Now for the most important test. "Can you read me?"

"Loud and clear," Laserka replied. "Those magical black tights you wear will provide protection against radiation?"

"Land warrior technology," Bolan answered, running toward cover nearer to where Mahklov could land the Hind. "I've dealt with enough NBC situations to make antiradiation shielding a part of my uniform. Without a mask and gloves, though, it won't provide much defense against nerve gas."

"You're not leaving the party so soon," Kroz said as he jogged into the open.

"The truck first, then you and I will have words," Bolan told him. "Besides, there are still Iron Hammer gunmen on the premises."

The Hind roared overhead, its impressive bulk enhanced by the mottled desert camouflage that it wore on its back. Mahklov lowered the giant craft, and Bolan hauled himself up into the passenger section. Kroz looked at the warrior as he boarded the monstrous airship.

"Police the area. And if Laserka comes to harm, you'll never learn the answer to your question," Bolan warned.

"My beef is with you, not her," Kroz replied. "Go stop that bastard Dagroych!"

The Mi-24 swung into the sky.

KAYA LASERKA FED her VEPR another magazine and looked for more targets.

Barbara Price contacted her over their communications net from Stony Man Farm.

"Thermal contacts to your north," Price warned.

Laserka pivoted and triggered the full-auto rifle, punching shots into the rotting crops. A scream of dying pain cut the air as surprised gunmen scrambled. "Thanks, Barb."

"We spend enough on this real-time satellite coverage, might as well use it to help our allies," Price told her. "We've got thirty down and returning to ambient temperature. Except for the two trying to flank you, it looks as if the situation is back under control."

"Only if you're not counting Dagroych's runaway truck bomb," Laserka returned. "Any update on Bennorin yet?"

"Anomalous communication tags," Price said. "Best we can guess, Bennorin *is* inside Chechnya," she explained.

Laserka opened fire on one of the two remaining gunmen circling her. Her initial burst had knocked his legs out from under him, but she quickly followed up with a second salvo of rifle fire that opened his rib cage.

"Inside Chechnya?" Laserka asked. "But Kroz told Cooper that he had set up accommodations for a safehouse in London."

"Kroz believed that Bennorin was doing that. I don't feel that Kroz was lying," Price said. "These guys might do unspeakable things for ideology and to exercise their blood lust, but too many of them are honorable and won't lie when promised a good scrap."

Laserka's brow furrowed. "So Bennorin dropped red herrings so we wouldn't be able to find him. Sounds like typical KGB spymaster bullshit, hiding in plain sight and all that."

"We picked up a burst of communication just before Dagroych went after the truck, and we believe that might have been Bennorin," Price said. "The signal hadn't been up for long, but my team is triangulating it."

"It helps that you have eyes in the sky right above us," Laserka noted.

"Our satellites and computers aren't magical," Price returned. "We just happened to luck out and catch Dagroych's conversation with Bennorin."

The last of the Iron Hammer assassins in the crops took that moment to lunge into view. His rifle was empty from his previous misses, so he cocked the weapon over his head with the intent to smash the buttstock into Laserka. She triggered her VEPR and excavated his belly with a half dozen 123-grain spoon-nosed bullets moving at twice the speed of sound. The dying Chechen missed her by a yard, his legs still in motion from his savagery-fueled momentum, and he ended his career of terrorism with broken stalks of dead wheat folded over his corpse.

Laserka took a deep breath, then looked back toward the farm. "You're certain that there are no more combatants on the scene?"

"There's still Kroz," Price told her. "I know that Cooper's promised him a fair fight…"

"No way," Laserka answered. "Certainly he's deserved a cheap death, but the man went toe-to-toe with Cooper twice, and walked away once. He also managed to survive an entire compound full of Iron Hammer gunmen shooting at him."

"Then there's option two," Price said. "We've narrowed down the location of Bennorin's cell phone."

Laserka paused. "And it's within walking distance?"

"Driving distance," Price corrected. "The next farm over. You have a set of wheels?"

Laserka glanced toward the tractor surrounded by corpses and her lips turned up into a smile.

"I've got the closest thing to a tank for a hundred kilometers."

Laserka rushed toward the farm machine in a dead run.

## CHAPTER TWENTY-ONE

Dagroych had one advantage in the waste-laden transport, and that was the volatility of his lethal cargo. A powerful bullet penetrating the back would cause a gusher of contamination that would turn the highway he traveled into a deadly wasteland. Hundreds of Chechens used this road every day, and the effects of the poisonous radiation would cause irreparable health damage. It was less of a catastrophe than an explosion detonating in the middle of the oil storage tanks of Grozny, but he knew that the man in the helicopter pursuing him would never allow that kind of a risk to noncombatants. With his pedal to the metal, Dagroych accelerated toward the city, glad that the vehicle had been gassed up. There was an off-road motorcycle in the back with which he could set the timer and escape the blast radius of the improvised gamma bomb.

Of course, at that point, the American would have his hands full in an effort to disarm the two-and-a-half-ton truck bomb laced with nearly a half ton of radioactive medical waste before it exploded. With 220 pounds of octogen plastic explosives packed between the drums to bring it up to a full 500 kilograms, the dirty bomb would be a world-class threat that would rupture oil containers for hundreds of yards. In the wake of the blast, spilled petroleum would be ignited to cause a fire that would threaten to engulf the city. Fire department responders coming to the scene would succumb to lethal levels of radiation poisoning, provided they even could penetrate the edge of the blazing conflagration. The flames would take irradiated ash and turn it into a blanket of deadly smoke that would blanket an entire city. More than 200,000 lives would be forever changed by gene-damaging particles inhaled from the inferno.

There was only one option that the American could take, and while he was insane enough to attempt it, Dagroych knew that if he tried to get the helicopter to land on the cab, the struggle would still be enough to crash the truck and detonate the superbomb in the back. The 500-kilogram death burst wouldn't take out a pipeline, but it would turn a ten kilometer section of an important road into an impassable terrain, and if Dagroych was lucky, he'd die instantly. Those downwind of the blast wouldn't be so lucky as airborne radioactive particles would travel much farther, bringing a plague of radiation poisoning that would induce cancers and brain damage across the region, albeit in a less than ideal form than having an oil fire's already toxic smoke further contaminated and mixed with airborne waste particles.

"Are you crazy enough to try this, American?" Dagroych asked as he dropped the hammer on the accelerator, the big diesel engine rocketing the truck forward, climbing past 130 kph. "Because at this speed, all you're going to do is wreck the transportation infrastructure of Chechnya by detonating my little truck bomb. I know it's going to be a hard choice, allowing a city to die quickly, or strangle a nation by a disruption of travel, but there's no way you'll be able to take me down."

Dagroych shook his head. He'd started talking as if the big American in the helicopter could hear him. While the farm and the truck had been under constant orbital surveillance, there was no way that their electronic ears had the capacity to listen to Dagroych's spoken words. Still, it felt good to issue the challenge as he guided the multiton truck for its appointment with the apocalypse in Grozny. Kroz had spoken of how the American was a sorcerer, smarter, stronger and faster than any of his opponents and able to bring down impossible odds. That might have been the truth, but Dagroych and his radioactive cargo had written a whole new definition of "unstoppable" in the dictionary. The diesel-powered juggernaut would be difficult for police small arms to stop with its heavy metal frame and massive ten-cylinder engine. Throw in the fear of accidentally releasing a cloud of death with a stray bullet, and no one would stop this juggernaut.

"Slow down!" came a bellow from the loudspeaker on the Mi-24 Hind. "You have one chance to surrender!"

Dagroych looked at the American as he stood in the side door of the speeding, reptilian aircraft. He smiled, then flipped the Executioner the finger. "I'm never stopping! I'm a runaway train of doom!"

The winds whipping past the cab tore his words

from his mouth, but the single-digit salute was all the answer that the American would need. Dagroych flinched as the fender of his car struck a small Yugoslavian compact car. The lesser vehicle careened into the roadside as if it were a spinning top, its frame compressed as it landed nose-first in a roadside field.

Other drivers swerved, seeing the hurtling vehicle bearing down on them. Dagroych adjusted his steering and felt the bumps of the sedans as he plowed past them. Their paths deflected, they caromed wildly off of the road. Some had been skilled enough to stop their radically altered course, but still more ended up like the first car, crushed against rocks or wrapped around trees.

Dagroych, drunk with the power he wielded, pounded the horn. The Armageddon Express was on schedule, and the next stop was the single greatest petrochemical disaster in Asian history. He roared with glee as he jammed the accelerator to the floor.

MACK BOLAN WATCHED as a half dozen cars were destroyed by Dagroych in his insane charge toward the city of Grozny.

"We have to blow that animal away, Cooper!" Mahklov shouted from the cockpit. "Give me the go-ahead, and I'll let him have a burst of 14.5 mm ammo."

"Negative!" Bolan said, looking at the crushed vehicles scattered at the roadside. The wake of the madman's express run to the city filled the warrior with a level of dread that had rarely been matched before. By the inactivity that had been calculated to save lives, at least three people had been murdered as they lost the war of physics between a two-and-a-half-ton truck and their thousand-pound automobiles. Dagroych was drunk on murder, and his nightcap was going to be the devastation of an entire city, followed by the economic collapse of two countries.

"Put me closer, over the bed of the truck!" Bolan ordered.

Mahklov looked over his shoulder, stunned by the proposal. It was part of a long-standing state of shock at the current crisis. The American had already told him about the plan to climb aboard the runaway truck. Now, having seen the metal juggernaut obliterate half a dozen cars and maybe twice that many lives, the soldier was dead set on seeing his plan come to fruition. With a steady hand, he swung the war bird closer to the transport and its apocalyptic cargo. The Hind had more than enough velocity to keep up with a diesel truck, but the kind of pilot skill needed to hold the chopper steady over a swerving two-and-a-half-ton meat grinder was something that Mahklov didn't know he had. They were charging along, eating ground at a rate of 72 mph. One misstep on the American's part, and the Chechen federal government would need mops to collect his remains off the highway.

Mahklov finally understood the big American who braced himself in the passenger compartment. He had stripped out of his camouflage uniform, and now was clad in his body-hugging blacksuit and war harness, with a hazmat hood and thick gloves covering his head and hands. He no longer was an elite commando on a dangerous antiterrorism mission. He was a living embodiment of night, sawn from the black void of space.

The Executioner tensed his leg muscles, preparing

for the leap that could either put him in a position to stop Dagroych's death charge, or reduce him to a lique-fied smear if he missed the back of the truck. Through the heavy leaden glass visor, Mahklov saw him wink.

"Keep her steady, Wayid," he said. "I'll be back."

Mahklov returned his attention to his task, his hands steadied by a surge of confidence. The American's in-spiration had calmed him, silenced the doubts in his mind, and he pushed the throttle on the Hind's massive engines to keep pace with the diesel doom truck along-side them. Dagroych laughed, waving his middle fin-ger at the Chechen pilot, but the Mi-24 didn't waver. Out of his peripheral vision, he caught the black blur of a human form fly from the passenger compartment. That was Mahklov's cue to pull up and away from the truck, a prayer for the American's safety on his lips.

IN THE BRIEF MOMENT that he was in the air between the Russian combat helicopter and the renegade Dagroych's truck, Bolan experienced a heartbeat of the purest free-dom that he had felt. The last time he had been so un-encumbered by the oppression of Earth's gravity, he was riding a space shuttle. The roaring winds that as-saulted his ears had grown silent, as well, and Bolan ma-neuvered his arms and legs to steer himself on the wind. With a shift of his weight, he aimed himself ahead of the truck's cab, knowing that air resistance would slow him as effectively as a parachute. That was why the world had gone silent, because he had been stopped in mid-leap, the forward momentum imparted on him by the he-licopter torn away as he collided with the atmosphere.

The two-and-a-half-ton truck, blistering down the

blacktop at close to 80 mph, caught up with Bolan as he fell to the Earth's longing embrace. His lightning-fast reflexes pulled in his legs before the roof of Dagroych's cab could guillotine them off, and a drop of his shoulder plunged him into the canvas covering of the transport's bed. The military-grade fabric was strong, but had enough slack that when Bolan landed, his skeletal structure didn't compress under the hammer blow that struck him. The canvas split under the Executioner's weight and with a twist of his torso, he prevented the shattering of his bones on the bed of the truck with a roll.

The impact with the back of the truck was not lethal, nor was it crippling, but Bolan lay on the floorboards, hunched against the 500 kilogram dirty bomb, recovering his strength and coordination. His shoulder and back were livid with the abuse that they had absorbed. Once again, his superb agility and physical conditioning had turned an almost suicidal action into a survivable stunt, and he willed his arm to brace on the wooden slat seat so that he could drag himself to his feet. In the cab, through the torn fabric cargo cover, Bolan could see Dagroych stare at him with a slack jaw.

The Russian had to have been under the impression that Bolan was a superhero, complete with the power of wingless flight. That hadn't been the case, though. The Executioner simply knew how to fall with style.

"You had your chance to stop," Bolan snarled, giving in to his anger. He turned Dagroych's callous murders of Chechen drivers into a jolt of controlled rage that negated the signals of pain and stress on his body. Adrenaline fed achy muscles, endorphins released in his bloodstream numbing him to the exhaustion and beating that his body had taken over the past few days. "Now, you get stopped."

Dagroych brought up a handgun and triggered it, 9 mm bullets leaping through the back window of the cab. Bolan's blacksuit and the chest-conforming sheath of Kevlar and ceramic trauma plates absorbed the Makarov rounds' relatively weak impacts, stopping their penetration with enough efficiency to prevent bruising on his ribs. The rounds would have stung if the Executioner had not been riding on his body's natural chemical reaction to danger and pain. Bolan lunged, leaping the distance between the bed and cab in a single bound.

Dagroych wrenched the steering wheel, and centrifugal force jammed the warrior against one side of the broken window, the high-tech polymers pushed to their limits as shattered shards of glass tried to penetrate and lacerate Bolan's arm. Only the hard knock of the metal window frame on Bolan's shoulder penetrated the haze of endorphins running wild in his bloodstream. Dagroych exploded with a single laugh.

"Falling down, American?" Dagroych cackled, maintaining the breakneck pace of the doom load.

Bolan grabbed a handful of seat belt and used it as leverage to brace himself. Then with a surge of strength, he kicked both feet through the broken window. Dagroych recoiled, swerving hard, Bolan's heels only striking the Russian's shoulder.

"Missed!" Dagroych shouted, but he realized that Bolan's kick hadn't been meant for his head. The Executioner's lithe body slid through the shattered rear window of the cab and deposited him in the passenger seat with snakelike speed and agility. Dagroych yelped in surprise and stabbed his pistol at Bolan, but an iron grasp wrapped around Dagroych's wrist. The gun was jammed hard into the seat and its bullets punched harmlessly through cushions, springs and floorboards. With the handgun jammed into the seat, Bolan brought down all his weight, focused behind his knee, on the Russian's pinned forearm. Bones snapped like twigs, and Dagroych roared in agony. He released the steering wheel. The Executioner had anticipated the reflexive reaction of his opponent, and his hand lashed out, seizing the wheel and holding the truck's course stable.

"You bastard!" Dagroych sputtered, foaming at the mouth as uncontrollable pain and fury seized him. Unlike Bolan's disciplined surrender to rage in order to minimize the effects of pain and mortality on his body, Dagroych lashed out in blind hatred. His first punch was so wild that Bolan didn't even need to flinch to avoid it, and a follow-up blow was delivered by the Russian's broken arm. That hit proved less than spectacular as the flopping hand at the end of the limb delivered a rubbery, open-handed slap.

Bolan seized the shattered limb and pulled hard. The combination of twisted and shattered bones grinding against each other and tearing muscle turned the truck cab into a wailing chamber that threatened to drive a spike of deafening sound into Bolan's brain. Having only one hand free to manhandle Dagroych, he brought his knee up under the man's armpit, shocking the cluster of nerves and blood vessels there with enough force to choke off his cry of pain. Bile bubbled over Dagroych's lips as unfocused eyes darted around the cab. The soldier utilized the steering wheel as a brace to pull him into a brain-scrambling forearm blow that rocked Dagroych's head on his shoulders.

"Bastard…" the Russian cursed through vomit splattered lips.

"Hit the road, pal," Bolan growled, popping open the driver's door. Another kick and the Curved Knife commander was sucked out onto the road. With the loss of his weight on the gas, the two-and-a-half-ton lurched, losing some speed. The Executioner didn't have time to see Dagroych's fate, and he twisted into the driver's seat and grabbed the wheel with both hands. The truck lurched as if it were a wild ox, trying to break its reins. Bolan's arm muscles drew cable-tight, and he fought against wild momentum, jamming on the brake in an effort to control its deceleration. He had seen for certain that it would take a considerable amount of centrifugal force to destabilize the improvised radiation bomb in the bed, but if the transport flipped over, that would mean the end of the damage control that Bolan had wanted. Wheels screeched and smoked, and the brakes seemed to lose pressure, the pedal gone slack and spongy beneath his foot.

Bolan grabbed the emergency brake and pulled on it, holding the lever in a white-knuckled grasp beneath the heavy rubber gloves. Two and a half tons of ramp-aging steel skidded and swayed on the road, and Bolan sighted more traffic on the nighttime highway. Rather than fight the out-of-control momentum, Bolan disengaged the emergency brake and stepped on the gas, accelerating into the slide.

Now the steering wheel became responsive to the Executioner's touch and he narrowly avoided wrecking a pickup in an oncoming lane. He worked the emergency brake again, bleeding more velocity, and with the clutch, he downshifted to further hamper the transport's forward movement. So far, he'd dropped from eighty to twenty miles an hour, and with a yank on the emergency brake, he stopped the truck, letting it coast and slide onto the shoulder of the highway.

The Mi-24 Hind swooped overhead, then extended its landing gear.

"Cooper?" Mahklov asked over the radio.

"I'm alive," Bolan replied. "I'm going to need someone to guard this thing."

"Sure, no problem," Mahklov said. "I just received word from Laserka. Your people located Bennorin. He's at a neighboring farm, and she's on her way to deal with him with Kroz in tow."

Bolan took a deep breath. He looked at his belt unit, and realized that the wire to the comm link on the common hands-free set had disconnected from his secure link to Laserka. It had stayed in place on the supplementary transceiver that had kept him in touch with Mahklov. He pushed the wire back in, but Laserka had apparently gone off-line. With a lurch, he dragged himself out of the driver's seat.

"Do you want me to fly you back? Or lend you the Hind?" Mahklov asked.

"No. There's a motorcycle in the back," Bolan replied. "You might need the firepower of this bird to secure the truck."

"Motorcycle... You just jumped onto the truck while we were going 130 kilometers an hour!" Mahklov said. "And you're going to rattle your spine on that thing?"

Bolan climbed into the bed. "Stay in the cockpit. I wouldn't want you exposed to the waste."

Mahklov gulped. "That was the most amazing thing I'd ever seen."

Bolan dragged the motorcycle out of the bed and fired it up. It was a Ural off-road bike design, lighter and less strength intensive than the big Wolf road machine he'd used in Moscow only the night before. His shoulders sagged for a moment as he fought off the urge to catalog the combat he'd been through in the past twenty-four hours. "That was pretty crazy, wasn't it?"

"I'd say it was epic," Mahklov said.

Bolan smiled under his radiation hood. "And we're not even done yet."

The motorcycle snarled to life, and Bolan rocketed off toward Bennorin's farm.

KAYA LASERKA HATED that she had to endure Kroz's presence on the side of the rolling tractor, especially since the truce between Bolan and him was only for them. Sure, she'd declined the opportunity to take a cheap shot at him, and she wasn't stupid enough to go after Bennorin's farm all by herself. She just didn't like the fact that she had to be a chauffeur for the devil at a maximum of 40 kph. Only the great size of the wheels and the high clearance of the tractor's carriage enabled them to maintain that top speed, but the idea of riding a tank in on the Russian spymaster had been deflated by the sloth of its ground movement.

Kroz's complaints weren't inspiring love and affection, either. "You want me to hop down and push, perhaps?"

"You can walk if you want to," Laserka growled.

Kroz chuckled. "Lady, you do realize that we're one big, fat target for anyone with a weapon that can hit the side of a barn."

"The thought just crossed my mind," Laserka returned. "It seemed like a good idea at the time."

Kroz shook his head. "We're making enough noise that we've completely lost the element of surprise. I'm not even sure why I agreed to come."

"Kaya?" Bolan's voice came over her headset.

"Cooper," Laserka responded. "What's that sound on your end?"

"I'm on a motorcycle heading for the farm. You told Barbara that you were taking a tractor there?" Bolan asked.

"It's the fastest wheels we could get our hands on. Granted, it's not a motorbike, but we're making good time across the fields," Laserka returned.

"Good time if you've got only one leg," Kroz complained.

"I hear that you have a hitchhiker," Bolan said.

"Yes, it's your sparring partner," Laserka answered. "He said he wanted in on Bennorin's finish. Especially since his presence turned everything he said into a lie."

"Except for the fact that I want a shot at killing

Cooper," Kroz added. "He can hear me through your microphone, right?"

"Yes, I can," Bolan informed her. "Let Kroz know we're almost finished with this."

Laserka relayed the message, or at least most of it when she saw a puff of smoke in the distance. Her words trailed off and she recognized the incoming warhead, an RPG rocket. She hurled herself off of the driver's seat and landed in the long grass. Kroz was hot on her heels as the 77 mm warhead impacted with the growling tractor. The antiarmor round turned the farm machinery into a twisted mass of burning wreckage, mutilated metal raining down on her body. Fortunately, the pieces that landed on her were only slightly heavier than coins, but she knew that her shoulders and back were going to be a mass of bruises. She looked over at Kroz, who scooped up an assault rifle that had fallen from the tractor.

"We need to reach cover," Kroz told her. "They'll know that we survived that hit."

Laserka drew her Makarov. All she had were her handguns, the rifle left behind somewhere in the blazing pile of wreckage. Gunfire crackled in the distance, and stalks of long grass toppled as bullets cut through them across the hundreds of yards. Kroz grabbed her shoulder and dragged her toward a ditch while Bennorin's bodyguards laid down streams of death to catch them. Another rocket-propelled grenade arced into the ground, just a little behind the tractor, but close enough to batter Laserka's ears.

They were sitting ducks in the ditch, and within a few moments, the man with the RPG-7 would have the range and trajectory needed to rain high-explosive fragmentation warheads onto their position. They couldn't move, though, as rifle-armed marksmen maintained the pressure with precision accuracy. She couldn't help but think that the depression that they huddled in was nothing more than a a shallow grave.

"Laserka!" Bolan called out. "Are you all right?"

"We're pinned down," she answered with a pained whimper. "There's no way out of this."

The snarl of a motorcycle engine rose over the chatter of automatic-weapons fire. "Don't worry, Kaya. I have a plan."

A shadow leaped into the air behind their hiding spot, the solitary headlight in the middle of its mass betraying its identity as a Ural off-road motorcycle. The RPG gunner had to have seen the bike because the smoky finger of a rocket-propelled warhead sizzled under the arc of the leaping vehicle.

Mack Bolan had drawn Bennorin's fire away from Laserka and Kroz, outracing the explosive arrow of doom on his iron steed. It was time for the Smyernet Consortium and their Curved Knife assassins to receive their judgment.

## CHAPTER TWENTY-TWO

The Executioner landed the motorcycle, its knobby off-road tires catching in the grass and loose dirt and rocketing him forward toward the farmhouse. Zigging and zagging, he weaved the bike so deftly and swiftly that the enemy riflemen had nothing to gauge his position with. Bolan's random steering kept him several feet ahead of the arcs of their autofire. He knew that his luck wouldn't hold out, no matter how maneuverable he was, but by the time he'd gone within 150 yards of the house, Laserka and Kroz opened up to provide him with covering fire. The headlight on his motorcycle had made him a living bull's-eye. Now Kroz had returned the favor with his rifle, pouring bullets into Bennorin's farmhouse with withering accuracy. Split between the muzzle flash of their former comrade and the burning, baleful eye of the oncoming motorbike, Bennorin's protectors dithered. That was all that Bolan needed to close the rest of the distance.

He spotted a solid mound of dirt and aimed for it, accelerating to top speed. The bike skyrocketed off the jump and Bolan kicked the motorcycle forward, shoving it like a missile at a window crammed with Russian riflemen. They tried to nail the Executioner in midflight, but their bullets deflected off the 250-pound frame of the off-road bike. The machine obliterated the window and tore through the defenders behind it. In the meantime, arms and legs spread to catch the wind, Bolan maneuvered himself so that he slowed his flight. Just before he hit the shattered window frame, he tucked himself into a human ball and somersaulted into the building. Sure enough, one of Bennorin's armed defenders was there to catch his fall, the motorcycle having shattered enough of the Russian's skeleton to make him into a suitable cushion to decelerate.

"He's inside!" came a cry of dismay. "The bastard's inside!"

Bolan came out of his tumble, Desert Eagle clamped in his fist. The next day would hurt like hell, but for now, the warrior had work to do and conspirators to exterminate. The muzzle of the big Israeli handgun tracked to a stunned gunman whose face had been slashed open by a shard of flying glass. Bolan gave him a Magnum pill to ease his suffering, the bullet catching him just above the sternum, blowing his heart into two free-floating pieces. Having eliminated that threat, Bolan hooked the stock of a fallen Kalashnikov with his foot and kicked it into the air. The rifle spun into his hand and Bolan snatched it to his body. With a spin, he was out of the path of an oncoming storm of automatic weapons fire by Bennorin's defenders.

The engine of the crashed motorcycle snorted and growled as it idled, a human corpse ground into the fork that should have held the front wheel. The noise let the Executioner know that there was still fuel in the tank, so he whipped around the corner and emptied the Desert Eagle. Fat .44-inch holes sprouted in the fuel bladder, each hole turning into a fountain of amber gasoline. Before the irony of using a fuel explosive on the conspirator who would have destroyed Russia's important oil supplies could come to full focus in Bolan's mind, he swept the frame of the motorcycle with the borrowed AK-47. Steel-core bullets sparked on gasoline-soaked steel and in an instant, the wreckage strewed halfway where the big bike had landed blossomed into an inferno. Screams of terror erupted throughout the house as tongues of flame lashed at Curved Knife gunmen.

The eruption of fire had cleared out the corridor in a gout of superheated death, and that gave the black-suited warrior all the space he needed to advance toward a set of stairs leading to the second floor. Shocked and thrown into disarray, the enemy gunmen on this level had a new focus—the blaze. Some were still bearing fresh burns from the flash of flame, while others who had not been filled with elemental panic quickly turned their attention to putting out the conflagration. Bolan took the stairs four at a time, his long legs pumping up the steps to the second floor where a Russian guard lurched into view.

The second-floor sentry swung the stock of his rifle like an ax, and the folding steel tubes sliced the air with a deadly whistle. The blow barely missed Bolan's head as he ducked, and the weapon jammed hard into the wall, sticking there from the force of the attack. Bolan speared the Russian in the gut with the muzzle of his rifle, but didn't pull the trigger. It was enough that the hardened steel tube and sharp muzzle brake had broken ribs with its impact, and it pried the gunman away from the top of the steps. Unarmed and staggered, Bennorin's guardian tried to step back into hand-to-hand conflict, but a neck-breaking kick connected with his jaw. The Russian poured down the stairs, his head connected to his shoulders at an unnatural angle.

A second gunman saw the folly of hand-to-hand combat, and wisely chose to sweep the top of the stairs with a withering burst of autofire Bolan had dropped prone, however, the raging storm of lead and fire billowing so close to his downed position that he felt the heat of the slugs against his blacksuited shoulders. Bolan pivoted his rifle toward the cautious shooter and fired parallel to the floor. The man's ankles and shins disappeared under the full-auto onslaught. The agony of losing his legs didn't last long as he fell face-first into the extended burst. Bolan's bullets tore into his head and shoulders, churning the organs of his chest to stew.

No one else seemed in a rush to come out on the second floor of the farmhouse, but from the sounds of things, there was still some kick in the gunmen downstairs. Bolan plucked the last of his concussion grenades off his harness and waited until a shadow moved at the bottom of the stairs. He released the high-volume, bright-flashing minibomb to let it bounce down the steps.

"Aw fuck me!" came a curse in Russian a moment before the grenade detonated and knocked the foul-mouthed operative for a loop. Groans of agony and confusion erupted downstairs, and Bolan swung around to see their condition. There were three men, all of them blinded and deafened by the flash-bang. These three had enough training and presence of mind to hold on to their weapons, meaning that the window of opportunity for Bolan to take them down with minimal fuss was disappearing with each heartbeat. Bolan let the empty Kalashnikov drop to the floor and he transitioned to the full Beretta 93R machine pistol. A trio of 3-round bursts hacked the stunned riflemen in the head and neck, ending their threat before they could recover their senses.

A handgun round smacked between Bolan's shoulder blades, its sudden impact forcing him to sidestep. Unfortunately, at the top of the steps, his foot sought support in open air. The toll of combat, even with a body charged with adrenaline, had been too much for the Executioner. He tumbled down the steps. The Kevlar and trauma plates under Bolan's blacksuit, the same thing that stopped the surprise bullet, came to his rescue again, protecting him from shattering his ribs as he rebounded off the railing and flopped onto the floor. For the second time in as many minutes, the bodies of the dead also aided in cushioning his fall.

The Executioner had held on to his Beretta in the topple down the steps and he swung his point of aim upward. A figure shifted in the darkness, and Bolan lit him up with a triburst, 9 mm Parabellum sizzlers slicing the air around the shadow.

"Shit!" was the only reward that Bolan received, and he knew that he had missed. The man at the top of the steps disappeared, and the warrior dumped the spent magazine from his Beretta, replacing it with another 20-round stick.

"Bennorin!" Bolan challenged.

"Fuck you and die, American!" came the response. "I've come too far to be taken down by you!"

"It's not just me you're dealing with, Bennorin," Bolan said. "Even your own man Kroz decided to tag along to see you dead."

"The thick-headed fool is probably holding a grudge for the misinformation I'd fed him," Bennorin answered. "So you're the force of nature I've spent my career hiding from. It was pretty easy to get the drop on you once."

"One bullet and a flight of stairs, and it still hasn't taken the fight out of me yet," Bolan taunted. "I'd heard rumors that you boasted about conducting operations under my nose."

"It helped that you were dealing with overly flamboyant and noticeable comrades at the time," Bennorin said. "Our paths had bumped, but never really crossed."

"It looks like your legend ends tonight, Bennorin," Bolan said. He retrieved a Kalashnikov from one of the corpses at the bottom of the steps and walked into the smoldering hallway. Above him, floorboards creaked as Bennorin moved. He tried to step softly, but the warrior was able to triangulate the man's position.

"Or yours," Bennorin answered. "I'd come here to fake you out. I figured that hiding right under your nose, I'd be able to escape your notice, at least until Kroz's information led you on a wild-goose chase back to London."

"The plan would have worked, but you just had to

goad Dagroych into the bombing run on Grozny," Bolan said. "So you hoped to make a profit on the oil-speculation market as well as insure a seat for yourself at the new Soviet table?"

Bennorin laughed. "I'd always prided myself on being flexible in my planning. I guess I let my greed get to me."

The ceiling erupted, bullets searing from the second floor. Bennorin had gotten hold of an AKM, as well, and the steel-cored penetrators roared down at Bolan. The warrior's legs launched him out of the way of the firestorm as Bennorin's initial estimate of his position through the floor had been off by one yard. His fore-arm had been opened up by a stray bullet that had enough penetration to rend the blacksuit's remarkable polymer fibers. Bolan triggered his captured Kalash-nikov, and he raked the ceiling a few feet back from the holes torn by incoming fire.

Bennorin cursed again, and Bolan knew that his aim hadn't been true enough to end this particular fight. A Curved Knife gunman staggered into the corridor with the Executioner, covered in blood and mouthing some-thing. Bolan whirled to deal with the man, but he col-lapsed, already riddled with slugs from Kroz's weapon. The Russian traitor and Laserka were visible outside the window.

"Finish this, Cooper!" Kroz yelled. "I'm tired of waiting for you!"

Bolan charged up the stairs. The sound of his pound-ing feet alerted Bennorin to movement, but the warrior reached the top of the steps on his belly, not standing. By taking the low road, he avoided catching the snarl of Kalashnikov fire from the Russian spymaster. In the darkened shadows of the second story, Bennorin's muzzle flash illuminated his position and Bolan triggered his rifle. The AK jammed empty, which meant that there was no way he could reload the empty rifle in time to take out Bennorin. He let the long gun drop and pushed his Beretta out in front of him with his other hand.

Bennorin had to have run out of ammo for his rifle, as well, because the flare of a Makarov flashed in the shadows. Bolan winced as his body armor stopped another of the relatively weak Makarov rounds, and he responded with the more authoritative Parabellum payload of his machine pistol. Bennorin jerked violently as the high-velocity hollowpoint rounds ripped into his flesh, coring his heart and lungs. Bolan triggered two more 3-round bursts into the man, walking fire up his chest, and finished him off with a final trio of bullets that punched into his face.

The Russian spymaster collapsed on the carpet, leaking lifeblood in an ever growing puddle. Bolan took a moment to check his pulse. He reached out with his instincts in the smothering postbattle silence. Things felt finished, but just to make certain, he dipped the corpse's fingertips in its own blood and pressed them against a piece of stationery. A little research would give the Executioner some advanced data for the next time a conspiracy wanted to revive the bad old days of the KGB and their dominion over the Russian people.

"Cooper!" Kroz called out.

"Hold on!" Bolan said, letting the blood dry on the

paper. He folded it up and inserted it into a plastic bag he kept on hand for securing evidence. He pocketed the plastic-preserved slip and walked down the stairs. There wasn't a part of him that didn't elicit a dull throb.

And Kroz wanted a round-three match with him.

KROZ LIT A CIGARETTE, taking a deep breath. Two farms had been littered with corpses in the past half hour, and there was still the challenge that he had made to the American. With Bennorin's death, the Curved Knife and the Smyernet Consortium had been crippled, if not destroyed, which meant that Kroz was now freed from the fear of reprisals by his fellow conspirators. However, there was still the nagging knowledge that he had survived two intense battles with the American, and would have been given a free pass to walk away and never be heard from again.

Kroz knew that he couldn't stay below the American's radar for long. There were only so many jobs in the world for someone with Spetsnaz covert operations training, and all of them would bring him to odds with the forces of law and order. There would still be the possibility that he'd catch a bullet from a police officer in the commission of his new duties, but the truth was, Kroz was just a little too good for such lesser combatants. Sooner or later, the trail of dead behind him would draw the American's attention, and once again, the conflict would be joined.

Kroz was doomed to make this confrontation one way or another. There would never be a better opportunity, he calculated. The American had been fighting hard for the past five days, engaging in skirmishes from London to the outskirts of Grozny. He had to be running on empty, and the slow gait he carried himself with confirmed that suspicion.

Bolan met his eye. "You ready?"

Kroz raised an eyebrow, then looked over at Laserka. "I just fired this up. I figure that I'd give you five minutes to recharge."

"You don't have to do this, Cooper," Laserka said. "Let him walk, and Russian Intelligence will grab him later."

"He knows all the tricks that RIS has," Bolan replied. He unbuckled his battle harness and it dropped to the dirt with a thud. Blood trickled from the rifle bullet laceration on his forearm. Laserka saw the injury and pulled some gauze from a first-aid kit.

"You're insane. You've been wounded," she told him.

"Which is exactly why Kroz is sticking around," Bolan returned. "Isn't that right?"

Kroz chuckled. "Perhaps. Forty-pound battle harness?"

"It gets lighter the more ammunition I use, but that's how much it weighs on average," Bolan replied. "I'm almost as fast with it as I am without it, I've worn that junk for so long."

Kroz took the cigarette from between his lips and flicked it away into the dirt. "That's bullshit, Cooper."

Bolan bent and tossed the harness toward Kroz, who caught it with a grunt. "The Beretta and Desert Eagle, combined with their full ammunition loads, come out to twelve pounds alone."

Kroz let the harness of holsters and pouches drop

to the dirt. It hadn't weighed as much as the American had said, at least by his estimation, but then the man had exhausted several rifle magazines and three grenades in this night's battle. His stomach churned. It could have been a bluff, but if it was, it was starting to work.

"Bare-handed," Bolan said. "The purest form of combat."

Kroz flexed his fists, then twisted his head, popping neck tendons. "I'm still fresh. I've had days to rest up since our last tussle. You had fights in Moscow and the airport before this confrontation. I'm not buying your bullshit."

The corner of Bolan's mouth turned up. "You don't have to buy it."

Kroz's confidence waned even more at the cocky smirk. He fought to dismiss it. It was just a ploy on the part of an experienced combatant to get inside his enemy's head. The bluff would fill him with doubt and make him too cautious. In battles like this, caution was a hindrance, because fighters spent too much time second-guessing tactics rather than operating within the moment. He closed his eyes and took a deep breath, concentrating to cleanse his mind. When his eyes opened, he smiled. "Nice try, Cooper. But as you Americans say, I haven't just fallen off the turnip wagon. You're trying to put me off my game."

"You already are off your usual battle plan," Bolan said, starting to circle around Kroz. "You're a half step too slow. Trust me, I've been in more battles than you've even read about. I've plotted your five most effective opening moves, and I have counters for every one of them. I'll even be nice to you and warn you against your fourth option. That's the one that will hurt the most when I turn it back on you."

Kroz grunted, then launched himself into the air in a classic jump kick. Bolan pivoted out of the path of his spearing foot and grabbed him by the ankle. Kroz tried to pull his leg back, but Bolan yanked on his ankle and flexed his shoulder into the Russian's crotch. Testicles crushed, Kroz wailed in agony before Bolan turned, using the leverage of his shoulder to slam his opponent's head and neck into the dirt. The jolt of his skull bouncing off the ground folded Kroz into a fetal ball, made possible as the Executioner released his ankle.

"Why wouldn't you listen to the voice of experience?" Bolan asked, stepping back.

Kroz crawled to his hands and knees, spitting bile that had crept up into his mouth. His head swam from the collision with the ground, and there seemed to be an atom bomb detonating continuously between his legs. Tears flowed down his cheeks unbidden, and he looked over his shoulder at Bolan. "Lucky…guess…"

"I've never been a man who was interested in inflicting pain for pain's sake. You're still invited to surrender. If you don't, the next chance you get will have to be accompanied by a decade of physical therapy if you even want to be able to scratch yourself with what's left of your arm," Bolan told him.

Kroz exploded to his feet, anger getting the better of him. He lunged, intending to put the point of his elbow through his opponent's face. Instead, the American caught the Russian's limb, immobilizing it. He swung his other hand over Kroz's fist, then wheeled, using their combined weight to straighten the Russian's arm. Too late Kroz realized that the American's prediction was about to come true again. Kroz hurtled face-first into the side of the farmhouse, his body stopped cold, but Bolan's spin continued on. His elbow cracked and bent in reverse. Blood cascaded from his broken nose and torn lips from where his face met unyielding wall.

"Sorcerer," Kroz sputtered. "Fucking...sorcerer."

Bolan shrugged. "Last chance, because by now, you've lost patience for a fair fight, and I'll end up twisting your head off your neck."

Kroz turned and spit blood onto the dirt at Bolan's feet. "What are you, a mind reader?"

"Just a veteran of too many of these fights," Bolan answered. Kroz could see a softening in his adversary's face. "And you've made your decision, haven't you?"

"You'll have to be quick about it," Kroz told him. "Otherwise, I'll at least put a bullet into your girlfriend Laserka."

Bolan frowned. "Your funeral. Literally."

Kroz leaped, but this time it was away from the Executioner and toward the holsters and ammunition pouches left in the dirt. Reaching out with his good hand, he wrapped his fingers around the handle of the massive .44 Magnum Desert Eagle in its quick-draw leather. Laserka looked on, her jaw dropping at the swiftness of Kroz's movements as the powerful handgun slipped from the holster. Fingers sank into the flesh around Kroz's right ear, nails tearing skin and twisting the Russian around reflexively. The Desert Eagle in his hand was locked into place, but his first shot was wide and wild, missing Laserka by five feet. Meanwhile, Bolan's other hand cupped under Kroz's chin.

"Fuck you, Cooper!" Kroz shouted, wrestling to aim the Magnum pistol at Laserka. Bolan's clawing fingers raked away from the torn flap of Kroz's dangling ear and pressed against the back of his head. With a twist, the Russian felt his neck turned hard to the point of cramping, Bolan's muscular grasp tightening around his skull. Kroz's second shot sank into the dirt in front of Laserka's feet, and she was already running away from this nightmarish situation. Trying to hit a running woman with the American holding him in a headlock would be almost impossible, and once again, the man had interfered with every move Kroz had planned.

It had to have been telepathy or some form of war magic. That was all Kroz could think of as he leveled the Desert Eagle at Laserka's fleeing figure.

Bolan's powerful arms flexed, and Kroz saw the world whip past his vision as if he were being spun at a 100 mph. Something ugly crunched, but Kroz didn't feel anything wrong with his body. "I am not your judge," Bolan said. "I am your judgment."

Spine severed, his head hanging on to the rest of his body by only the skin and muscle of his neck, Kroz dropped into the dirt. He wanted to breathe, but his central nervous system no longer sent the impulse to his lungs to suck in breath. His eyes glazed over, blurring the image of Bolan as he loomed over his dying form. Drool and blood pooled around Kroz's mouth.

"I told you so," Bolan said sadly. He bent over and plucked the Desert Eagle from numb fingers. "Blink if you don't want to spend an hour dying."

Kroz blinked, just about the only thing he could do with his neck shattered.

The .44 Magnum roared, and the last of Vitaly's and Catherine's murderers was dead.

# The Executioner®
## Don Pendleton's
## DANGEROUS TIDES

A wave of terror strikes the high seas....

The large cruise ship was designed for luxury and relaxation...until rogue sailors seized it. And when Mack Bolan infiltrates the vessel, he learns that it's a testing ground for a sinister chemical weapon. Up against ruthless pirates, compromised antiterrorist units and the delicate balance of international relations, the Executioner must tread lightly—and become deadlier still.

GOLD EAGLE®

*Available August wherever books are sold.*

www.readgoldeagle.blogspot.com

GEX369

# ROGUE ANGEL™

## AleX Archer
## FOOTPRINTS

**The search for a legendary creature has never been deadlier....**

When her longtime friend claims to have evidence of Bigfoot's existence, archaeologist Annja Creed can't resist checking it out for herself. But when she arrives at the destination, her friend is nowhere in sight. The search for Sasquatch turns into a rescue mission, and Annja has only her instincts to guide her in a forest full of predators, scavengers and spirits.

**Available September wherever books are sold.**

The search for a legendary creature has never been deadlier...

ROGUE ANGEL™
AleX Archer
FOOTPRINTS

GOLD EAGLE®

**www.readgoldeagle.blogspot.com**

GRA20

# JAMES AXLER

# DEATH LANDS

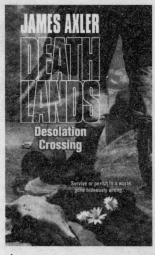

## Desolation Crossing

Survive or perish in a world gone hideously wrong....

The legend of the trader returns in the simmering dust bowl of the Badlands, the past calling out to Armorer J. B. Dix. Her name is Eula, young, silent, lethal and part of a new trading convoy quick to invite Ryan Cawdor and his band on a journey across the hostile terrain. But high-tech hardware and friendly words don't tell the real story behind a vendetta that is years in the making.

### *Available July wherever books are sold.*